BLACK SOIL
WHITE BREAD

MADELEINE D'ESTE

'Black soil produces white bread.'

Norwegian Proverb

'Time present and time past

Are both perhaps present in time future

And time future contained in time past.'

~ **Burnt Norton - T.S. Eliot**

'…the absence of the Witch does not invalidate the spell.'

'Long Years Apart' - Emily Dickinson

Table of Contents

Chapter One
EMPTINESS

1972 – AGNES

Agnes tripped in a divot and rolled her ankle. She tumbled onto the dewy grass and her two notebooks spilled from her handbag. She cursed her shoes and her lack of foresight. Platform sandals were the worst possible footwear for running across a paddock in the dark.

She glanced back over the flat quiet fields. The house was a faraway speck of light. But it was still too close.

"Where are you going?" said a voice in her ear.

Agnes gasped. She clutched her books to her chest and spun around but there was no one there. Then, in the distance, something was glowing in the feeble moonlight. Something yellow. A blond head.

She was not as clever as she thought.

Scrambling to her feet, Agnes broke into a run. Through paddocks, under barbed wire fences and along dirt roads, ignoring the rubbing ankle straps and blisters on the balls of her feet, until she reached the township of Braidwood.

At the train station, the bearded station master eyed her with suspicion when she asked for a single ticket to Sydney. Strangers were rare in a small town and the locals would know all about the farmhouse. She smiled sweetly as she handed over the fare and smoothed her sweat-dampened hair. The man didn't smile back and wiped his fingers with a handkerchief as she walked away.

For twenty arduous minutes, she paced the platform on aching feet and flinched at every sound. When the train arrived, she scrambled aboard but fidgeted in her seat until the doors closed. Only when the whistle blew and the train rolled from the station did Agnes finally exhale. She collapsed into the bench seat and stroked her two notebooks sitting beside her. The train picked up speed and she settled in for the journey home. Dawn peeked over the hills outside the window and the houses dwindled into open fields.

Then, standing by the tracks, she saw him. The blond figure waved at her and Agnes's heart began to race all over again.

She was a fool.

They would never let her get away so easily.

2018 – NANCY

Chew, chew
Where are you?
Sister, sister
Black and blue.

Three small girls in knee-length school uniforms sang. Above their heads, orange bunting fluttered from every maple tree and lamppost down Station Street. They squealed as they sprinted past the bakery.

'Last one gets gobbled up by Agnes,' called out the girl with the swinging black plaits. Her freckled friend leaped over a crack in the footpath.

From her bakery doorway, Nancy squinted into the golden afternoon sunshine. The three girls, like beetles with their oversized backpacks, scurried away. She pushed her slippery glasses back into place. Agnes? Did that little girl say Agnes? She looked again but the girls were already half-way down the street, out of earshot.

Stepping back inside the faded Victorian two-storey building, Nancy flipped the sign to 'Closed' and pulled down the roller blind. With a sigh, she trudged across the black and white linoleum floor and stacked the four iron chairs on top of the two tables. Next stop was the till, and on the way she passed the glass display cabinet fully stocked with golden scones, vanilla slices and coffee scrolls. It was a similar story on the wall, the bread racks were heavy with unsold baguettes, white block loaves and speckled multi-grain rolls.

She pressed the tally button on the grey cash register with a clunk and sighed again. $5.70. Four hours in a hot kitchen, mixing and kneading while the rest of the world slept, for a grand total of three customers. And yet this was her best day's takings to date.

Until three months ago, Nancy had lived thirty-eight years without even knowing she had a Great Aunt Agnes. Sickness and death often brought families back together. Sometimes.

Arriving in Hopetoun with a key and a letter from her family

9

solicitor, it had taken a month of hard work to reopen the bakery and make the flat upstairs liveable. Without money for repairs, Nancy had to do the best she could on her own.

Inside the shop from dawn til dusk, she spoke to no one. After sweeping away the years of dust and neglect, there were recipes to be tested and a kitchen to be reorganised. The paint on the outside walls still flaked like a sunburnt nose but the cobwebs were gone and the front window sparkled. Now, four weeks after the anticlimactic reopening of *Bittesby Bakery*, Nancy spent her days standing at the counter. Alone and waiting for the tinkle of the shop bell, the hours crawled by and there was nothing to drown out her thoughts of the past. Her new venture hadn't filled the Grant-shaped hole in her heart.

The vanilla slices looked lonely. Nancy lifted a square out of the display cabinet and took a bite. The crisp light pastry shattered inside her mouth, followed by a rush of gooey creamy custard with a hint of fragrant vanilla. It was good, damn good, even if she did say so herself. So where were her customers?

She stepped out onto Station Street again and took another bite. Not many people in Melbourne knew about the inner-city suburb of Hopetoun. Tucked away, Hopetoun felt like a trip back in time, a corner of village life in the midst of a metropolis. Her bakery sat on its own, but only a few hundred metres past the main shops and on the path to the train station and the primary school. Hopetoun locals traipsed by each day, in their suits and trainers or pushing high-end strollers in yoga pants, but no one stopped to buy.

Nancy's hand was suddenly empty. The vanilla slice lay in her stomach like a stone but without a second thought, she stepped back inside for another.

'Stop.'

She slapped her hand and instead, piled all the leftover baked goods into a cardboard tray. There was no point saving them, by morning, they'd be stale.

Twelve-feet above her head, a fluorescent tube spluttered from the pressed-tin ceiling, dipping the room into shadow. The exhaust fan in the wall slowed like a propeller and Nancy's shoulders dropped.

'Stupid wiring,' she grumbled. She dumped the tray on the laminex counter and pushed through the swing door, heading for the ramshackle sheds in the backyard. A warm fridge full of spoiled milk and butter was the last thing she needed.

When she was halfway through the door, a sharp knuckle rapped on the shop door.

'Hello!' the knocker called. 'Hello?'

Nancy rolled her eyes but with five dollars in the till, she couldn't afford to turn away a customer. She plodded back through the shop and opened the door to an angular woman with violet streaked hair.

'The sign says I'm closed but don't worry about it,' she said, forcing a welcoming smile onto her face. Every day was a little easier but dealing with people didn't come naturally to Nancy. 'What can I get you?'

'Finally,' the purple-haired woman said and reached out her hand, a row of silver bangles jangling from her wrist. 'I've been trying to get in contact with you for weeks.'

'I'm here every day, except Sundays. Open 7 to 3,' Nancy said, shaking the woman's hand then pointing to the opening hours sign on the door. 'What can I help you with? A loaf of bread? Something for afternoon tea?'

'I've seen the lights on upstairs after-hours but no one ever seems to be home when I knock. Some people might think you're avoiding me.' She smiled coldly, revealing incisors as sharp as her cheekbones.

'Baker's hours are pretty unsociable.'

'Of course. You'd have your plate full getting this place back up and running. After so many years.' The woman slinked her way through the half open door and inside the shop. 'You haven't changed it much at all. How is business by the way?'

'Can't complain,' Nancy lied. She kept her voice light as she eyed the stranger closely. If she didn't want bread, what *did* the woman want? 'Always room for improvement though.'

'Starting out is so hard. Especially in this economy. I remember my first year. You wouldn't believe the mistakes I made.' The woman squeezed Nancy's forearm with a chuckle. Nancy tried not to flinch as her bangles grated together. 'And of course, you are extra brave.'

Nancy frowned. 'I am?'

Before she could ask another question, the woman interrupted with a gasp. 'How rude of me, I haven't introduced myself. I'm Stella.'

'Nancy.'

'I know and I'm here to help you.' She clapped her hands together and clasped them in front of her chest. 'Have you heard about the Autumn Festival this Saturday? You'll have seen the streamers of course? And you got the flyers?'

Nancy shrugged apologetically and Stella handed her a slip of paper.

'The Festival is the annual Community day organised by the Traders Association. I'm one of the Five. The Committee, sorry—we call it the Five. The Festival has been held every autumn since puss was a kitten. A day to show our appreciation for our good fortune and welcome the winter rains. It's a bit of fun and all the local business owners get behind it. We set up little stalls outside our shops and the Green is all decked out. More stalls and a stage for live music. Petting zoos. Face painting. All that jazz.'

Nancy glanced at the clock ticking over Stella's shoulder, her milk curdling in the dark fridge in the kitchen behind her.

'You have to join. I mean…we'd love it if you joined us. There's a meeting tomorrow night at the Railway? The pub on the corner? If you're free, come along. The more the merrier. Please say you'll come?'

Stella's dark eyes sparkled as she took hold of Nancy's hand again. Her soft skin hummed like a tuning fork and Nancy fought the urge to yank her hand away. 'Sure. Sounds good,' she mumbled in reply.

'Must dash. A million last minute details to organise. We'll see you tomorrow at the pub.' This seemed to be a statement of fact rather than a question.

'Thanks. Before you go…' Nancy gestured to the cardboard

tray. 'Can I interest you in a scone or a coffee scroll? My compliments.'

'How kind. But you know what they say about sugar.' Stella strode out the door with a wave. 'We'll see you tomorrow.'

Closing the door behind her, Nancy exhaled. She'd never been one for parties but networking and self-promotion were a necessary evil. It was only a few fellow shop-keepers in a pub and the bakery wouldn't last until winter if things didn't change soon.

Pushing her reluctance aside, there were more important and pressing things to worry about, like her fuse box and her butter.

Heading out through the swing door, Nancy bustled past the galley kitchen with its stone-cold baker's oven and glass-fronted fridge. The shed keys hung from a hook on the wall underneath three framed certificates. Royal Melbourne Show blue-ribbon first-prize awards in the name of Agnes Bittesby; two prizes for bread and one for scones. The awards, over thirty years old, were yellowing behind the glass.

Out the rickety screen backdoor, Nancy followed the broken concrete path into the rusty-roofed creeper-covered wooden shed. The thick padlock opened with a clunk, and using her phone's torch, she spread light over the mouldy boxes, broken chairs and a bent bicycle. Through the dim musty air, she inched along a narrow pathway through the junk towards the fuse box, sitting on the back wall adjoining the main house.

Wiping aside the fresh cobwebs, Nancy flipped open the box and stared blankly at the dials, switches and fuses. Rewiring the house was high on her list of repairs, although the list was growing longer every day. She chewed her lip and pulled out a random fuse with a snap.

'Just a matter of logic.' She adjusted her glasses and twirled the wire-wrapped plastic puzzle-piece around in her fingers. Everything appeared fine, although she wasn't exactly an electrician. She flicked all the black switches off and clicked the fuse back into place. When she turned the switches on again, the needles jumped to life. Electricity was flowing into the main part of the house again.

She clapped her hands with delight. Her milk and butter were safe. Then on her left, something scurried amongst the mildewed boxes. Nancy stopped her celebrating and shuddered.

Small claws scampered through the clutter. She followed the sound with her torchlight and scanned the walls for any holes into the main house. Rodents were the last thing she needed in a food business.

As she bounced the light around the shed, a dark-brown rat the size of her hand jumped out of a tea chest and ran over her feet. She yelped and flinched, then lost her balance and tumbled into the wall. The wall shuddered, dislodging something from behind a stud. The object landed on the ground with a dull thump.

Whatever it was, it was dense and lifeless, and once she convinced herself it wasn't another rat, Nancy leaned over and picked up the dusty old jar sealed with red wax. She wiped the unlabelled bottle, about the size of a pickle jar, on her already filthy black tunic and shone the torch inside. Clumps of blonde, brown and red hair filled the bottom of the jar, along with a rusty four-inch nail and an assortment of tiny yellowed bones. Nancy gulped.

'Chicken bones,' she said to herself until she recognised a knuckle-bone. 'Plastic. It has to be plastic.'

She rubbed the back of her neck. Part of her desperately wanted to put the jar back and pretend she never found it. Another part of her itched to examine it more closely, in the full light of day. Or should she call the police? Double check that the bones weren't human? If they were—what were they doing in Agnes's shed? Before she could dial Triple 0, her thoughts were interrupted by a soft soothing murmur, the whispering of dreams in her ears. The strange and comforting lullaby lit a flame inside of her. Life tingled through her veins and her mind became as clear as a summer sky. Then, out of the corner of her eye, she glimpsed another object hanging

14

halfway down the wall behind the joists. It was a book. Her heart vaulted in her chest.

Had she finally found it?

She eased the navy-blue school notebook out of the wall cavity and hungrily opened the pages. 'Agnes Bittesby 1971' written in flowery copperplate on the inside cover, the type of handwriting no longer taught in schools. She licked her lips as she touched the dog-eared pages, fat with stains and ruled with faint blue lines and margins. Since the first moment she saw Agnes's awards on the wall, she'd hoped she'd find a recipe book. She'd turned the house upside down looking but all she'd found was towering stacks of newspapers from the 1990s and a collection of western paperbacks. She feared the recipes had been lost, locked inside Agnes's head. Until now.

She clapped and grinned widely. This called for tea.

With the jar and the book cradled close to her chest, Nancy skipped over fifty years' worth of junk and out the door. She left the cloudy jar on the rusty iron-lace outdoor table and took the book inside with her.

As her foot touched the first creaking step up to her flat, there was a loud thump on the shop door. Nancy froze, hoping if she was quiet they'd just go away. But a second knock followed quickly after, this time more clumsy and violent.

With a sigh, Nancy turned back to answer the door, and as she passed through the bakery galley kitchen, she opened the door of the cold oven and slid the notebook safely inside.

A dark shape was pressed against the window blind and Nancy hoped it wasn't Stella again. She tugged at the cord and the blind flickered up like an old movie reel. The glass was condensed with hot breath, and a face with bared teeth and wild hair was pushed up against the window.

Nancy flinched.

'I'm closed,' she yelled through the glass, pointing at the sign.

The sun ravaged face squinted back at her. It was a woman with large eyes and teeth too big for her mouth, dressed in an oversized man's pinstriped suit.

'You. Why are you here?' The woman snarled with cracked lips.

'This is my shop,' Nancy replied through the door.

'You look just like her but fat. Where is she?' The woman squinted. 'Tell her I want to see her.'

'Agnes?' Nancy blinked. 'Do you know Agnes?'

'She's been calling to me.'

Nancy frowned and unlocked the door. A rush of warm air blew inside, tinged with unwashed clothes and body odour.

'How?' Nancy asked.

The woman grunted to herself in the doorway and stared down at her ripped and stained trainers in silence. Nancy waited but the woman, who seemed lost somewhere in memory or thought, said nothing.

Nancy grabbed the tray of leftover baked goods. Perhaps a snack would entice her to say more. 'Would you like a scone?'

The woman snatched an iced coffee scroll and shoved it in her mouth. 'Not as good as hers,' she said in between squelching bites, her big teeth smeared with half chewed dough.

Nancy cringed. She knew it was true. But tomorrow would be different. She had all of Agnes's secrets now. Her famous recipes would live again.

'What did you mean about Agnes calling to you?'

'Got any more?'

'Take as many as you want.'

The woman fished a blue plastic shopping bag out of her pocket. 'Chew. Chew. Where are you? Bones. Teeth. Sister stew,' she muttered as she loaded her bag with scrolls and scones. When her bag was full, she shuffled towards the open shop door.

'Wait. Tell me about…'

The woman ignored Nancy and disappeared out into the street.

'Wait.' Nancy followed her onto the footpath and watched her lurch towards the train station, and probably onto the bottle shop around the corner on Salisbury Street. What did the

16

homeless woman mean about Agnes? Her great aunt couldn't possibly be talking to her.

Looking out in the late afternoon sun, she noticed a dark smear on her glasses right over the woman's head. She wiped her lenses on a clean spot on her black tunic but the grey smudge was still there. It hovered around the homeless woman like a hood made of clouds. Nancy rubbed her eyes. She blinked and squinched and when she checked once again the fogginess was gone, but so was the woman.

Back inside, Nancy locked the door and took a moment to savour the silence. Next stop was the bakery kitchen. She wrenched open the oven and with the book in her hands, she shimmied her shoulders in a celebratory dance. She darted up the creaking stairs, two at a time, and switched on the kettle. Once armed with her enormous blue striped mug of Earl Grey, she returned to the backyard, heading for the table on the patchy grass beside a dead lemon tree.

She picked up the dusty pickle jar to clear the table. This time she noticed a dried yellow crust lying along the bottom of the glass. She swivelled it in her hand, considering the bones once again but eventually setting it aside for the real prize, Agnes's book.

Her heart pattered as she opened the cover and skimmed through the yellowed pages with tiny notes and doodles tucked into the margins. The recipe names were unusual: *Fat Rascals, Cold Dog* and *Imp Cakes*, and more were in unfamiliar tongues. There was one photo of Agnes she'd found in a suitcase. A black and white image of a young woman in a nip-waisted dress, her chin held high posing before the Eiffel Tower. The real story of her aunt's life was a blank page but she now imagined Agnes travelling the world and collecting recipes before settling in Hopetoun to open a bakery.

One particular recipe took Nancy's fancy. *Chocolate Fou.* Chocolate; everyone liked chocolate. This could be *the* recipe to bring all her aunt's customers back. Nancy scoured the ingredients list; cocoa, cinnamon, butter. Nothing out of the ordinary and everything available on her pantry shelves.

Nancy's skin tingled. She settled back in her chair and pictured all her customers queueing around the block. Bittesby Bakery would once again become famous, and this time for her *Chocolate Fou.*

For the first night in months, Nancy drifted to sleep with a lightness in her chest. For the moment, the hollowness was gone, her grieving over Grant finally quietened. They said time healed all wounds but perhaps hope was a short cut.

She stirred from her sleep as a chill crawled in under the covers. Her sleep-heavy eyes caught glimpse of a shape looming in her bedroom doorway.

With a gasp, she scrambled upright and lunged for her phone, accidentally knocking her glasses off the bedside table. They skittered across the floor and under the wardrobe.

Her heart thumped. She reached for the lamp and clicked the switch but the light wouldn't come on. Nancy squinted across the dim room, making out the blurry figure of a teenaged girl with long hair, white t-shirt and baggy jeans.

'Who's there?' she demanded but with a betraying wobble in her voice. 'What are you doing in my house?'

The girl hid her face in her hands. At first, Nancy thought she was crying until she started to speak.

'One, two, three...' The girl counted steadily, her hands never leaving her face. 'Four, five, six...'

The girl seemed to shimmer in the doorway.

'I want you to leave! Get out now!'

'Ten, eleven, twelve.'

'This isn't funny. I'm calling the police.'

Swallowing down her fear, Nancy swung out of bed while the translucent girl continued counting.

'Thirteen, fourteen, fifteen...'

There was a familiar smell in the air; the chalky sweet scent of lolly bananas. Nancy rubbed her nose and then her eyes. It must be the stress.

'Eighteen, nineteen, twenty.'

18

As soon as the girl reached the number twenty, she vanished. Completely. The doorway was empty.

'What the…'

Nancy swooped down to grab her glasses from under the wardrobe and then switched on every light in the room. She searched behind her bedroom door and inside the big wardrobe. Finding nothing out of the ordinary, she checked the rest of the flat.

There was no one in the bathroom, the lounge room or the tiny kitchen.

Nancy padded downstairs and rattled all the doors. Everything was locked tight and nothing appeared out of place.

When she thought she was safe and her shoulders had softened, Nancy suddenly flinched again and she scampered back upstairs. She didn't breathe again until she found the recipe book, sitting on the opposite bedside table, exactly where she left it. She covered her mouth with her hand, then stroked the navy-blue cardboard cover lovingly and slipped back into bed.

'Who are you?' she whispered as her heartbeat slowed and sleep dragged her under again. She wasn't entirely sure what she meant.

When her alarm sounded, it was still pitch black outside. With a grunt, Nancy headed for the small bathroom, last renovated before the invention of rock and roll. At the basin, she splashed her face and scooped her unruly hair back into a low bun. In the bright light, she inspected the lenses on her glasses, the thick black frames were her only concession to fashion. Without a scratch to be seen, Nancy put her glasses on and shrugged. The night visit from the girl in the doorway must have been a dream.

She climbed into her white chef's double-breasted shirt and sucked in her tummy to fasten the buttons. Running a bakery was hazardous for her waistline. Today after closing the shop, she'd take a walk rather than her usual nap on the couch.

Last stop was the toilet. When she wiped, red smeared

across the white toilet paper. Rolling her eyes, she leaned down to riffle through the bathroom cabinet for a pad. With all the recent upheaval in her life, she'd lost track of her cycle. Not that it mattered any more. Generally, a woman needed a lover to get pregnant.

Yawning, with the notebook tucked under her arm, Nancy trudged down the stairs to the shop. After switching on the kettle, she moved to the big oven and turned the worn dial to 200'C. The oven always reminded her of a hungry mouth, open and waiting to be fed. Underneath the tea towels, her bowls of proven dough were as puffy as clouds. She cast a handful of white flour over the bench, rolled up her sleeves and began to shape the loaves.

The rest of the world was deathly quiet while Nancy worked, the rhythmic tick of the white-faced clock and her thoughts were her only companions. She'd placed the notebook up on a high shelf and glanced up at it every few minutes. 'I'll get to you soon,' she said aloud.

The order of work was always the same, bread first and then the sweet treats. By five A.M., the trays of scrolls and scones were in the oven and the golden loaves of bread were cooling on racks. Now it was time for the *Chocolate Fou,* and with a slightly sweaty hand, she took the book down from its place on the shelf. Carefully she measured out the cocoa, melted butter and cinnamon into a cauldron-sized metal mixing bowl. But when she reached the next line of instructions, she paused, and chewed her lip as she underlined the words with her fingertip.

Stir the bowl thirteen times only, then let the mixture rest under a dark moon for thirteen minutes exactly. Preferably during a red tide.

Nancy grimaced. Had Agnes's mind already started to decline when she wrote these recipes?

Outside the window, the sky was still black and Nancy knew nothing about phases of the moons. With a shiver, she stepped out into the backyard and looked up. She only noticed the moon when it was extraordinarily big or mysterious. Wisps of clouds drifted across the sky but there was no moon, and the inner city light pollution masked all but a handful of the brightest stars. She rubbed her chin. If it worked for award-winning Aunt Agnes...

Back inside the kitchen, she stirred the bowl thirteen times as instructed and returned to the backyard, placing the bowl on the outdoor table under the night sky then setting the timer on her phone.

She had no messages or alerts, not even a text from her mum. While she waited, her fingers automatically scrolled for her voicemail and pulled up a saved message. His last message. She knew she should delete it; it wasn't helpful to hold onto it—but it was all she had left of him. They'd taken everything else away. She listened to his voice again and her heart broke for the ten thousandth time.

Thirteen minutes passed quickly. Once the chime rang, she hurried the bowl back inside and poured the dark-brown batter into the pans. The three full trays were then slotted into the hot waiting oven.

It was already past six, time to prepare the shop and fire up the white Italian coffee machine, the only new investment she'd made in the business—it was Melbourne after all. Then the two small cafe tables were set out and the shelves stacked with fresh bread. As she worked, the aroma of spicy cinnamon and rich chocolate trickled in under the door from the kitchen. Her belly fluttered. She wished the smell of temptation would travel further, flowing out the front door to be picked up by the wind and carried along the streets of Hopetoun.

The old oven buzzed and Nancy rushed through the swing door, slipped on an oven mitt and reached into the hot oven. But as she slid out the tray, she scorched her bare wrist against the rack. In her excitement, she'd only pulled the mitt on halfway. She yelped and dropped the first tray with a clang. Muffins tumbled out and smashed onto the linoleum floor.

'Shit,' she squealed as chocolate crumbs spilled everywhere. She squatted down and scraped five broken muffins up off the floor. With a sigh, she stuck a crumb in her mouth and the *Chocolate Fou* exploded into her mouth.

'Woah.'

She reeled back on her haunches as the flavour caressed her tongue, then melted away. Velvety chocolate, richer than she'd ever tasted before, followed by the smoky woody warmth of cinnamon. Her own baking was good but this was something else, bordering on erotic.

She gripped her hands into fists, fighting the urge to shovel up all the crumbs and pour them into her mouth. 'You little beauty, Aunty Agnes.'

Nancy had an idea.

By seven o'clock, dawn was peeping through the maple trees and Nancy was on the footpath outside the shop with a tray in her bandaged hand.

'Free sample? A little bit of chocolate to start the day?' She said to every passer-by, smiling so wide her face ached.

They ignored her. The early morning commuters in suits or gym gear focused solely on their screens, their ears plugged with white earbuds. One sweaty faced dad with a stroller waved as he jogged past, but he didn't stop.

Eventually an apple-shaped woman in her fifties hesitated. Nancy lifted the tray in the air to spread the scent.

'You're from in there?' the woman said warily. Dressed in a bank teller's geometric print uniform, she had the face of someone who knew disappointment.

'Under new management,' Nancy explained. She made a mental note to make a sign later.

The woman pursed her lips. 'I guess a little taste won't hurt,' she said.

'They're really good,' Nancy added. 'And it *is* Friday.'

The woman picked up a chunk of muffin and slipped it into her mouth. Her eyes closed and Nancy held her breath until she heard a tell-tale little moan escape from the woman's throat.

The woman grabbed for her purse.

'I'll take four.'

Chapter Two
MADNESS

2018 – NANCY

Suddenly it was three o'clock. Closing time. Today there'd been no clock-watching or leaning over the counter or crossing her fingers as each pedestrian passed by. And for once Nancy was looking forward to checking the tally on the cash register.

The shop bell tinkled. Again.

A slim red-haired woman in active wear bustled inside. 'Any more of the chocolate muffins?'

'Sorry,' Nancy said with a half-shrug. 'I sold out at lunchtime.'

'Oh no,' the woman tossed her flame-coloured hair. 'Will you have more tomorrow?'

'Absolutely.'

After today, Nancy'd be mad not to bake the *Fou* again.

'I guess while I'm here…' As she scanned the glass display case, a chubby bearded man in brown corduroy trousers slipped in and waited patiently behind her. 'Ooh coffee scrolls. And a couple of fruit scones for the kids. And a loaf of multi-grain. Has to be better than that plastic rubbish from Freshworx.'

'Sliced for toast?'

'Please.'

Nancy glided over to the rack and grabbed the bread, leaving only a single unsold loaf behind. She hummed as she pushed the loaf through the rumbling slicer, but watched her fingers closely. Her bandaged wrist still smarted and no one wanted blood-splattered bread.

'There'll be chocolate muffins tomorrow?' the woman said as Nancy handed over her purchases. 'Promise?'

'Cross my heart.'

'I'll hold you to that.' Her phone rang and the woman answered as she headed out the door. 'Jen. You'll never guess where I am…The bakery on Station Street…I know…I never believed the stories anyway.'

Nancy frowned briefly but quickly replaced it with a friendly face and turned to the man waiting in the check shirt.

'Sorry for the wait,' she said. This was a new phrase for her and she liked the way it rolled off her tongue. Her smile was coming easier too and she didn't even feel tired. 'What can I get for you?'

'Did I overhear you say that all the chocolate things are gone?' he said. 'What a shame. I heard they were rather good.'

'Sorry. Tomorrow?' She shrugged. 'If you don't mind me asking, how did you hear about them?'

'This morning, there was a woman groaning obscenely in my shop. I went to throw her out, thinking all kinds of strange things. Then I saw what she was eating. And I had to know more. And here I am. But sadly I'm too late.'

Nancy chuckled. The man had one of those boyish faces which needed a beard to be taken seriously.

'Miles Nancarrow.' He placed his hand on his chest. 'Station Street Books. Dealer in stories and tales.'

'Nancy. Nice to meet you,' she said, then gestured to the display case. 'No chocolate, but can I interest you in something else?'

There were only two iced coffee scrolls and three plain scones left. Miles placed a finger to his lips. His nose whistled as he breathed. 'A scroll please. My nan would murder me if she heard that I was eating anyone else's scones.'

She bundled a scroll into a bag. 'Actually I've been meaning to come in and visit your shop.'

'Aah a fellow bookworm,' he said. 'What's your poison?'

'I love a good mystery.'

'Don't we all?'

Nancy smoothed back a few wayward strands of hair and laughed, the sound a little more girlish than she expected.

'Just this afternoon…' he said.

Miles continued to talk. The diffused afternoon light streamed through the shop window, surrounding him. Nancy nodded along, until from out of nowhere, a shadow descended over his head and landed, floating around his shoulders.

In an instant, Nancy was transported back to her childhood: a Sunday afternoon at a local Greek street festival. A round-faced woman who told fortunes, not from cards or a crystal ball, but from the swirls of leftover coffee grounds in the bottom of tiny white cups. Predictions of marriage, babies and misfortune from the shapes in the dregs. Nine-year-old Nancy had been so engrossed her father had to yank her away by the arm.

She blinked several times but the fog didn't move, yet everything else was crisply focused. Like yesterday—the homeless woman who claimed to know Agnes. Nancy lifted her glasses and rubbed her eyes. It *had* been a long day.

'...a big box of old cosy mystery paperbacks. Classics. Perfect for an autumn evening with a glass of Shiraz. You must come in and have a look.' He handed over a five-dollar note. 'I presume you'll taking part in tomorrow's festivities?'

Nancy gave him the bagged scroll and his change with a gulp. In all of today's bustle, she'd forgotten about the Autumn Festival. 'Stella came to see me yesterday and filled me in.'

'She invited you to tonight's Association meeting?'

Nancy nodded.

'Excellent. Because I have a feeling that your marvellous chocolate thing ...what do you call it?'

'*Chocolate Fou.*'

'Right.' Miles raised an eyebrow. 'Interesting. And somewhat appropriate. Anyway, if the rumours are true your *Chocolate Fou* will be a welcome addition to the Festival. Especially by me.' He rubbed his rounded belly. 'So you'll be coming along to the meeting at the Railway tonight? All in all, the Traders are a good group. Some of them are a little odd, but then again, aren't we all in our own little ways?'

'I wouldn't be able to stay for long,' Nancy said, surprising herself.

'Of course. The hordes of Hopetoun need their chocolate bright and early. I don't envy your work hours.'

Nancy flipped open the counter and followed him towards the shop door.

'Tell you what,' he said. 'I'll bring along a selection of

paperbacks for you tonight. I have a sixth sense for books.'

'Now I'm curious.'

'That settles it. Until tonight, Miss Nancy.' And with a little salute of his white paper bag, Miles left, and she locked the door behind him. She turned the sign to closed and leaned against the shop door with a satisfied sigh.

Untying her apron, she headed up the creaking stairs to her bedroom, changing into her baggiest t-shirt and her only clean pair of leggings. Rummaging through her suitcase under the bed, she pulled out her brilliantly-white, barely-worn runners and a baseball cap. Back downstairs, she put the leftover scones and the last coffee scroll in a bag and left the house through the back door with a flutter in her belly. It worked yesterday, but would this entice the woman to tell her more about Agnes today?

The gate in the side fence led into a narrow bluestone alley, built in the days of stables and dunny men. Nancy stepped gingerly over the uneven cobbles, then turned down into Station Street, passing the three empty shops alongside hers. All three had dirty windows and only one had an official real estate agent's sign. The other two *For Lease* signs were faded and handwritten on scraps of paper.

The first amber leaves of the season fluttered onto the footpath. In the distance, a chime and a recorded voice announced the next train at Hopetoun Station. After the abandoned shops and a handful of gentrified terrace houses, the busier end of Station Street began. Six shops sat underneath a forest-green Victorian awning fringed with iron lace work; a hairdresser, an accountant and Couple a Cinos cafe. A locksmith, then Miles's Station Street Books and finally, on the corner of Salisbury Street, sat the hipster Morning & Mocha cafe, and every single shop window had an Autumn Festival poster on prominent display.

Along the street, Nancy scoured every face and park bench, looking for the woman. She crossed the road and took the underpass under the railway line to Linlithgow Street on the city side of Hopetoun. On this side, coloured umbrellas shaded the footpath. Groups of fashionably-dressed people nursed craft beers or tapped on laptops while well-groomed dogs rested at their feet. Still no sign of the woman.

A train approached and Nancy covered her ears against the clanging bells of the boom gates. The gates lowered and as the traffic stopped, Nancy wove through the waiting cars across the road towards the Green—the quaintly named large park abutting the railway line.

The buzz of the inner city melted away as soon as she passed under the first set of leafy thick-trunked European trees. The footpath was flanked with neat garden beds, blazing with orange blooms. In the distance, past the War Memorial, the hazard lights of a flatbed truck flashed in an open field of manicured grass. Three men in hi-vis vests were unpacking equipment while another two were slotting poles and building scaffolding. The preparations for tomorrow's Festival were in full swing.

Then Nancy finally spotted the woman, dressed in the same suit and ripped sneakers on a bench, and made a bee-line straight for her.

'Hello,' Nancy said cautiously.

The woman sucked wine from a silver cask bag. 'What do you want?'

'Are you hungry?' Nancy offered her the paper bag, holding her breath against the stink of booze and dirty clothes. 'I wanted to talk to you.'

The woman scowled. 'I don't want them if she made them.'

'Do you mean Agnes?'

The woman nodded and picked at her scabby lips.

'I promise you, it was me.'

'Is she gone?' the woman whispered like a fragile child.

'Kind of.'

'Noooo!' the woman wailed. 'Nooooo!'

She sucked a long draught from the nozzle of the wine bag, then scrubbed her face with her hands and cried out again.

Nancy glanced around the park, the paper bag still gripped in her hand. 'It's alright,' she said, stroking the air, not knowing what else to do.

'Noooo!'

The woman's moan echoed across the quiet park. The workmen setting up the Festival stage stopped and stared.

A dark-haired man burst out of the bushes. 'What's going on here?'

Nancy jumped.

'Jackie?' The thirty-something man was dressed in a Council worker's khaki shirt and shorts. 'You alright?'

'She's gone!' Jackie whimpered. 'She left without telling me the truth.'

'Who?' the man frowned.

Nancy winced. 'I think she means my Great-Aunt Agnes. She's not dead. She's only—'

'Is this lady upsetting you?' The man glared at Nancy, sizing her up and down.

'Yeah, you. Go away,' Jackie snarled.

'I didn't…' Nancy stammered and held out the paper bag. 'I wanted to give her these.'

Jackie covered her head with her hands and yowled. 'Go away. Go away!'

'It's OK, Jackie, love,' he said placing a hand on her shoulder. 'She's leaving. Aren't you, lady?'

'But I need to talk to—'

'Just go alright.' His dark eyes were as hard as coal. 'She doesn't need your help.'

Without another word, Nancy turned and scurried away, her pulse thundering in her ears. It was all too familiar. Shunned and threatened, it was happening to her again.

Dumping the unwanted paper bag in the nearest bin, Nancy's shoulders slumped. It didn't make sense. Jackie seemed to hate Agnes but got upset when she thought she was dead. The woman was obviously troubled. Maybe Nancy should forget the whole thing. But for some reason, she couldn't. Jackie knew something. But what?

1992 – JACKIE

'But Mum, it's Saturday night,' Jackie whined. 'I have plans y'know. I was going to the movies with Michelle.' She leaned against the bathroom doorframe, her arms folded tightly against her skinny chest.

'I don't ask much of you. This is important to Ray.' Her mum lined her lips with burgundy in the mirror.

'Like I give a shit about your boyfriend,' Jackie mumbled.

'We're not having this conversation now.' Her mum tossed the lip-liner into her glomesh clutch purse. 'I told you about this last week. Anyway, you can go another time.'

'*Tank Girl* finishes this week. Mum! It's so unfair. Why do I always get stuck with them?'

A car horn blasted from outside the house.

'He's here. There's money for a pizza next to the phone. I shouldn't be too late.' Her mum kissed her on the forehead and wrapped Jackie in a L'Air du Temps hug.

As her mum closed the door, Jackie stuck out her lip and kicked the skirting board with her bare foot. Why was her life so disappointing and boring?

An hour later, Jackie was on the couch. Baby-sitting wouldn't be so bad if only her sisters would sit quietly in front of their video and leave her alone. But no.

'Play a game with us,' Molly pleaded. Her youngest sister was five years old with flaming red hair and no front teeth.

'Go away,' Jackie grunted. She was busy reading the dirty bits in her mum's Cleo magazine as she finished off the last slice of Hawaiian. 'Watch your video. Or I'll send you to bed.'

'It's scary. I don't like the witches.'

'Come on. You never play with us any more,' said Bridget and tugged at Jackie's hair. The older of the two, Bridget was seven with long chestnut brown curls.

The girls giggled as Jackie swatted her hand away. 'Piss off,' she moaned and pulled the magazine closer to her face.

With a grin, her two sisters jumped up on the couch and started to tickle her, their breath sweet with the scent of lolly bananas. Jackie squealed and writhed, then curled into a ball as their little fingers dug into her ribs.

'Alright. Alright.' Jackie raised her hands in surrender. 'How about Hide and Seek?'

'Yay!' The two girls leaped off her, then bounced up and down on the rug, their curls springing in the air. At least with Hide and Seek she'd get a few moment's peace to finish the article on the big O.

'I'll count to one hundred and then come and find you.'

'No, you won't.' Molly giggled. 'I'm the best at hiding.'

At the time, Jackie didn't realise how true Molly's words were.

2018 – NANCY

Nancy returned home and plodded up the stairs to her empty cold flat. Her supposed new life Hopetoun was turning into a big mistake. Why had she moved here? She knew the answer to the question. One very important reason.

She paced the short hallway, her fingers threaded through her hair, her breathing painful in her throat. Grant. With him gone, there had been no reason to stay in Sydney. The dying wish from her grandmother was an opportunity to start a new life. A new home, a new business, a chance to forget. Ha.

Grant. His chin and the stubborn sprout of hair which defied even a five-blade razor. The way his smooth dry hands caressed her neck. The sharp sting of his sports deodorant when his body heated up. His animal grunts. Her lungs ached. Six long months without him.

Her grip on him was loosening, his face, his smell, his touch fading like a leaf shrivelling in the sun. His ghost was slipping through her fingers and memories were all she had. How long until there was only dust?

Tears coursed down her cheeks and she bit down on a wail. Her face burned red-hot as she held her breath, smothering the hurt inside until her lungs ran low, and she wilted against the wall.

When she finally pulled herself upright, the mantelpiece clock showed quarter past six. Nancy flopped down on the couch with a puff of dust and changed her mind about going to the Festival meeting. Her phone buzzed and vibrated across the surface of the spindly-legged coffee table. She ignored it and wished she'd kept those coffee scrolls. The call stopped.

'Good. Go away,' she said and it immediately started ringing again.

Sighing, she reached over and turned her phone face up. She sighed again, and answered it.

'Where have you been?' the familiar voice blasted. Mum.

'My phone was in the other room,' Nancy lied.

'For the past two weeks? You're not still moping, are you?'

'The bakery takes up a lot of time, Mum. Where are you now?'

'Borroloola. About a thousand Ks out of Darwin.' After Nancy's grandmother's death, her mother had used her bequest to buy the freedom of a campervan while Nancy, it appeared, had inherited a mess of responsibilities. 'Have you been to see Aunt Agnes?'

'I'm going on Sunday. I presume she's fine. I haven't heard anything from them.'

'You need to visit her regularly. Your gran's will was very specific.'

'So *caring* after fifty years of silence,' Nancy grumbled.

'Families can be complicated.'

'Not the word I would've used.'

Her mum continued talking, some story about her grey nomad friends who'd gone missing in the Simpson Desert. Half-listening, Nancy glanced lovingly at the recipe book on the coffee table. For some unknown reason, she felt compelled to keep the recipe book a secret.

As her mum rabbited on further, Jackie sprang back into Nancy's thoughts. She needed to know more about Agnes. Nancy knew first-hand how it felt to be the subject of lies and gossip.

'Have you remembered anything else Gran said about Agnes?' Nancy cleared her throat. 'Anything strange?'

'She was *artistic*.' Her mother said the word like it was an insult. 'I heard she ran with a very peculiar crowd. My father definitely disapproved.'

Nancy pictured her permanently scowling grandfather, a man who drained the life and laughter from every room he entered.

'He stopped Gran from talking to her own sister? Controlling bastard.'

'Nancy! Show some respect. That's my father you're talking about. We don't know the full story.'

Nancy grimaced as questions wormed inside her head. Who did have the answers? Perhaps someone else local. Someone from the Traders Association? 'I have to go, Mum. I promise I'll visit Agnes on Sunday. But call me if you remember anything else about Agnes's past. Anything.'

'I don't see why it matters. She's a frail old lady now. Everyone else is dead. The past is the past.'

'Indulge me, Mum.'

Mother and daughter said their goodbyes and she groaned up off the couch, headed for the bathroom. Time to find some answers. She washed away her dried tears, scooped her wayward brown hair into a top knot and with a smear of terracotta lipstick, she was ready to face the Festival Committee.

As she stepped outside and locked the back door, Nancy stopped dead. Something shifted in the twilit garden behind her. She spun around. Shadows and dark shapes loomed in all directions. It was the murky hour between day and night when the light played tricks.

'Who's there?' she called into the gloom. The light bulb above the back door had blown—another maintenance chore on her long list.

She fumbled inside her handbag for her phone. Finding the button, the bright torch beam waved across the overgrown backyard and a pair of shining eyes reflected back at her.

She jumped.

The eyes were too low to the ground.

Was it a child? Or perhaps someone on their knees?

With a gulp, she steeled herself and inched up the garden path. She crept forward stealthily until a huge black dog emerged from the shadows.

'Good dog,' she stammered, gripping her phone with white knuckles.

Camouflaged by the falling night, the shaggy dog stood very still. It didn't snarl or bark. Underneath its plate-sized paws were piles of disturbed earth and grass.

'What have you been doing, doggie?' Nancy scolded.

Dolefully, the dog bowed his wiry head and backed away from the holes. Something white glimmered amongst the soil and weeds and Nancy's breath snagged in her throat. She peered closer and poked the object with her toe. It was long and thin, a bleached-out grey in the torch light.

'You burying your bones in my backyard?'

With a roll of its lolling pink tongue, the dog skulked away. He disappeared into the thick mass of creepers along the flimsy back fence and was gone. She turned back and hovered over the hole in the dirt, shaking her head as she stared at the bone.

How long had Agnes's house been vacant again? A year or more? An abandoned house was the perfect place for a dog to hide his bones, she told herself. That's all. There was nothing more to it. And definitely nothing sinister.

Grimacing, Nancy left the uncovered bones and continued out the side gate, down the laneway and along Station Street towards the Railway Hotel.

The art deco red-brick pub sat on the crossroads overlooking the train line, glossy green tiles wrapped around the outside walls. She squeezed past the huddle of exiled smokers on the footpath to the main glass door and stepped into a warm fug of beer.

She'd forgotten it was Friday night. The pub heaved with perfume-soaked women and men with their ties at half-mast. From a stool in the corner, a waif-like singer strummed an acoustic guitar, the roar of the after-work crowd drowning out her tunes.

Faced with the noise and a sea of unfamiliar faces, the Festival meeting suddenly seemed like a bad idea. No one had spotted her yet and Nancy glanced back at the door. Retiring to the couch at home with a book and a family block of Old Gold was still an option. Yet all the answers to her questions about Agnes could be here.

'Nancy.'

She slapped on a smile before she turned to see Stella and her shock of violet streaked hair. 'Sorry I'm late.'

'You're just in time,' Stella said with a cold hand on

Nancy's shoulder, once again a faint pulse radiating from her fingers. 'But first I think a bottle of Sav Blanc is in order. Go on. Say you'll have a glass?'

Nancy half-shrugged. 'I'm not much of a drinker.'

Stella chuckled. 'Wish I could say the same. But we all have a devil on our shoulder, don't we?'

Nancy nodded weakly. One? She had more devils than she could count. Before she could reply, Stella was deftly navigating through the Friday drinkers to the bar and striking up an easy conversation with the Hemsworth-lookalike barman. Nancy fidgeted as she waited, her attention darted around the room until she saw another familiar face, one with a scowl. The gruff council worker from the Green was standing alone at the bar. She dropped her head and pretended to scan her phone.

Stella reappeared with a bottle in a silver bucket. 'This way. I'm so glad you could come.'

She followed Stella down a corridor with red patterned carpet and into a smaller private room with a long table in the centre. At least fifteen people were crammed into the small space—they were mainly grey-haired but a few younger ones were scattered among them—all chatting, smiling and laughing. Wine glasses and empty beer pots covered the table, and in the centre sat the remnants of a well picked at cheese platter. Nancy loosened her tight grip on her handbag. The rowdy room was warm and welcoming. She suddenly felt silly about her reservations. These people were her neighbours, her peers, her customers. What was she worried about?

'This is Nancy, everyone,' Stella announced as they stepped through the doorway.

'It's her. From the bakery,' someone hissed.

'She looks exactly like her,' said another and the conversation in the room stopped dead.

There were two camps in the awkward silence. The older people folded their arms tightly and glared, while the bewildered younger people shrugged. Only one person grinned directly at Nancy; a woman with short grey hair wearing lilac glasses and a matching polar fleece. But for some reason the woman's beaming smile was equally disconcerting.

Gulping, Nancy finally spotted a familiar face. Miles was sitting half way down the table between two stern female faces; a thirty-something blonde with a youthful ponytail and a small silver-haired woman all in black. He didn't look up to meet her eyes.

All of a sudden, Nancy's vision clouded like a bathroom mirror. Mist wrapped itself around their heads, all three faces obscured. She glanced up at Stella as a similar snake-shaped fog draped around her neck. She blinked in rapid succession, and as quickly as it arrived, the blur lifted.

Finally, Stella broke the chill in the air. 'Thank you for coming along tonight,' she said quietly in Nancy's ear. 'We love to welcome new blood to the Association. And to the community.'

'I'm not sure everyone is as keen as you.'

Stella swatted the air. 'Don't mind them. They'll warm up.' She shoved a very full glass of white wine into Nancy's hand and then marched to the front of the room. 'Everyone. Let's begin,' she announced. 'Where did I put my list?'

Nancy took a hasty sip and skulked to the closest empty chair, unfortunately positioned at the head of the table where everyone could see her clearly.

'Preparations are all on track,' Stella said, referring to a clipboard in her hand. 'The stage is already set up in the Green. Ah, Danny, there you are. Everything good from your end?'

'Ready to go,' rumbled a deep male voice from behind Nancy. Danny turned out to be the dark-eyed man from the Green. He shot her another icy sideways glance and she shrunk back into her chair.

'Excellent. The Community Rubbish Clean-Ups start from 8 o'clock. Fred will be leading the efforts around St. Bart's and Neha's patch is by the railway line. See Fred or Neha if you'd like to join in.'

A white man with sparse grey hair and a brown-skinned woman nodded their heads.

'The official speeches will begin from midday. Then the judging of the corn-growing...' Stella continued on, outlining the run sheet for the day, before moving onto Health and Safety obligations. Nancy shuffled in her chair as the older woman in black glowered at her from further down the table. She simmered with frustration, yet glanced down and took another sip of wine.

'Now, I trust everyone has their stalls ready to go. Please be on time this year. That means you, Janet.'

'I told you someone broke in and interfered with my alarm,' Janet, the woman with the lilac glasses, said. 'But I have my surveillance system in place now. So everything will be hunky dory.'

Stella pressed on. 'The forecast is for a sunny morning with a cool change in the early afternoon. Brace yourselves for anything. We all know what Melbourne can be like.'

'Autumn is finally here,' said Miles. 'About time.'

'Thankfully. After the scorching summer we've had,' Stella said.

'We can't have another dry year,' muttered the scowling silver-haired woman.

'We've done an extra flyer drop at the new apartment blocks, so if the weather is fine we should get lots of new people coming along this year.' Stella rapped her knuckles on the wooden table top and knocks rang around the room as others followed her.

'If there are no other questions...' Stella paused to glance around the room. '...let's raise our glasses. To a successful Autumn Festival and the bountiful rains of winter.'

'Hear, hear!' Everyone charged their glasses and raised them in the air. Despite the prickles running down her spine, Nancy joined them.

With Stella's toast, the formalities seemed to be over and the Traders Association members turned back to their individual groups, leaving Nancy all alone at the head of the long table. After a sip or two in silence, she placed her wine glass down and grabbed her handbag. No one would notice if she slipped away. Except perhaps the mumbling woman in black who hadn't taken her eyes off her since she entered the room.

Nancy made a lunge for the door but her escape route was blocked by the Community Clean-Up couple; the South Asian woman and the grey-headed man. 'Pleasure to meet you finally. Nancy, isn't it?' The woman extended her nut-brown hand. 'I'm Neha and this is my husband, Fred.'

Nancy shifted back onto her heels as the couple inched a little too close.

Fred spoke next. 'We've been past the bakery on our evening walks. Good to see the old place up and running again.'

'Thank you,' Nancy replied. 'I haven't seen you come in?'

'Oh. Yes.' Fred cleared his throat. 'I've been meaning to.' His voice had a slight European twang, Dutch perhaps.

'Have you lived in Hopetoun long?' Nancy said.

'Moved here in the 70s,' Fred said. 'It's a very different place these days.'

Her belly fluttered. If he lived here in the 1970s…?

She leaned in. 'So Fred, did you know—.'

Her question was interrupted by a strong grip on her elbow. Stella. 'Sorry, Fred. Can I steal Nancy away?'

Nancy started to protest, but Stella dragged her away, her mouth still hanging half open. They stopped behind Miles and the other two women seated at the table.

'Let me introduce you to a few people. This is Dajana, Miles and my mother, Mafalda,' Stella said.

'We've met,' said Miles with a friendly nod.

The trim, toned and blonde Dajana sized Nancy up and down. 'Right,' she said flatly. 'Welcome. Where have you come from?'

Nancy sucked in her stomach. 'Sydney.'

'You left those beautiful beaches for this dump?'

'I've never really been much of a beach person. My skin's pale as a ghost.' Nancy laughed feebly at her own joke. The smooth-faced Dajana stared back at her as though she were mad, and all the while Stella's mother Mafalda said nothing, her lips pressed into a colourless line.

Miles jumped in. 'What do you have planned for the festivities tomorrow, Nancy? Your scroll was delicious, by the way.'

'Was it one of Agnes's old recipes?' asked Mafalda, a hint of Italian heritage in her voice.

'No, my own,' Nancy said. 'I'm not sure what to bake. This is my first Autumn Festival. Any suggestions?'

'Something for the children?' Stella offered.

'Is that a good idea?' Mafalda said, flinching.

Miles rubbed his chin. 'Something autumnal. Perhaps a flourless orange cake?'

'Orange would match the streamers,' Dajana said.

'Or ginger?' Stella said.

'Cinnamon would be safer,' Mafalda said disapprovingly.

Nancy chewed on her fingertip as they threw ideas at her. One particular recipe of Agnes's immediately came to mind and a warm glow swept over her. Although if the *Chocolate Fou* was any indication, any of her aunt's recipes would be a big hit. 'I have an idea.'

Stella clapped. 'I'm sure it will be perfect.'

'Excuse me Stella, may I have a quiet word?' A tall elderly man interrupted them. Despite his years, his face was still handsome and his posture straight.

'Certainly, Russell,' she replied.

She rolled her eyes at Nancy and the others, and before following him into the corner, she whispered behind her hand. 'Russell is probably going to tell me off about something.'

Once Stella had gone, Dajana stood up, made her own excuses and strode away. Nancy was left shuffling her feet under Mafalda's persistent iron glare.

Like Fred and Russell, Mafalda was of a similar age to Agnes. But before Nancy gathered up the courage to interrogate the old woman, Mafalda also stood up and left the table without a word.

Nancy sighed through clenched teeth. Miles patted the seat next to him and she reluctantly sat down. He fanned three paperbacks out on the tabletop like a croupier. 'Tell me I'm right.'

'I haven't read this one!' She pounced on one book and immediately started reading the back cover blurb. Then she reached for her purse but he stopped her with a wave of his hand.

'When you've finished, we should get together to discuss it. Perhaps over a glass of Sav Blanc.'

Despite herself, Nancy blushed.

Miles leaned in and lowered his voice. 'You're rather fascinating, you know.'

Nancy guffawed. 'You don't even know me.'

'So very brave.'

She stopped short and squinted. 'Stella said the same thing.'

'I want to know all about you.'

'What do you mean?' She wrung her hands in her lap. How did Miles know about what she left behind in Sydney?

'Your decision to take over…after everything. Most people wouldn't have the guts.' He studied her face but unlike Mafalda's cold scrutiny, Miles's gaze was curious. 'You don't know, do you?'

Nancy shook her head, frowning.

'How interesting,' he said and licked his lips. 'You came here without knowing anything about it?'

'I have no idea what you're talking about.'

'The Sheridan girls?'

She shrugged. 'Are they famous?'

'The missing girls?'

'I don't understand.'

Miles pulled his buzzing phone from his pocket. 'I'm really sorry but I have to take this. I've been desperately hunting down this first edition Dickens for months now.' He turned away and answered. 'Miles Nancarrow. Ah, Mr Fossington, we finally get a chance to speak. How was Tuscany?'

Miles stepped away from the table, leaving Nancy alone.

What did he mean?

All the other Association members were clustered together

deep in their own conversations. Nancy tugged at her collar, the warm room felt suddenly stifling. She grabbed for her phone. Sheridan girls? Is that what he said? She started to type the name but then stopped. Not here, not in this room, full of strangers and prying eyes. Dread dragged on her stomach like concrete. She needed to be alone.

As she was halfway out the door, Stella grabbed her arm. 'Leaving so soon?'

She winced. 'The early bird bakes the bread.'

'I don't know how you do it,' Stella said with a shudder. 'We'll see you tomorrow.'

Nancy left without speaking to anyone else. She pushed through a side exit door onto the footpath and into the cool evening air. After sucking in a thankful breath, she started for home.

'Wait!' Miles yelled and rushed over, his phone pressed to his thigh. 'You're leaving already?'

'Remember Hopetoun needs its chocolate. But I have to ask...what did you mean about those missing girls? What does it have to do with me?'

Miles paused. There was a mischievous turn to his mouth which Nancy didn't like.

'They all think she was involved.'

'Who?'

'Agnes. Your great aunt. They think she murdered them.'

His words were a kick to the face.

'Stay. Let me tell you more. I won't be a moment. Yes, sorry Mr Fossington. How about Monday evening...'

With nothing but *murder* in her ears, Nancy blindly crossed the road and headed home in a daze.

Chapter Three
LEMON AND BONES

2018 – NANCY

Her Great Aunt Agnes a killer? How was that even remotely possible? They all must be mad. Nancy's head roiled as she trudged home along the dark deserted street.

Did the rest of her family know about these rumours? Did her dead gran send her to Hopetoun like a sucker? Her mum would have warned her, wouldn't she? If she knew. Although families were strange things and hers was no exception.

The five-minute walk passed in a blur and before she knew it, Nancy was outside her shop door. Agnes's shop door. She gulped. Did the murders happen right here? What about the ghostly counting girl in her bedroom doorway last night? Was there a connection? What secrets lived inside the walls of this house?

She rummaged inside her bag for her keys and her fingers brushed against a smooth rectangular piece of cardboard. With a frown, she pulled the business card out and went to the kerb to read it under the yellow street light. *Janet Egloff. Optometrist.* How did this get into her bag? With a shrug, she shoved the card back inside and found her keys.

Heading straight upstairs, Nancy switched on the kettle and pulled out her laptop. A search for the 'Sheridan Girls Hopetoun' produced eight pages of results.

Nancy chewed her lip as she clicked into the highest ranking result from The Daily Herald Archive. She held her breath.

No sign of the missing Sheridan Girls – 9 March 1992

It has been three days since the disappearance of Bridget (7) and Molly (5) Sheridan from their home in Hopetoun and there is still no sign of the girls.

'Yet again, we ask the public for any information on the whereabouts of the two little girls,' Detective

Simone Lennart said in a press conference today. 'Their mother and older sister miss them desperately and everyone wants them home safe. Anyone with information should contact Crimestoppers or Triple 0.'

Detective Lennart refused to comment on speculation about the involvement of the girls' father in their disappearance. Neil Sheridan (39) estranged from his family, is currently living in Auckland.

'We are keeping an open mind to all possibilities.'

Nancy leaned back in her kitchen chair. There was no mention of Agnes at all. She rubbed her eyebrow, pushed her glasses back into place and continued into the next article from the Herald Archive.

Missing Sheridan Girls – 'I'd never hurt my girls' Father says – 11 March 1992

Neil Sheridan has denied any involvement with the disappearance of his two daughters, Bridget and Molly Sheridan, after a lengthy interview with the investigating detectives.

In a press conference today after leaving St Kilda Road Police Station, Mr Sheridan said, 'I'm devastated. As soon as I heard the terrible news I came as quickly as I could from Auckland. I haven't slept, I've been out all night looking myself. Someone must know something. If you have any information, please come forward.'

When questioned about a possible custody dispute, Mr Sheridan added, 'My ex-wife and I have had our difficulties. Divorce is bloody hard as anyone who's been through it knows but I would never do anything to hurt my girls. No way.'

There have be no sightings of the two girls since Saturday night. Bridget Sheridan (7) is approximately 120cm tall with long curly brown hair and brown eyes and was last seen wearing a pink tracksuit top with white piping, blue jeans and white sneakers. Molly Sheridan (5) is approximately 110cm tall, missing her two front teeth with shoulder length red hair, brown eyes and freckles and was last seen wearing white pyjamas with a lollipop pattern and a purple terry-towelling dressing gown. Anyone with information should contact Crimestoppers or call Triple 0.

Still nothing about her Aunt. Why had the locals pointed the finger at Agnes? Had she done something to make them suspect her?

Police announce reward for any information on missing Sheridan sisters – 3 April 1992
Today Victoria Police announced a $10,000 reward for any information leading to an arrest in connection with the missing sisters Bridget and Molly Sheridan. The girls aged 7 and 5 were last seen at their home in Hopetoun on Saturday 5 March. Anyone with information should call Crimestoppers or call Triple 0.

Nancy slurped at her tea. It appeared the official story had nothing to do with Agnes. It was time to delve a little deeper. Further down the search results, Nancy found a blog post on the site 'UnsolvedAU – Australia's most comprehensive true crime chronicle.'

The Mystery of the Sheridan Sisters: who covered it up? By Sorrel Nurick
In 1992, I was in Grade 3 and the story of the missing Sheridan girls was our own local bogeyman tale. Their abduction was headline news every night. Their smiling faces stared out from flyers papered all over Melbourne and from every newspaper stand and television screen.
And 20 years later, they have still never been found.
At first everyone suspected the father, in another of

those child custody kidnappings which were all the rage in the '80s and '90s. But the police found nothing to pin on the dad.

There was evidence and rumours of police searching properties in the Hopetoun area, especially the property of a 'well-known but never convicted' child predator but charges were never laid.

After studying all the evidence, I have a theory of my own. The Victoria Police in the '90s was riddled with corruption and connections to organised crime. High ranking Masons operated in positions of power…

Masonic conspiracies? Nancy sighed and rubbed her eyes. At least it wasn't satanic cults or witches. But searches on local properties? Did the police come here to the shop and that's what started the rumours? But why, why here?

Before moving to Hopetoun, Nancy had searched for Agnes Bittesby but she'd only found a physiotherapist in Wellington and a teacher in Fayetteville, somewhere in America. It appeared that the internet didn't hold the answer to everything.

Nancy pushed back her chair and drummed her fingers on the tabletop. People always needed someone to blame, often twisting the facts to frame someone vulnerable, especially a woman on her own. Human nature never changed. Even Nancy knew how it felt to be the scapegoat.

She tried searching Agnes's name again and this time, Nancy clicked ahead to the fifth page of search results. A thumbnail of a photograph from the early 1970s appeared, a group of people on the sandstone steps of a courthouse. An older woman, a smirk on her foxy face, stood in the centre dressed in a tweed suit and pearls, and over her left shoulder, in the background was a familiar face, a young Agnes in a flowing gauzy dress. The caption read 'Lorna Gaskill acquitted.'

Bang!

Nancy jerked up from her laptop. She froze, one ear tilted towards the open door and the dark hallway. All she could hear

45

was the droning whine of the ancient fridge downstairs in the bakery.

She bolted to her feet.

Crash.

A shatter of breaking glass.

Nancy grabbed the stone pestle from the kitchen bench—finally a use for the heavy tool—and headed for the noise.

Half way down the stairs, she stopped. The floorboard under her foot groaned, her palm clammy as she gripped the pestle tighter. What the hell was she doing? Why hadn't she stayed upstairs and called the police? She grimaced. The closest phone was the landline in the bakery kitchen. Her mobile was still inside her bag somewhere upstairs.

She tip-toed down another step.

Clang!

The strike of metal on metal came from the bakery kitchen.

Nancy crept further down the stairs, her heartbeat walloping in her ears.

Thud.

Something hit the wall. She gasped and flinched, imagining the dent in the plaster, and gripped the chunk of stone until her knuckles were white.

She hurried down the last few steps to the ground floor and darted into the bakery kitchen, yanking the push-button phone handset off the wall. With the cord stretched tight, she hid below the counter and hit Triple 0.

'Police, please,' she whispered.

'You are calling from Hopetoun, Melbourne?' the operator asked. '36 Station Street.'

'Yes,' Nancy said cautiously. 'Oh yeah, caller ID. That's right. Someone's breaking into my shop. Bittesby Bread. Right now.'

'Are you safe?' the operator replied. 'Are there any children on the premises?'

A voice yelled from the shopfront behind the swinging door. 'Where are they?'

The intruder was a woman?

46

'Where are they?' the woman screeched. 'There must be more.'

Nancy clutched the pestle in her hand and dropped the handset.

'Where have you hidden them?' This wasn't the voice of a young aggressive junkie, it was throaty and mature, and reminded Nancy of her own mother.

Nancy sucked in a courageous breath and inched through the swinging door into the shop front.

Cold air whistled through the hole in the broken glass door. The roller blind was torn, hanging lopsided and banging in the breeze. Amber streetlight stretched across the room while a dark shape rummaged behind the counter.

Her pestle held up high, Nancy stood to her full height. 'There's no money,' she said calmly.

The woman, apple-shaped and short, lifted her head. Her face still hidden in the dark. 'Where are they?'

'Who?'

'You know. You can't hide them from me!'

'I don't understand.'

'I need them. I need more of them,' she said, her voice more shrill with each demand. 'Get me more.'

The woman turned and the weak yellow light revealed her face. It was Nancy's first customer from yesterday, the bank teller.

'Where are they? Make me more!' the woman shrieked.

Nancy blinked. 'Sorry?'

'The chocolate muffins.' The woman's eyes bulged with desperation. 'More. Bring me more. I need them.'

'I don't have any right now,' Nancy said, maintaining a polite and steady tone. 'But I can bake more. Come back in the morning. I'll have them ready for you. As many as you want.'

'No. Now,' the woman babbled. Her eyes darted every which way, shifting so fast they almost shook inside her head. 'I ate them all. All four. I was going to share them with the others but they kept calling to me. All day. More. More. Then they were gone.' She scraped her hands down her face, digging

47

gouges in her skin with her nails. 'But they didn't shut up. I tried to sleep but I needed more. Bring them to me. Now.'

The woman dragged streaks of blood down her cheeks, and Nancy's breathing rasped.

'There must be more!'

She lunged at Nancy with her bloodied fingers.

Nancy stepped back. She stumbled, falling backwards and clunking her head against the iron leg of a table.

'Ow!' She grabbed the base of her skull and dropped the pestle, the lump of stone landing on her foot before it thumped to the floor. 'Fuck.'

The woman loomed over her. 'Give them to me. Now!'

With one hand clutching her head and a throbbing big toe, Nancy scuttled back and fumbled on the floor until she found her pestle. She wrapped her fingers around the cool stone then hesitated. The woman was clearly having a psychotic episode, it wouldn't be right to hit her.

The woman grabbed hold of Nancy's hair and screamed into her face. 'Hurry. I need them now!'

Nancy tried to push the woman away with her free hand when she was blinded by white torchlight.

'Police,' said a gruff male voice and two sets of heavy boots crunched through the broken glass.

The woman took no notice, her fingers stayed laced through Nancy's hair. 'Make me more.'

'She's in here!' Nancy yelled and dropped the pestle to the floor. She tried to yank away from the woman's grasp, but only managed to tear strands of hair from her scalp.

'Police. Don't move,' said a female officer.

Someone found the light switch and the tubes of fluorescent lighting flickered on above their heads. Two uniformed cops stood by the door, a tall white bald man and a young Asian woman with her hair tied in a sleek bun.

'Blimey,' the male said. His blond bushy eyebrows drooped over his crinkled eyelids. His female partner gave him a dirty look. He cleared his throat and spoke again in a more authoritative voice. 'What's going on here?'

'Police. Good. About time,' the intruder said. 'You make her promise, Officer. Arrest her. Force her.'

'Alright,' the male cop said calmly as he inched forward. 'What's your name, love?'

'I need more. She said there'd be more. But I know she's lying.'

Nancy straightened up her glasses and saw the intruder for the first time clearly in the light. The wrung-out middle-aged woman she'd met on the footpath this morning was gone. Now her cheeks were twitching and streaked with blood while her eyes bulged like boiled eggs. Jekyll and Hyde was just a story, wasn't it?

'Let the lady stand up.' With a subtle move, the policeman—his badge said 'Constable Kurt Brouwer'— positioned himself between Nancy and her intruder. He managed to edge the woman ever so slightly towards the door. 'Move back please. Is there someone we can call? Someone who can come and get you?'

The woman started to sob.

The female officer helped Nancy to her feet, Constable Johanna Trinh according to her badge. 'Are you the occupant?' Trinh said without smiling. 'Are you OK? I can call an ambulance?'

'I'll live,' Nancy replied.

'Do you know her?' Trinh said in a low voice.

'She came into the shop yesterday. But I don't know her name.'

'Come on now, Lorraine,' the bald officer said and took the woman's elbow gently but firmly. 'Let's go get your hands bandaged-up.'

'She's probably off her medication,' Nancy whispered to Trinh as Lorraine muttered and wept.

'We'll get her looked at.'

'Thank you,' Nancy said.

Trinh jotted down Nancy's details in her small notebook and handed over a business card. 'Please come down to the station tomorrow and make a statement.'

'I don't want to make a fuss. But I guess I'll need a report for the insurance. Is Sunday OK?'

'Sooner is better.'

Nancy nodded. Trinh joined Brouwer and the two officers pushed Lorraine through the front door towards the police car at the kerb.

'Give me more! Bring me more,' Lorraine screeched as they guided her down the footpath.

Inside the shop, Nancy rubbed the back of her neck as she stared at the mess, although it was nothing a glazier and a broom couldn't solve. The white faced clock on the wall said it was five to one. She sighed. Even once she'd cleaned all this up, her head would be too full of murder, burglars and ghosts to sleep tonight. She tapped the policewoman's business card against her bottom lip. There was one little mystery she might be able to solve tonight.

'Constable Trinh? Before you go,' she called out of the broken window. 'Can I ask you about something? Inside?'

'One moment,' she called over her shoulder as they helped Lorraine into the back seat.

First Jackie and now Lorraine. Coincidence? Or was something attracting troubled women to her shop?

Trinh poked back through the broken door. 'What can I help with?'

'It's probably nothing. It's outside.'

Trinh's face remained passive. 'Is it urgent? We have to deal with Lorraine first. I can't leave my partner alone.'

'Are you a local? Did you grow up around here?' Nancy asked.

'Footscray girl,' the policewoman replied. 'Is that relevant?'

Nancy swallowed. Close enough.

'I found a stray dog out in the backyard. Digging around,' she blurted. 'It looked like bones under the dirt.'

'Any reason to think they might be suspicious?'

Either she was a good actor or Trinh knew nothing about Agnes and the rumours. Would her middle-aged partner at the car have come to a different conclusion?

50

Nancy shrugged. 'I just moved in.'

The bald cop yelled from the car at the kerb. 'Trinh. Come on. Let's go.'

She waved in reply then turned back to Nancy. 'This house is fairly old. And I've heard there were cattle sale yards and abattoirs all around here back in the day. We'll come by tomorrow and take a look.'

'It's probably nothing like you say,' Nancy forced a chuckle. 'Sometimes you have some weird thoughts in the dark.'

'Are you sure you don't want a doctor?'

'I'll be fine.'

'Goodnight, Miss Grakowski.' Trinh walked away and Nancy crept up beside the broken door to watch them leave.

Her partner was standing on the nature strip, looking up at the house. 'What did she want?' he said as Trinh came down the path towards the patrol car.

'Nothing. What are you looking at?'

'I never thought I'd be back here again. The witch house.'

Nancy's mouth fell open.

'What?' Trinh scoffed.

'The Sheridan girls? Surely you remember that. We tried our damnedest but we could never pin it on the old woman. She looks exactly like her. I couldn't believe my eyes when we first walked in.' He shuddered. 'Let's get out of here.'

This time, Trinh paused and turned back. As Nancy ducked into the shadows out of sight, Trinh began to sing to herself. Like the school girls in the street a few days earlier. 'Chew. Chew. Where are you? Bones, teeth. Sister stew.'

The young cop climbed into the patrol car and they drove away.

Three hours later, a sheet of plywood covered the broken shop window and all the glass had been swept away. Nancy had finished her workaday breads and was sliding them into the hot oven. But as she cleaned and kneaded, her head churned.

51

Agnes. Child-killer. Witch house. Ridiculous. Had someone put acid in the Hopetoun water supply?

It was Saturday—Autumn Festival day—and Nancy reached for Agnes's book. This was her chance to prove them all wrong. The Bittesby Bakery was under new management and defamatory rumours were no longer allowed.

The book instantly opened to the right page; a recipe for Imp Breads. Autumnal and spiced with ginger and cinnamon, the biscuits were perfect for the Festival, especially for children. Nancy ran her finger down the handwritten ingredients list, ticking each item off one by one until she reached lemon zest. Nancy tsked. She didn't stock lemons in the pantry, or upstairs in her own kitchen and the ancient tree in the backyard looked dead.

Where would she find lemons at four o'clock in the morning? She screwed up her face, weighing up all the possible substitutions, until she saw a tiny asterisk and a footnote in pencil. *Preferably Meyer lemons. Best lemons at 34 Birch Street.*

She grimaced again. Like any normal person, the people at 34 Birch Street would be asleep now. But Agnes's recipe needed lemons. She couldn't just turn up at the house and steal them. Could she? A grin started to spread across her face. Could she? It wouldn't hurt to go for a walk and look? Lemon trees were common in Hopetoun, there had to be at least one fruiting lemon tree leaning over a fence somewhere.

String bag in hand, Nancy headed out into the night. At four in the morning, the Hopetoun nightlife consisted of a possum leaping from fence to tree, a lone taxi cruising down Salisbury Street and a wobbly possibly drunk cyclist humming to himself.

Night walks were one of Nancy's favourite things. Unlike other sensible women, she found traipsing around the empty dark streets calming. Tonight was no exception. The quiet felt right and she breathed it in deeply. She crossed Salisbury Street and passed Freshworx, the overpriced mini-supermarket with pictures of juicy fresh fruit and plump vegetables on the windows, the type you'd never find inside on the shelves.

Victorian-era sandstone warehouses lined the western side of the train tracks, and on the hill, streets of narrow one-storey worker's cottages. Hopetoun's industrial past was long gone, businesses and factories finding cheaper land elsewhere, replaced by advertising agencies and architecturally designed apartments. Luckily, there were just enough tumbledown renovator's delights and colourful residents left to spoil a total gentrification.

A dog's bark echoed through the streets as Nancy turned the corner into Birch Street. Cars were packed in, bumper to bumper, on both sides of the cramped road. High heels clomped on concrete behind her and Nancy scampered to hide under an overgrown wattle tree. From her hidey-hole, she watched a woman teeter on stilettos down the centre of the road, her house keys jangling from her hand. When she heard the slam of a front door, Nancy came back out to continue her search.

Like all the other houses in the street, the freestanding weatherboard Number 34 was dark. Surrounded by knee-high sun-bleached weeds, the roof on the front verandah sagged like a frown. A faded and peeling For Sale sign was nailed to the fence, next to a letterbox overflowing with junk mail. And worst of all, there was no sign of a lemon tree.

Nancy sighed then looked closer. The front left window was nailed-up with chipboard, like her own shop. Surely, the house was vacant.

Edging the gate open, she crept down the footpath. She skirted around the left side of the house to find a six-foot wooden fence blocking the path to the backyard. She stretched up on tip-toes and peered over the fence into a wild grassy backyard, and just beyond the Hills Hoist, she spied the famous lemon tree, heaving with ripe fruit.

As she let go of her grip, the rickety fence swayed. She searched up and down for a way through but the fence was solid; the gate must be on the other side of the house.

She couldn't turn away now. If the recipe was going to be a success she had to make it exactly as Agnes instructed. The lemons called to her, tugging at her heart and head. A lullaby, a yearning, a deliciously soft caress. All her problems and questions dissolved. The lemons on the tree became her whole world.

She grabbed hold of the flimsy fence again, and a few steps further down, a loose paling rattled. She slid the loose plank like a windscreen wiper, opening up a gap in the fence. The yellow lemons glowed in the distance and she licked her lips. But was the gap wide enough?

Sucking in her stomach, Nancy forced herself through the hole. She tripped on the horizontal paling at her feet and tumbled towards the concrete like a sack of potatoes, rolling her ankle and losing her glasses from her nose.

She cursed and rubbed her ankle, then something scurried inside the house alongside her. She froze, listening closely but the thump of her blood was too loud. Rats, had to be rats. An empty house like this would be riddled with the little bastards. Convincing herself, she picked up her glasses and made a dash for the tree.

The branches were straining with fist-sized lemons. Nancy loaded five into her string bag without even making a dent in the crop. With her bag full, she turned to the other side of the house to look for the gate, not wanting to tempt fate with a second squeeze through the derelict fence.

As she turned, she flinched. The gate was open and someone was standing there, watching her, blocking her only way out. Reality slapped her across the face. Seriously? What was she doing here? Raiding a lemon tree in the middle of the night? She gulped and prepared herself to hand over her stolen goods. Then the wave of longing swept over her again and she hid the bag behind her back.

'You!' the silhouette yelled. It was Jackie, the woman from the park, in a stained t-shirt and bare legs. 'Why are you here?'

Nancy put her hands in the air, the bag of lemons swinging from her elbow.

'Who sent you?' Jackie roared. 'It was her, wasn't it? She sent you.'

'No one...' Nancy lied and fumbled in her coat pockets for money. 'I-I-I needed some lemons.'

Once again, Jackie's face was blurred by a cloud. Nancy squinted. How many times had this happened to her now? It must be a trick of the light. Or a brain tumour.

Jackie inched forward. 'It's so thin,' she whispered as she clutched fistfuls of air. 'I can almost remember.'

'I'm sorry.' Nancy pressed her hand against her breast bone. 'I'll pay for them. I forgot my purse but I'll come back tomorrow.'

'I can't. I almost can. But I can't.' Jackie grabbed at her temples. 'She's there. She's stopping it. Why won't she let me go?'

'I'll leave the lemons,' Nancy lowered her voice, suddenly remembering the neighbours. She didn't want to encounter the police twice in one night.

'It wasn't my fault, was it?' Jackie's eyes were as wide as full moons. Her anger now replaced with a pure frightened innocence.

'No, it wasn't,' Nancy cooed but she had no idea what Jackie was talking about.

Jackie huffed and turned on her heel. She padded away on bare feet through the gate and disappeared out of sight, leaving Nancy alone in the back garden with her swag of lemons.

Her whole body slumped. Tomorrow, she'd come back with cash for the lemons and a hamper of bread and goodies.

Bread? She'd forgotten all about her bread in the oven at the bakery. She made a dash for the gate and launched into an awkward shuffling run down Birch Street, dodging overhanging branches and wheelie-bins until she came to a skidding stop. In her haste, she'd blindly run the wrong way.

Birch Street was a no-through road. The end of the street narrowed to a footpath and then a wooden staircase up to an overpass above the train lines. She had no idea where the path led and time was ticking away. There was probably smoke billowing from her kitchen right now, the oven filled with trays of blackened bread.

Footsteps crunched on the gravel by the train tracks and Nancy pulled her bag of lemons tightly against her chest. A figure in a hoodie appeared under the underpass, walking backwards and dragging something heavy. It looked like a sack, leaving a thin trail on the ground behind it, a white stripe which gleamed under the floodlights. Was it sand? Or sugar? Or drugs?

From the shadows, Nancy watched intently until the figure stopped and lifted their head in her direction. Suppressing a gasp, she darted back onto Birch Street and hurried in the direction of home. The right way this time.

Power-walking down the empty Salisbury Street and around the corner, her mind whirled with riddles and unanswered questions. Her belly quivered as she glimpsed her shop in the distance, imagining the burnt bread inside. Until she saw a big black shape loitering outside her door.

'What now?' she muttered, clenching her fists. But nearing the door, her shoulders softened. She recognised the black shaggy shape.

The dog trotted over to meet her, nudging her gently with its wet nose.

'You again?' she chuckled, patting its wiry head. 'What do you want, Wolfie?'

The giant dog jogged alongside her until they reached the shop door. Nancy sniffed the air for smoke, but unwashed dog was all she could smell.

'Time for you to go home, Wolfie,' she said as she pulled out her keys.

With a forlorn whimper, it looked up at her. She rubbed her hands through its thick fur until she found a medallion around its neck. The initial 'J.E' and a mobile number engraved on it.

'It's too early to call your owners now. Come on,' she said begrudgingly and entered the backyard from the side alleyway. 'Maybe you can keep the burglars away. Or the mad chocolate women.'

The dog darted inside the gate and made a bee-line for the back door, then it stopped and circled three times before curling up on the threadbare doormat. Nancy smiled as she squeezed past it and inside the door. Not everyone was frightened of Agnes's house.

She strode into the lit-up bakery kitchen where the recipe book sat waiting for her. With the lemons in her bag, she had everything she needed to bake the Imp Breads.

'I'm here,' she said aloud but she didn't quite know why, and then she got to work.

Chapter Four
HALF-TRUTHS

1972 – AGNES

A breath snagged in Agnes's throat. David was teetering on dangerous ground.

The crowd of long haired poets, innocent-eyed waifs and tie-wearing accountants sat open-mouthed. All crammed together on cushions and chairs in the lounge room of the sandstone farmhouse.

'I disagree,' said David, a bookish, scrappy-bearded man. 'The world is out of balance, of course, but we're better than that.'

From her cushion at the back beside the towering bookshelves, Agnes shuddered. The daily after-lunch debates used to be open lively affairs where opposing ideas were exchanged with good cheer. However, something had changed, and every day Lorna's glare and her grip on the group grew colder. Despite the bright sunshine outside, the darkness of winter was approaching.

David wagged a finger. 'We can't battle the evil in the world with more evil.'

'Evil?' Lorna raised an eyebrow and the temperature in the room plummeted. Small and dumpy, Lorna sat perched on a plush cushion in the centre of it all. In tweed and pearls, her dull brown hair shot with grey, she looked more like a country housewife than the 'salacious sorceress' portrayed in the Sydney papers. 'Who are you calling evil, David?'

'I didn't. If you'll let me…'

Agnes stared down at the Persian rug, her brown bobbed hair shielding her face. Why wouldn't David stay quiet?

'David, don't be naive,' Walter scoffed, his voice hardened by a Germanic accent. Tall and blond, and skilled at speaking with the dead, they called Walter the Alsatian behind his back. Agnes's pelvic sacral chakra fluttered whenever their eyes met and their gaze locked for a few seconds too long, but outside the orgies, Lorna's much younger husband was definitely off-limits. 'You think the world is good? Have you been living under a rock?'

Lorna took a drag from her cigarillo and nodded at her husband. 'Your mind is closed, David. Bricked up like the walls of a prison.'

'Not at all,' David said while he tugged at his shirt collar.

Lorna narrowed her beady eyes. 'You know better than me, do you, David?'

'I only wanted...'

Agnes wrung her hands. David had been living at the farmhouse for months, although not quite as long as Agnes, and he'd been present at the incident with Marjory. And Peter. He knows exactly what they are capable of. Did he really think they would let him win?

'Have you lived as long as I have?' Lorna continued. 'Have you seen anything beyond your suburban street and your books? Have you experienced everything the world has to offer? Hmm? What is our first principle, David?'

'Curiosity,' he choked.

'Good boy. Curiosity. We have a unique opportunity here. This land is rich with ancient wisdom yet free from the debris of European history. We have a chance to make something new. To take all that has been written, thousands of years of thought and rumination, and distil it into our own ways. A better way. A stronger way. We are impartial. We are curious. We are open.'

'Exactly, but what Walter is proposing— '

Lorna shook her head. 'David. You and your little ego. I've warned you before. If you can't open your mind to the possibilities—beyond the black and white simple-mindedness of good and evil—you'll have to leave us. You obviously don't have the intellect to understand what we're doing here. The grey is where the insight is.'

'I mean no disrespect.' His hand grabbed for his Adam's apple. 'I wanted to—'

Agnes bit down on the inside of her cheek, she flooded

David with telepathic messages, pleading with him to back down and apologise. In all truth, she didn't care much for the skinny know-it-all man but no one deserved Lorna's wrath.

'Lies, David. Every time you open your mouth, lies. You think you can fool me. I can smell your ambition from here. Oh, David, such mediocrity. Another white man desperate to take over. Desperate to shower us with your wisdom.'

'Jealousy,' Walter said with a curt nod.

Agnes picked at a loose thread on her sleeve. The only jealousy she'd encountered had come from the person in the centre of the room, smoking. While Lorna was always encouraging, in recent weeks there'd been a poisonous undercurrent behind her words. Especially whenever Agnes mentioned her books.

'You see me here in the centre and want to be me.' Lorna waved her small hand around the room. 'You want all our friends to look up to you. You talk of goodness and purity but in reality, you crave power. Grubby dirty power. You disappoint me, David. I had high hopes for you. But you're just like the rest of the sheep out there. Walter, escort David out.'

'But...' David's eyes widened.

'With pleasure, my love.' Walter stretched to his full height and grasped David by the shoulder.

'Lorna. I-I-I.' David yanked his shoulder but Walter's grip stayed firm.

Agnes lurched forward, stopping herself just before her lips opened to protest.

Lorna held up her hand. Cigarillo smoke coiled up into the high ceiling. 'No more, David.'

'Please, Lorna. Forgive me. I didn't mean to. Please don't.'

With her left hand, Lorna twirled her fingers in an elaborate dance. The fluttering of her hand ended with a direct point of her index finger at David. He collapsed into Walter's waiting arms.

The room turned into a statue garden as Walter dragged the unconscious David out of the room. Dread swirled around the room, merging with the expelled breaths and cigarette smoke, coating their clothes and skin.

Sitting quietly with the others, Agnes squinched at Lorna. Did her fingers hold real power? Or was it the sleight of hand tricks of a sideshow charlatan? As soon as the thought flitted through her mind, Lorna's eyes met hers and a cold draft whistled across her shoulders. Instantly Agnes collected her defences and shielded herself with a circle of white impenetrable light.

Before she met Lorna, Agnes had never kept a thought to herself. Every ripple in her mind flowed out into the world through her mouth. She was artistic and convinced herself this was all part of the territory. But in her lonely moments of truthfulness, she knew it wasn't just the simple desire to be heard and acknowledged, it came from a stranger deeper place. As long as Agnes could remember, her days had been peppered with vivid dreams, imaginary friends and bizarre coincidences. Mrs Hoolihan from down the road said she was touched by the fey. Her sister Pamela called her mad. Uptight bitch.

'Anyone else agree with David? Anyone?' Lorna pointed at a long-haired boy with doe eyes and buck teeth. 'You?

The pretty boy, one of Lorna's pets, shook his head with a coquettish smile.

'If you disagree with Walter and myself feel free to leave. In fact, I encourage it.' Lorna scoured the room, her glare like dark ice. 'Your negativity only infects the rest of us. And I will not stand for it.'

Lorna was right about infection but David was not the cause. Like love, fear changed a person and Agnes was sick of being scared.

'Friends,' Lorna said, the syrup returning to her voice. Agnes noted that Lorna never said 'disciple' in front of the others. 'Don't let David's disloyalty affect you. Let it be a reminder. We must all be vigilant and watch out for those who don't belong. Those who wish to tear us down. We, my friends, we all must remain strong and true to our principles.'

Her onlooking devotees, the painters, lawyers and society wives, all nodded and murmured in agreement. Was Agnes the

61

only one who felt the menace?

Lorna carried on. 'Let's move onto the next reading. Roger. I'm sure you have something fascinating and well-considered for us.'

Roger flushed red as he cleared his throat and began to speak. Agnes took the opportunity to scramble up from her cushion and skulk away, as best she could in platform sandals. Once she stepped through the door, she exhaled and her belly softened. Until a hand firmly gripped her upper arm.

'Leaving so soon?' Walter asked.

Agnes dragged her gaze away from his golden-flecked blue eyes. 'I need a little air. I have a terrible headache.'

Walter scrutinised her. 'Don't let David's dissent upset you.'

'I know,' she sighed, her fingers gracing her temples. 'Sometimes the energy overwhelms me.'

'I'll ask Lorna to speak to you later. You need to prepare your defences better. You, of all people, must protect your gift.'

'And it's not just David. I received some bad news today.'

'We know,' Walter said.

The envelope had already been torn open, and presumably read, when Agnes received it at breakfast this morning.

'But there is a silver lining,' he went on. 'Your windfall will be put to good use here at the farmhouse. You should reply today and organise for the money to be sent here as soon as possible.'

Agnes nodded in reply and he let go of her arm slowly.

Without looking back, she clomped across the corridor through the door onto the wide shady verandah until Roger's voice was a murmur in the distance. She ignored the view of the sun-bleached paddocks and found a love seat in a dark far corner and pulled out the letter secured inside her bra.

The letter was from Lewis and DeHavilland from Mountsorrel, a firm of solicitors in England, and for the fourth time today, Agnes ran her fingers over the thick paper and embossed letterhead. Handwritten and crossed-out forwarding addresses covered the envelope, but somehow the letter had

62

finally found her here in Braidwood. Mr Wraxall had written to notify Agnes of an inheritance from her great aunt, a gift of £2,000. She smiled as she folded the letter.

Suddenly, Agnes was a woman with options.

2018 – NANCY

The last batch of gingerbread Imps went into Nancy's oven at half past six. The squat golden figures beamed up at her with their raisin smiles as she slid the trays inside.

Her oven full, Nancy trudged upstairs to splash water on her face.

'Look at you,' she said to the bathroom mirror, tapping the purple bags under her eyes and slapping her double chins with the back of her hand. She put on a clean black tunic, brushed her unruly hair and coiled it up on top of her head.

With a second glance in the mirror and a defeated shrug, she slapped on some lipstick and headed back downstairs.

The chocolate muffins were cooling on the racks and before she could stop herself, she grabbed one and popped it in her mouth. With the lemons fiasco, she'd been running late when she started on the *Chocolate Fou,* and after her sleepless night, she'd lost count of the number of stirs. The warm muffin crumbled in her mouth. It was good. It was great. But not as groan-inducing as yesterday's batch. Nancy shook it off. On Monday morning, she'd follow the instructions to the letter. For the Imps she'd been truer to the recipe, even using a black handled knife and a red cloth, finding a stash of bright red tea towels in the back corner of the pantry.

The scent of the baking Imps wafted out from the kitchen into the shop front, ginger and cinnamon with a hint of stolen lemon. Nancy switched on the chrome coffee machine, opened the chipboard-covered front door and went out onto the footpath to finish her *Chocolate Fou.*

The spiked steeple of St. Bart's was silhouetted in the distance as the first tendrils of daylight stretched over the hill. The moment didn't last long, Nancy's peace was rudely interrupted by thoughts of Agnes and the Sheridan girls.

'All ready for the big day?' said a voice. It was Danny, the man from the Green in his khaki Council uniform.

Nancy's stomach dropped. Why was he here? He must know about her midnight visit to Jackie. She braced herself for another reprimand.

'We didn't get a chance to meet properly yesterday. I'm Danny,' he said, this time with a wide white grin. He reached out a calloused hand.

She wiped the muffin crumbs away and shook his hand like a wet rag. 'Nancy,' she mumbled. Why was he so friendly all of a sudden?

Danny produced a reusable coffee cup from his backpack. 'Your coffee machine on?'

'Absolutely.' she said. He nodded as he handed over a blue and green plastic cup and followed her inside the shop. 'What can I get you?'

'Macchiato.' He leaned leisurely over the counter as Nancy took the helm behind the espresso machine.

'Sugar?'

'Nah, I keep away from the stuff.'

Nancy glanced down to grind the beans but his gaze never left her face, she could feel the heat of his dark-eyed stare. She wished she could duck under the counter and hide.

'You're a new arrival, right? What made you decide to move to Hopetoun? Aside from this place.'

'Nothing in particular,' she said.

'There must be something else. Let me guess. Divorce?'

'Not quite.'

Why was everyone so interested in her background? City people weren't usually so nosy.

'Redundancy?'

Plumes of steam rose into the air as Nancy frothed the milk and half-shrugged.

'What kind of work did you do?'

'Insurance.'

He chuckled and patted his uniformed chest. 'Corporate law.'

'Really?' Nancy baulked. 'You were a suit?'

'Escaped with my sanity. Just. But only after they sucked my spirit dry for ten long years.'

Nancy tapped the jug against the counter three times before

pouring out a dash of hot milk.

'I finally listened to what's in here.' He tapped his chest again. 'Now I couldn't be happier. I'm back to my roots, so to speak. Well, as much as I can.'

Inspecting his face closely, she made a guess at his heritage but she wasn't sure how to ask without causing offence.

Nancy cleared her throat, she'd had enough of the spotlight. 'You left the corporate world to join the Council? And the Traders Association?'

'Nah, I only look after the Green. I'm not one of the them. Thank God.' He shuddered and then grimaced. 'Interesting bunch of people.'

'What do you mean?' She tilted her head as she handed him his coffee.

He stiffened, then drifted away and seemed to leave the room entirely. After a moment he blinked, took his cup from her hand and abruptly changed the subject.

'So you're Agnes's niece, right?'

'Great niece.'

'Hmm.'

'You know her?'

'Only by reputation. There was a bit of trouble here, eh?'

'The glazier couldn't come until later this morning.'

He looked back blankly, then nodded when he noticed the chipboard. 'I meant before. Yonks ago when Agnes was here. What happened to the door? Someone break in?'

'Kind of. A woman having a funny turn. Harmless really. The police came and took her off to hospital.'

'It wasn't Jackie, was it?' His voice quickly turned serious.

Nancy swallowed hard, then shook her head. 'How well do you know Jackie?'

He shrugged. 'How well do we know anyone? Even ourselves. *A lie which half the truth is ever the blackest of lies.*'

Poetry at six o'clock on a Saturday morning? Who *was* this guy?

'Look, about yesterday,' he continued. 'Maybe we got off on the wrong foot. When I found out who you were it all made sense. The bakery reopening probably brought back all kinds of bad memories for Jackie. What do they call it these days? Triggering?'

Triggering? What *was* the connection between Jackie and Agnes? And if Nancy had triggered something in Jackie, appearing in her backyard in the middle of the night must have completely terrified her.

'Tell me. What happened back then?'

The oven timer in the kitchen buzzed and Nancy jumped.

'Wait one second.' She turned and rushed for the swinging door into the kitchen.

'I've got to go,' he said. 'I'll see you down at the Green later. Yeah?'

Half-way through the door, she stopped. He couldn't leave now, she needed to know more about Jackie and Agnes but the gingerbread came first. Before she could call out again to stop him, Danny was gone.

Throwing her hands up in the air, she hurried for the oven and opened the door. Rows of little golden faces with raisin smiles looked up at her. For a moment, she forgot Agnes and grinned back. She couldn't wait to hand the Imps out to the local kids.

With the gingerbread Imps lined up and cooling, Nancy went back into the shop. What had Danny meant about the Traders Association? Every conversation seemed to produce five more questions.

A stack of coins and a scrap of paper lay on the counter, '*half truths*' written on the back in blue biro.

Nancy stared at the word, then crushed the paper into a ball and tossed it in the bin.

Half-Truth Hopetoun.

Enough already. It was time for answers.

Her sleepless night called for something stronger than Irish Breakfast. With a triple espresso humming in her veins, the wire racks were now stocked with crusty bread, the glass cabinet filled with *Chocolate Fou* and sticky-iced scrolls. With everything in place, Nancy headed outside.

Saturday had broken into a vibrantly blue-skied autumn day. A gentle breeze fluttered the orange bunting on the telephone poles and trees, and set adrift the first yellow leaves of autumn.

Squatting down on the footpath, Nancy took the coloured chalk she'd found with the red tea-towels down the back of the cupboard, and drew hopscotch squares and arrows pointing towards the shop. She sketched out gingerbread men and wrote *'you can't catch me'*, *'free for kids'* and *'Autumn Festival special'* on the concrete.

By eight o'clock, the children started coming.

'Mummy. Mummy. Look,' said a little boy no more than four. His face painted with orange and black stripes like a tiger, he sprinted for the shop with a greedy grin.

His mother glanced up from her phone a moment too late and shrieked, 'No! Davin! No!'

She dashed after him and scooped him up in her arms, pulling him close to her chest. The boy screeched and Nancy stood by, saying nothing as snot and tears dribbled down the pre-schooler's face, washing away his tiger whiskers.

'I said. No.'

The mother marched away with the writhing boy in her arms. His screams echoed all the way down Station Street, even the bells of the boom gate and the metallic squeal of an approaching train couldn't drown him out.

Yesterday, the boy's mother's reaction would have baffled Nancy, but today she understood why.

Luckily, not everyone was frightened. As the hours passed, the footpath grew busier with prams, children and yappy dogs on leashes, and Nancy stood by her shop door, placing a golden Imp into every outstretched little hand.

'Say *thank you*,' reminded the parents, as the kids immediately crunched into the gingerbread arms, legs and heads.

'Thank you,' they muttered through crumb-filled mouths.

Nancy's smile came freely today, despite her eventful night

and the worries squirming around in her head, she chatted effortlessly with her customers, churning out lattes and cappuccinos, and packing bags of rolls and sliced bread. Today was the day she finally enticed some familiar faces inside, people she'd watched walk right by her shop every day. Yet each time she convinced herself that this was a new beginning and that the rumours about Agnes were old news, the next person sneered in her face, spat on the footpath or stomped straight past her with their nose in the air.

The crowds were dwindling by two o'clock, just a few cheeky teenagers came through the door to collect their free gingerbread men. At two-thirty, Nancy wiped the chalk signs off the footpath and hid away the remaining Imps for Jackie.

Her phone had been vibrating in her pocket all day but she'd been too busy to check her messages. Until now.

She gasped. There were four missed calls, all from Willowmere Residential Home.

'Nancy Grakowski returning your call,' she said in a fluster. 'Is she alright?'

'Finally,' the care home receptionist sighed like a disappointed parent. 'She's calm now but your great-aunt was extremely agitated today. Unusually so.'

'What happened?'

'Can you come to visit her?'

Nancy clenched her jaw. 'Now?'

Ordinarily Sundays were reserved for visiting Agnes. Grant used to call her rigid and uptight, teasing her about her huffs when her plans got disrupted. But she already had the rest of the day laid out—first she'd close the shop, then head down to the Festival hub at the Green to search for answers. Someone must know what actually happened to Agnes. In her later years Agnes had apparently become a recluse, but before her illness took over she must have been friendly with someone in Hopetoun. Unravel some lies, apologise to Jackie and squeeze in a nap—Saturday was all booked up. Until now.

'The nurse tells me she's resting at the moment. She had quite a disturbed night.'

'Join the club,' Nancy muttered.

'Later this afternoon would be better.'

'I'll be there about five o'clock.'

With a loud exhale, Nancy puffed out her cheeks and shoved her phone into her tunic pockets. Her nap would have to wait. She flipped the shop sign to 'Closed', ran a cursory brush through her hair and refreshed her lipstick before heading out the back door.

The screen door squealed open and the dog scrambled to its feet, long claws scraping on the concrete.

'Whoops,' she said with a wince as it licked her hand with a rough wet tongue. 'I forgot all about you. Poor thing.'

She searched through its fur for its identity tag and dialled the number. The call went to voicemail. 'Hello, my name is Nancy and I've found your dog. Please give me a call.' She turned back to her new friend. 'Sorry, Wolfie. It looks like you're stuck with me for a few more hours. Come for a walk?'

The long-legged dog trotted beside her along the path to the side fence, passing the holes in the dirt.

'They *are* your bones, aren't they, Wolfie?' He looked up at her with soft brown eyes but said nothing, of course. Nancy exhaled loudly. 'You're supposed to convince me.'

She opened the side gate but the dog sat back down, inside the fence like a sentinel.

'Suit yourself.'

She stepped out into the alley and headed for the Green, where she hoped she'd finally find some answers.

2018 – MELODY

Melody Magee was bored. Was she high when she agreed to pick up cigarette butts along the railway tracks on a Saturday morning? She kicked at the gravel with her toe and sighed dramatically but her mum was too busy filling garbage bags to notice.

Her mum owed her big time. Melody thought at least Tino would be here. Weren't his aunty and his gran supposed to be big in this Hopetoun community stuff? She'd overheard her mum saying they were part of the Five. Whatever that meant. The Clean-up was supposed to be the perfect chance for Melody to flirt with Tino. The first step in her plan to get him away from Prudence Chan. But Tino and his dimples were nowhere to be seen, and Melody was left alone wearing pink washing-up gloves with a bunch of boring oldies.

And if picking up chip packets and dog turd bags wasn't bad enough, now her phone battery was dead. Her tummy growled. Her mum owed her a pizza after all this and she hoped her brother hadn't scoffed all those chocolate muffins.

'You said it was only going to be for a few hours,' Melody said.

'Just another half an hour, Mel. There's so much to do.'

'You said that an hour ago. I'm cold.'

'Go over there. That blackberry bush. I can see a bunch of kebab wrappers and beer cans. Make yourself useful. Here. Take the tongs.'

Melody slumped and reluctantly took the rusty barbecue tongs. She trudged over to the nearby blackberry bush decorated with garbage like a Christmas tree.

'Train,' yelled the man with the embarrassing red knitted hat and the whole group stepped clear from the train line. Melody had to admit, it was kind of awesome to be standing so close to moving trains.

One small step forward and she'd be squished into oblivion onto the tracks. How much would a speeding hunk of metal smashing into your body hurt? Would you die instantly? Feel nothing and disappear into a pool of numbing blackness? Or would there be a moment of fierce all-consuming pain? A pain so intense you'd beg for death to come and take you.

For a split second, Melody teetered on her tip-toes as the Craigieburn line train hurtled towards her. It would be so easy, just lean a little bit further forward. But then the slipstream of the train blew her hair into her eyes and she jumped back. She couldn't die a virgin.

Once the train passed, the clean-up work started again and Melody noticed something pink stuck deep inside the straggly blackberry bush. She shoved aside the prickles and pulled out a small pink dirty sandal. Why were little kids always losing their shoes? Melody dumped the sandal into her garbage bag and took another step forward. This time her foot slipped and she rolled her ankle in a hole. She yelped but none of the others looked up.

Swearing under her breath, she looked closer. It was some type of animal burrow. Didn't the government poison rabbits like blackberry bushes? She kicked the hole with her boot and under the dirt, she glimpsed something white. It must be a chicken carcass. Some lazy bastard had tossed their leftovers from the chicken shop over the fence.

Melody squatted down, and wary of the prickles, stretched out and grabbed hold of the bone with her tongs. She pulled but the carcass stayed wedged in the ground. She tugged harder, and this time the bone came free but she sent herself tumbling backwards.

'Bastard,' she spat as she landed in the gravel.

Her mum rushed over. 'Are you alright, Mel? I told you...' Her mum gasped and covered her mouth with her leather gardening glove. 'What?'

Melody grumbled. She hated it when her mum called her Mel. Then she saw what her mum saw, and let go of the tongs with a squeal.

It wasn't from a roast chicken. It was way too big.

She'd been studying anatomy this semester.

It was a leg bone.

A human leg bone.

2018 – NANCY

Nancy strode into the Green. The footpaths were flanked with canvas market stalls and caravans, selling artisanal cheeses, handmade toys and wood-turned bowls. The sweet voice of a folk singer drifted from the stage. Above the grey-haired singer's head, the 'Hopetoun Autumn Festival' banner flapped angrily against the poles while slate-grey clouds rolled in from the south. The wind shifted and strengthened, carrying the aroma of roasting chestnuts, scented candles and grilling onions. Nancy shivered and pulled up her collar.

The only thing missing at the Festival was people.

A heavy cloud of embarrassment hung over the Green as Nancy counted three women, and one greyhound, browsing the stalls. It was a party where no-one had turned up.

Cringing, Nancy considered turning back home until a photograph on a stall caught her eye. A black and white snap of Station Street from the 1920s. The round-bellied stall-holder didn't even look up from his phone when she picked up the picture. The bakery was there, neat and tidy as a child on school photo day. The image was almost a hundred years old, taken long before even Agnes's time. Then again, when did Agnes first arrive in Hopetoun? And what compelled her to come to Melbourne in the first place? There was so much Nancy didn't know.

'Nancy!' Stella called and waved, and Nancy shivered again as Stella marched towards her.

The smudge reappeared in Nancy's vision, a snake-shaped cloud wrapping itself around Stella's long neck. Not again. She'd had eye floaters before but never this bad. Perhaps it was cataracts. Although to be fair, Nancy hadn't slept properly in days. She added a trip to the doctor to her list of chores.

'A little bird tells me your gingerbread men were quite the hit,' Stella said.

Nancy shrugged modestly. 'The kiddies seem to like them.'

Stella sighed. 'Unfortunately your good luck didn't extend down here.'

Behind them, the photography stall-holder yawned loudly.

Nancy offered a fake smile. 'Maybe they'll come later?'

'We had a few busy periods this morning. But no, I think this is it.' Stella puffed out her lips and exhaled. 'Even the corn growing competition was a flop. Three years ago, we had over twenty houses joining in. Today we had two entries. Two! We gave out free seeds and everything! And the Clean-Up groups aren't back yet. They're still out there, clearing out all the rubbish from the cemetery and along the train tracks. No one cares any more.'

'We're off, Stella. No point hanging around,' interrupted a woman in a long black apron with a bulgy potato-shaped nose. 'I've lost enough money already. You should refund the site fees. Either way, we won't be back next year.'

The woman trudged away and Stella scrubbed her forehead with her hand. 'It's a disaster. When I was a kid, Hopetoun was a really strong community. People looked out for each other, especially in bad times. Now all I see is strange faces.'

Nancy fidgeted with her coat buttons.

'I didn't mean you!' Stella grabbed her arm with a pained smile. With her sharp cheekbones and widened dark eyes, Stella's face was almost a grinning skeleton. 'You're practically one of us now.'

Behind her shoulder, Nancy glimpsed Stella's mother in the distance, standing at a lit brazier. Nancy's vision clouded again, a blot sitting on Mafalda's back like a piggybacked child.

Stella followed Nancy's gaze and turned. 'The Festival used to have a huge bonfire each year. But now, with Health and Safety and all the regulations, you need the fire brigade on stand-by and fifty million permits. It's not worth it. I used to love the sound of the flames roaring.'

'Was Agnes ever part of the Festival?'

Stella blinked. 'I wouldn't know.'

'But your mother would?'

She nodded. 'They were very close at one point. But something happened between them. They stopped talking years before the rumours started.'

'Do you know why?'

'She's never really talked much about Agnes.'

'Will she tell me anything? She doesn't seem to like me.'

'It can't hurt to try. She's a pussycat really. Not as tough as she likes to think.'

'Who is?' Nancy muttered to herself and left Stella for the brazier. She stopped alongside Mafalda clad in all black, and for a moment, they both stared at the red coals and said nothing.

Eventually Nancy cleared her throat. 'I was hoping to talk to you.'

Wrinkles rippled over Mafalda's olive-skinned forehead as she raised an eyebrow.

'About Agnes,' Nancy continued.

The old woman grumbled. She jabbed the coals with a stick, fiery sparks scattered in all directions.

'I understand you used to be friends.'

'A long time ago,' Mafalda finally said.

Nancy breathed again and clutched her hands together.

'I was hoping you could help me. There are all these rumours about her. Horrible terrible things. I moved here without knowing anything. I thought I was making a fresh start. Ha. Now I'm hearing all these stories but no one will tell me what happened.'

With a begrudging sigh, Mafalda beckoned Nancy over to a nearby park bench. Above the trees, the grey clouds thickened, darkening the sky. The wintry-side of autumn had arrived in the blink of an eye.

Mafalda folded her child-sized hands onto her lap. 'We were very different but somehow we became friends. We laughed so much.' She chuckled once, then seemed to catch herself, and returned to her stern expression again. 'She never mentioned family. I thought she was all alone in the world. I was surprised when I heard about you. But when I saw you. Peas in a pod.'

'Agnes and my grandmother fell out years ago. My mother doesn't even know the details.'

'Family can hurt you like no one else.'

'Tell me about her. Please.'

'When we met, I was only a young mother, not wise to the world. Agnes had so many stories, she'd lived a full life before she came to Hopetoun, sometimes I wondered if they were true. But then it all changed. She changed. I didn't understand at the time but now I know. She was sick.'

Mafalda tapped her temple.

'All of a sudden, her light was gone. She was scared. Worried about everything. She didn't sleep or eat. She would bake all night and then wander the streets in the dark.'

Nancy blinked. Maybe she and Agnes were more alike than she realised.

'I tried to talk to her, help her, but she wouldn't listen,' Mafalda said with a sigh. 'She said people were watching her house. I tried to convince her to speak to Father Matteo but she wouldn't listen.'

Mafalda could be right, dementia was sometimes a slow decline over many years. Why then was she wringing her hands in her lap so vigorously? Didn't they say that a vexed friend could turn into the bitterest of enemies?

'We fought over something silly. I can't remember what it was now. Then I had my own bad luck.' Mafalda tugged at the gold cross hanging between her breasts. 'She hid herself away. Shop girls sold her bread and no one else saw her for years. Then one day, the shop closed completely and I wondered if she was even still alive. A few months ago I heard she was in a hospital. I should have tried harder.' Her wrinkled hands twisted harder. She looked up. 'Next time you see her, will you pass on my best wishes?'

'She's not very lucid.'

'It's the feeling that counts. As you get older, your regrets are like stains you can't remove. You must learn to live with them.'

It appeared to be the familiar tale of a broken friendship, but there had to be more. Nothing Mafalda had said explained her animosity towards Nancy when she arrived. And there was one gaping hole in the story. One key event. 'What do you know about these rumours? About Agnes and the missing Sheridan

77

girls?'

The old woman rubbed her chin and drifted away. 'I don't know.'

'They called her a witch, didn't they?'

Fear flickered over Mafalda's face.

'You knew her,' Nancy pressed. 'It's sounds like you were close. Do you think she was capable of something like that?'

'I want to say no. But,' Mafalda replied, 'have you heard of Lorna Gaskill? You're probably too young.'

Nancy knew full well who Lorna Gaskill was. The triumphant woman in the courthouse photograph with Agnes she'd found online. Playing dumb, she shook her head.

Although there was no one within eavesdropping range, Mafalda lowered her voice. 'Lorna Gaskill was famous. Infamous. In all the papers. One Christmas when Agnes and I drank a little too much wine, she told me about the ceremonies in Lorna Gaskill's big house in the country. How they dabbled with demonic forces.'

Demons?

'I was scared. I remember the *strega* from my village as a little girl.'

With a strange gesture, Mafalda curled up her right middle and ring finger and pointed the other three fingers towards the grass. The first drops of rain splattered onto the plastic stall awnings behind them.

'Did you ever see her do anything?'

Mafalda shrugged.

'You said yourself, you wondered whether her stories were true,' Nancy said. 'She is a sick woman.'

'Who would lie about that? The devil is not something to be played with.'

'The only proof you have is a drunken story?'

'You're as big a fool as her if you ignore him,' Mafalda spat.

'You don't have any proof, do you?'

'Darkness is all around us. Can't you feel it? Look what happened here today? Where are all the people?'

Nancy squared her jaw. She was wasting her time.

'I know she had a dark past,' Mafalda said. 'And sometimes that's evidence enough.'

'Finally, the truth,' Nancy said and stood up to leave.

Mafalda reached out her hand. 'A word of advice from an old woman. We all want to protect our families but sometimes it blinds us.'

Nancy left Mafalda on the park bench.

Someone had to know the whole truth.

Lorna Gaskill

Early life

Lorna Elspeth Gaskill (nee Maver) (1911-1977) was born into a farming family in Dirranbandi, Queensland. Married at aged 17 to George Gaskill, she started to explore witchcraft and the occult after his death in Papua New Guinea in 1942.

She travelled to Great Britain and Europe in the late 1940s as a secretary to the spiritualist Aubrey Cross-Holt and returned to Australia in the early 1960s with her second husband Walter Becker (unknown).

Witch of Woollahra

From 1963, Gaskill organised regular occult discussion groups in Pyrmont and Potts Point, creating a following in the bohemian circles of Sydney. The Sydney media (1,2,3) called her the Witch of Woollahra and claimed Gaskill was the leader of a satanic cult, known for its rituals and orgies. In 1969, Gaskill claimed she was responsible for the delays to the Sydney Opera House construction, putting a hex on the project for 'creating a visual blight on the beautiful harbour'. In 1970, after a series of raids on her Surrey Hills home and charges of possession of indecent materials and fraud, her activities moved to a country house in Braidwood, New South Wales. The house was bequeathed to Gaskill by a wealthy acolyte, Gabriel Brett. Brett's family sued Gaskill for stealing the property from his heirs.

Trial and later years

A trial was held in the New South Wales Supreme Court from 11-13 April 1971. Represented by David Manning-Scott QC, rumoured to be another one of Gaskill's followers, Gaskill was acquitted of all charges. After the trial, Gaskill retired from public life to

Braidwood. She died in 1977.

2018 – NANCY

The automatic doors glided open. Nancy shook the rain from her coat and stepped into the quiet of the reception area of the Willowmere Residential Home. The walls were painted a muted linen colour, plush couches were placed in clusters for private sensitive conversations, and soft classical music played in the background. Although, despite vases of fresh flowers on every surface, the scent of disinfectant lingered. Willowmere was a hospital after all.

A cotton-haired old woman shuffled through reception with a nurse in pale blue hovering at her elbow. She inched past, each step achingly slow, and Nancy averted her eyes.

Tasteful decor like this and around the clock care wouldn't come cheap, but Nancy had never seen a single bill. Someone must be paying and she presumed her Gran's estate was keeping Agnes comfortable. Money was always the easiest way to appease guilt.

Once the old woman shambled past, Nancy headed for the reception desk where a male nurse with a buzzcut was leaning over the partition, gossiping with the plump receptionist.

'They reckon it's a child,' he hissed.

The receptionist glanced up. 'Can I help you?' She asked loudly, her glasses bouncing on a chain against her chest as she spoke. The male nurse skulked away.

'I'm Agnes Bittesby's great niece.'

'Miss Grakowski, isn't it? Nice to see you again.' Her voice was like honey, comforting but with a judgmental aftertaste. Her Gran was not the only one with a guilty conscience. Nancy promised herself, and her mother, she'd visit Agnes every Sunday. Agnes was the sole reason why Nancy had moved to Hopetoun and aside from her work in the bakery which was closed on Sundays, she had no excuses. Yet she regularly found compelling reasons not to spend one hour a week patiently holding an old woman's papery hand as she vacantly stared at the wall.

The receptionist lifted the telephone. 'Mariel? Miss Bittesby's niece is here.' She turned back. 'You know the way to her room, don't you?'

Nancy nodded and hoped she did. The winding corridors all looked so similar. Luckily after she turned a few vaguely familiar corners, she spotted Mariel, Agnes's short softly spoken Filipino nurse, standing outside the room waiting for her.

'Nancy. Good to see you,' Mariel said.

'Is she alright?'

'She had a rough night. But she's much calmer now. Be prepared though, she's very talkative today.'

Talkative could be a good thing. It could be her opportunity to get the truth from Agnes.

'Miss Bittesby,' Mariel announced as they stepped into the room. 'You have a visitor.'

Wrapped in a rose-coloured dressing gown, Great Aunt Agnes sat in front of a large window, overlooking a stretch of grass and a row of sage-coloured Australian willows. Her long white hair cascaded over her narrow shoulders and down to cover her breasts. Her hands grimly gripped the arms of her chair, the veins on the back of her hands engorged like thin blue snakes. Nancy rubbed her eyes. Again, the blur. This time around her aunt's head.

'Tell them to piss off,' Agnes spat. 'I don't need a new vacuum cleaner.'

'This is your niece, Nancy,' Mariel said calmly. 'Say hello.'

'I don't know anyone called Nancy,' Agnes snarled.

'Your niece. Nancy,' Mariel repeated slowly.

'Listen to me! I'm telling you I don't know anyone called Nancy!'

Mariel turned to give Nancy a half-shrug, and she smiled back weakly. Despite her condition, Agnes was right. Until two months ago, they'd never met before. They *were* complete strangers.

'And waitress, where's my White Russian? I've been waiting hours. And who stole my book. You, fatty over there.' She pointed at Nancy. 'Give me a cigarette? I'm gasping.'

'You're not allowed to smoke, Agnes.' Nancy sat down in

the visitor's chair beside her.

'In a nightclub? What crazy nonsense is this? This place is rubbish. I know a much nicer club in Marble Arch.' Agnes swept her long white hair off her shoulder with a grin and Nancy stifled a chuckle. Her great aunt's eyes sparkled, a similar blue to her own. Here was the lively Agnes, the Agnes Mafalda talked about. But was this the face of a child-killer?

As if she was eavesdropping on Nancy's thoughts, the old woman squinted at her. 'What have you been doing?' she said.

'Me? What? Nothing,' Nancy spluttered. 'Well, I've reopened your bakery.'

'My bakery?'

'Yes, your bakery.'

'What are you talking about? I'm an artist. A painter. I don't bake bread. Although I have to admit I can rustle up a rather delightful sponge if required. Waitress, get rid of this liar.'

Mariel shot Nancy a tiny knowing smile. Nancy slumped in her chair. How did the nurse do this every day? How did she have the strength to stare into her patient's faces and watch the fragility of life play out without blinking? Nancy was so weak, so keen to avoid the reality of decline and death, she practically had to nail herself to the chair.

Agnes went quiet and gnawed at her nails. Then tears began to roll down her face and the scent of fresh shit punched Nancy in the nose.

'Oh dear.' Mariel swooped in. 'Have we had an accident?'

The old woman wailed like a three-year-old and Nancy winced, not knowing where to look.

'Let's take care of you.' The small Filipino woman lifted the frail Agnes to her feet.

Feeling useless, Nancy jumped up out of her chair to help but the experienced nurse had Agnes halfway to the ensuite before Nancy took a step.

As the bathroom door closed, Nancy sighed and looked around the room. Specifically, she looked for a silver framed photograph she'd brought on her last visit. The picture of Agnes posing beside the Eiffel Tower. The room was as anonymous as a hotel, every keepsake Nancy brought from the flat seemed to be gone the next time she visited. She thought mementos might help.

Nancy went to the window. The rain had stopped but the green lawn was dark with shadows and fresh threatening clouds were marching in from the south. An iron-grey curtain had been closed across the sky like a formal announcement of the end of summer.

In her condition, would Nancy be able to get any history out of Agnes? Like her mum said, perhaps she should leave the past alone. But hadn't Agnes lived the last twenty-five years under a cloud of suspicion? Surely, she'd want to clear her own name, even now. As Nancy chewed on her lip, a black crow flew out of the willows, heading in her direction. The bird came nearer and nearer, without slowing, aiming straight for the window.

'No,' Nancy wheezed.

With a loud thump, the black bird collided with the glass. The lifeless body dropped out of sight and she raced forward, pressing her face against the window, peering into the garden bed below. Before she could spot the dead bird, the ensuite door opened and Nancy scrambled back to her seat.

Mariel helped Agnes back into the room. 'That's better, isn't it?'

Agnes mumbled to herself and gnawed on her fingers. Nancy watched her great aunt shuffle towards the bed, her heart still thumping and unasked questions tingling on her tongue. She needed to know more. But would she upset and confuse Agnes by dredging up the past?

'A little sleep before dinner?' Mariel asked.

Like a sleepy child, Agnes nodded. The nurse pulled aside the covers and helped her into bed.

As Mariel closed the blinds, Nancy got to her feet with a pained smile. It appeared her chance to probe Agnes had gone. 'I'll say good-bye then. I'll come and see you next week, Aunty Agnes.' She leaned over and kissed her soft cheek. Her questions would have to wait.

The old woman jerked forward from her pillows and

85

grabbed Nancy's hand tightly. 'What have you done?' she hissed.

'What do you mean?'

The old woman's bony fingers crushed Nancy's.

'It's all unravelling and it's your fault.'

'But I'm trying to help.'

'They're watching me. They know.'

Agnes let go of her grip and collapsed back into her stack of pillows.

'Who?' Nancy said. 'The police?'

'Why are you here, Pamela? Have you finally come to apologise?'

'I'm not Pamela, I'm Pamela's grand-daughter.'

'You look terrible. You never could keep away from the cakes, could you?' Agnes tutted. 'Have you finally left him? I never understood how you could live with that tyrant Walter.'

'Walter?' Nancy narrowed her eyes. 'Who's Walter?'

'You were always full of shit, Pamela. Get out. Sometimes the past needs to stay in the past.'

She swatted Nancy away with her hand and rolled over.

Nancy left the room more confused than ever. She dawdled along the corridor on her way back to reception, her head whirring.

'Out like a light,' Mariel said, catching up with Nancy.

Nancy exhaled. 'I don't know how you do it.'

The nurse shrugged. 'Like all of us, she has her good days and her bad days. There but for the grace of God...'

'Did something happen to provoke it?'

'Not that I'm aware of. Just in the last few days, she's been very restless.'

'Has anyone else been to visit?'

'Only you.'

'She seemed very confused.'

'There's always something in what my patients say. It might be jumbled up but there's always truth in there.'

Mariel stopped at an open door. 'See you next week.' She waved goodbye and disappeared into another patient's room.

'Half-truths.' Nancy muttered to herself as she trudged back to the entrance. 'But which part is true?'

Chapter Five
SUCCESSION

1972 – AGNES

Agnes retired to the farm house library. A cool respite against the warm afternoon, the walls were lined with musty smelling books from every tradition imaginable. She carefully selected three hardcover books, and with a notebook by her side, flicked through the pages and got to work.

When Agnes first met Lorna, she borrowed books one-by-one week-by-week from her private collection but when Lorna took possession of the Braidwood property and Agnes came with her, the library was where she spent most of her time; reading, learning, transforming. When she wasn't in the kitchen, of course.

Her mind and soul had turned from art to food. It all began at Lorna's early meetings in the Scout Hall in Randwick. Each person was expected to contribute and bring an offering to share at the end of the meeting. At first Agnes brought fruit. Her ability to burn water was legendary. But as she read more, especially the footnotes and marginalia which hinted at the ignored wisdom of the country folk, Agnes found herself drawn to baking.

Despite the first charred and gluey disasters, she persisted. With each recipe and the more she learned from Lorna and her books, the more she realised baking was magic. It was alchemy. And all the more powerful when combined with the right intentions, timings and tools.

One particular summer night in the midst of a long heatwave, Agnes brought a new recipe to the meeting: honey cakes. During the readings, the air in the Scout Hall was tense, and the ceremonies lacklustre, yet when the social part of the evening began, everyone gobbled up the honey cakes until there was not a single crumb left. The mood instantly lifted, the group joked like old friends and warm heartfelt smiles filled the room.

Lorna took Agnes by the hand. 'You have found your true path, my dear.'

Lorna knew the jovial mood was not spontaneous. After a few run-ins with a persistently lecherous older male member, Agnes had dosed her cakes, and now the entire group, with lavender and vervain. The honey and butter had been imbued with intentions of love and protection.

'You are a hearth witch,' Lorna announced.

Agnes laughed. 'It's the 1970s, Lorna! We've fought our way out of the kitchen.' Lorna had always insisted that the men do the so-called women's roles in the group and vice versa. Agnes never believed she would learn how to fix fuses but she had.

Lorna smiled wryly. 'You are a witch of the home. A cunning woman. Much more than a cleaner and maker of beds. I can feel it in your blood. It is your familial destiny.'

The label of hearth-witch was unsettling at first. A woman of the world, carefree and childless, Agnes didn't live by the rules of the suburban Australian housewife, not like her stuffy sister Pamela and her boorish husband Maurice. She wanted to be esoteric and exotic, she wasn't like the women she grew up with, she was special. But underneath, the word 'hearth witch' rang true in her heart. The energy of the earth, the angels and the universe radiated through her body whenever her hands were deep in dough.

With a hunger for knowledge, Agnes delved into every tradition and lifted every stone, both dark and light, until she created her own recipes based on her studies. The two recipe books, the right hand book for the light and the left hand book for the dark, were her magnum opus. At the time, Lorna's grip was still firm on her shoulder, and Agnes fully believed there was no wrong or right in dark and light. But when it came to practice, and testing out her creations, her intuition warned her of another side to the story, and eventually she contained herself only to the recipes in her right hand book. Like everyone, the darkness fascinated her, the powers to control and hurt tried to entice her with their seductive dance but fear held her back. She had the knowledge but lacked the courage to test the powers of the left book fully. Until the day when Lorna asked for her help, to further their cause. The day when it all started to unravel.

The library mantel clock struck five. Dinner was served at eight and her daily contribution of dessert was due on the table by half past nine. Agnes closed the books around her, and with her head ripe with ideas, she sketched out a new recipe for this evening's meal. Her mouth ran dry. This was the first time she'd ever planned to use her skills against Lorna.

That night at dinner, the red wine flowed freely but the room crackled with tension and the roast leg of lamb sat on the table barely touched. The laughter was forced, with a hysterical edge, as everyone desperately tried to prove they'd already forgotten about David. His usual chair was gone from the table but his absence was like a hole punched in the wall.

Except for Lorna and Walter. She sat at the head of the table like a queen in tweed, a cigarillo in one hand and a smirk on her face. The fatty smell of the lamb made Agnes's already nervous stomach churn. She picked at a few roast vegetables and tried not to glance at the clock on the wall.

With a wave of her hand, Lorna declared the main course was over, and the young pretty boys descended, clearing away the plates and cutlery. It was now time.

Sucking in a breath, Agnes left the long dining table for the kitchen. She swallowed hard as she wrenched open the ancient fridge door and pulled out a crystal punch bowl. Tonight's dessert was a trifle, layer upon layer of milk pudding, soaked golden cake and ruby-red fruit.

'Something new tonight?' Lorna asked as Agnes placed the bowl in the centre of the table. One of the coquettish boys ladled the pink and white pudding into bowls which were passed from person to person.

'I call it Shekinah's Delight.' Agnes tried to keep her voice from shaking. 'I was inspired by Kerry's reading on the

Kabbalah yesterday.'

Agnes nodded towards Kerry, a red-head barrister, who groaned with pleasure as she spooned the pudding past her fat lips. For a brief moment, Agnes forgot her ulterior motive.

'Some of the Oriental spices are impossible to get out here and so I had to improvise.'

'I can taste the truth and beauty. You've excelled yourself.' Lorna tucked in greedily, her face gleaming with delight.

Agnes gulped, and waited.

But it was a long time before everyone settled to bed. The pot and the wine kept the delirious merriment going until the early hours of the morning. Agnes ignored the orgies at the side of the room and dealt tarot, dosing herself up with Methedrine instead. She had a long night ahead of her.

Once everyone drifted off into their own rooms, Agnes lay on her bed staring into the ceiling, fully clothed. When the hall clock chimed three and the spell was at its strongest, she tip-toed barefoot down the hall, her platform sandals in her hand, her notebooks stowed carefully in her bag.

She closed the hefty wooden door as gently as she could and winced across the driveway gravel. When she hit the dewy grass, she strapped on her sandals and began to run.

Her train out of Braidwood was departing in less than two hours.

2018 – NANCY

'Ninety eight.'

The same spectral brown-haired girl stood at the foot of Nancy's bed, her hands covering her face.

'Ninety nine. One hundred.'

She dropped her hands. Her face was an unrecognisable grey shimmer.

Nancy squeezed her eyes shut, her breaths trapped in her throat.

'Ready or not. Here I come,' the girl sang. Then her voice changed, from playful to vicious. 'I'm coming for you, Nancy,' she said with a snarl. 'Ready or not. I'm coming.'

Nancy woke with a splutter. The glowing green digits of her alarm clock glared at her across the room. Three o'clock. She gasped and bolted upright. Then she remembered and sighed happily. It was Sunday. She snuggled back underneath the thin patchwork quilt and Wolfie gently snuffled from the floor at the end of the bed.

Thump.

Wolfie growled and scuttled up to its feet. Nancy grabbed her glasses from the bedside table and listened hard. The house was silent. Except for the sound of her own heartbeat.

Scratch. Scratch.

The sound, faint at first, was coming from the ground floor. With each passing second, the scratching grew louder and more furious. If Wolfie wasn't already growling in the doorway, she would've blamed the dog.

Scratch. Scratch. Scratch. Scratch.

Nancy swung out of bed and shivered with deja vu. Two nights in a row? She pulled her Blundstones on with shaking hands and threw a polar fleece over her pyjamas.

Scratch. Scratch. Scratch. Scratch. Scratch. Scratch.

The rough scratches were joined by a new noise, the thin squeal of something scraping glass. Wolfie stopped growling and began to whimper, the mournful cry making Nancy shudder. She slipped her phone into her pocket and joined the dog in the bedroom doorway. It nudged her with its wet nose.

'What is it?' She whispered and stroked the dog's quivering back. 'Is it the muffin woman again?'

Whatever it was, it was at the back windows and door. And it wanted to come inside.

'Come on,' she said and stepped out of the bedroom but the big timid dog stayed put in the doorway. She rolled her eyes and went into the upstairs kitchen in search of a weapon.

Where did she leave the pestle? Downstairs with her rolling pins, heavy saucepans and all the other suitable weapons? She wrenched open the cutlery drawer and grabbed a kitchen knife.

Scratch. Scratch. Scratch. Scratch. Scratch. Scratch. Scratch. Scratch. Scratch.

Clutching a paring knife in her first, Nancy inched down the stairs. Halfway down, she froze. The staircase led down to a narrow walkway between the bakery and the backdoor, and along the wall, chest-high windows looked out onto the backyard.

Through the glass, Nancy spotted movement outside.

'What the—' she gasped.

The backyard was crowded with children, kids of all ages and heights scratched at the back door and windows with their grubby little fingers. Their eyes staring vacantly.

Behind the scratching mob, more small sleepwalkers streamed into the garden. Blonde, brown, black and red heads dressed in pyjamas and nighties jostled for the door with hands outstretched. Yet their lips were still, the horde of children was completely silent.

Nancy slipped down the stairs one by one until she was standing by the back door. She reached out her hand. Should she open it? They were only children after all, but their cold stares and unnatural quiet made her insides quiver.

A girl with brown plaits pressed her face hard against the glass and tugged the door handle. The door rattled in its lock but luckily stayed firmly shut. Another forty children scrabbled at the weatherboards with their fingernails.

93

With trembling hands, Nancy grabbed her phone and dialled Triple 0. 'I need police,' she croaked, then coughed to clear the fear from her voice. 'Bittesby Bakery on Station Street in Hopetoun.'

'What's the situation?' the operator replied.

'It's a bit hard to explain. Hurry.'

Beside her, the door lurched, the wood flexing under the weight of the children desperate to get inside.

'Are you safe? Are there any children there?'

'Yes!'

'I'll send a team as soon as I can but there might be a wait. We've been flooded with reports of missing children.'

Nancy scrubbed her hand over her face. 'From Hopetoun? Then I know where the kids are. They're here in my backyard. Hurry. I don't know what to do.'

The call ended and she stood uselessly by the back door, watching. Why were the children here, and what did they want? Last night had been the first time Nancy had ever needed to call the police. Now two nights in a row. Was it a coincidence or was something drawing people to the house?

As the door started to bulge under the strain of the kids, there was a loud knock at the shop door.

'Thank god.' Nancy ran through the bakery kitchen into the shop and flung open the door to the same policewoman from the night before, the wiry Constable Trinh. Her bald partner with the blond bushy eyebrows loomed closely behind her. Nancy waved them inside. 'Hurry. This way.'

They followed her with clumping boots through the swinging door towards the back of the building. She stopped in front of the windows and exhaled loudly. 'I didn't know what to do.'

The glass was now finger-painted with blood. Skin and little fingernails torn and bleeding from scratching at the timber.

'Woah,' Trinh said.

The bald cop, Brouwer, gulped and crossed himself. 'This isn't natural.'

'Why are they here?' Trinh whispered.

'I don't know,' Nancy said. 'A noise woke me up. And then I came down and found this.'

Brouwer shook his head and wandered away with his phone in his hand. Trinh flicked the switch for the outside light but the backyard stayed dark.

Nancy winced. 'Remember, the bulb's blown.'

'Have they said anything to you?' Trinh asked.

'Not a word. And more are coming.'

Trinh and Nancy stood open-mouthed, watching the bloodied fingers scrape against the glass.

'They look like they're in some kind of trance,' Trinh said.

'But where are their parents?' Nancy asked.

Brouwer reappeared alongside them.

'How long til back-up gets here?' Trinh asked.

'You want me to call them?' he said sheepishly.

'Brouwer.' Trinh rolled her eyes and grabbed her two-way radio from her belt. 'We need back-up at the Bakery on Station Street. There's about fifty children here. Yes. You heard me right. Five-zero.'

Trinh walked away, continuing her conversation with the dispatcher, and Constable Brouwer sidled up to Nancy.

'What have you done?' he said, keeping his voice so low only she would hear.

'Me?' Nancy recoiled. 'You think I had something to do with this?'

'They say it's hereditary. You're just like her,' he spat.

Nancy glared back with hands on hips but before she could speak, Trinh returned with news.

'They're sending the first available units,' she said and Brouwer closed his mouth, pinching his lips into a thin white line.

Nancy ignored Brouwer's dirty looks. 'What if we made a loud noise? Maybe that'd wake them up.'

'Come on.' Brouwer folded his arms across his chest. 'You know how to break the spell.'

'Now is not the time for your mumbo-jumbo shit, Brouwer,'

Trinh said. 'We should wait for the others. They'll be here soon.'

Nancy ran to the kitchen and left the cops by the shuddering back door. She grabbed two of her largest baking sheets and darted back.

With a tray in each hand, she crashed them together like cymbals. Outside, a few heads looked up with alarm in their eyes, quickly bursting into tears, but the rest of the crowd continued grabbing for the door.

'Well, that didn't work,' Nancy said with a sigh.

'Do you have a garden hose?' Trinh said.

'They're only little kids. How about some tear gas too?'

Again, someone knocked on the shop door.

'Good. Back-up,' Trinh said.

Making another trip through the bakery kitchen and into the shop, Nancy opened the front door. A bearded man and a pointy-nosed woman with coats over their pyjamas stormed inside.

'What have you done with Hugo?' they shouted, shoving her aside and sending her crashing into the wall.

'Wait,' she wheezed. But the couple were already marching through the swinging bakery door. She caught her breath and took off after them, grumbling.

'Talk about rude.' Nancy said when she arrived at the back door. 'Excuse me? Is this the way you treat the public?' She asked the woman intruder who had her face pressed up against the glass. 'Hello?'

She didn't reply.

'They're not police.' Trinh shrugged.

'Who the hell are they then?'

'Hugo!' the woman said. 'Oh thank god.'

She lunged for the door handle.

'No!' Nancy cried.

Hugo's mother turned the key in the lock and flung the back door wide open. An avalanche of small bodies flooded in through the gap and the silent children swarmed around them. With dull eyes, they reached out with blood-stained hands to grab things unseen. The five adults were struck dumb while the stampede into the house continued, and they barrelled down the narrow passage towards the bakery kitchen.

'Shut the door!' Nancy screamed. The woman was wading through the river of children and picked up a skinny brown-haired boy by the armpits.

Using all their weight, Nancy and Trinh heaved and slammed the back door shut, luckily without catching any small fingers in the door. Half the children were left outside, mauling at the walls and glass, trying to get in.

The little boy writhed in his mother's arms, clawing at her face with broken fingernails, scoring three long scratches down her cheek.

'It's Mummy. Ow. Stop it.'

Hugo's father hurried up to the mother and son, enveloping them both in a hug. 'I should've listened to you. I should never have let him take one.' The couple turned and shot Nancy a look of disgust.

Outside, the clouds opened. Sheets of fat raindrops splattered onto the heads of the children and the backyard turned into a deafening cacophony of cries as they all woke from their trance at once. The rain began to soak into their thin night clothes and twenty scared and cold children whined for their mothers.

Behind the wailing crowd, two new uniformed police officers and a group of parents in raincoats dashed into the back yard.

A din of crashing metal came from the bakery kitchen and Nancy pushed past the reunited family to investigate. Still staring with lifeless eyes, the children were tearing open the cupboard doors, tipping drawers upside down and scooping the contents onto the floor. A bag of flour had ripped and a cloud of white dust showered across the room.

A little girl with auburn ringlets stopped and turned. Her face, caked with a layer of flour, was ghostly white and as she stared blankly into Nancy's eyes, Nancy shivered.

'Water?' Trinh yelled.

Dodging the ransacking children, Nancy grabbed hold of the spray bottle on a shelf above the oven. She squirted a mist of water into the air, over the heads of the kids.

One by one, as the droplets of water dampened their foreheads, the kids stopped. Their grabbing hands dropped to their sides as they blinked and woke from their sleepwalking. Their faces twisted in confusion and the water turned their floured skin and hair to glue.

Nancy continued spraying until all the kids were screaming for Mummy and Daddy. She liked the children better when they were quiet and robotic, and clamped her hands over her ears.

Suddenly the chaos doubled as adults rushed into the kitchen from all directions. Blue uniformed cops, plain clothed social workers with I.D. badges swinging round their necks and angry parents stormed inside, all shouting, all trying to calm the distressed flour-covered children.

Her house filled with yelling strangers, Nancy stood in the middle all alone, gawking at the mess.

'Holy water?' sneered Brouwer, sidling up to her. The empty spray bottle still hanging from her trigger finger.

Nancy blinked. 'Tap water with a bit of salt.'

A skinny woman with a razor sharp bob wrenched at Nancy's arm with long fake nails. 'Witch,' she hissed and was quickly joined by another two women.

The three surrounded her.

'Why isn't she in cuffs?' a chubby brown-skinned mother spat at Brouwer. The bald cop turned without a word and walked away.

'I didn't do anything,' Nancy said feebly. 'They were here when I woke up.'

'I told you she was a witch,' said the third mother, her blonde hair piled haphazardly in a red scrunchie. 'Just like the other one.'

Trinh appeared. 'That's enough, ladies. Take your hands off her, please. It's been a stressful night for everyone. Find your kids and take them home.'

'I want to make a complaint,' the scrunchie lady said, her

eyes like slits.

'There'll be plenty of time for that tomorrow. Get your little ones to bed.'

The three scowling mothers disappeared into the crowd and Nancy retreated from the bedlam, taking a seat on the stairs and laying her head in her hands.

A fresh panic stabbed her in the ribs. She scrambled to her feet and bolted upstairs to the kitchen. Was this how the parents downstairs felt? She reached the kitchen doorway, then let out a sigh. There it was. Sitting on the table exactly where she'd left it. 'I'm sorry,' she said. She took the recipe book in her arms and stroked the front cover.

A little whimper came from under the table and Nancy bent down to see the big black dog curled up underneath.

'Coward,' she chuckled.

Footsteps trudged up the stairs, someone in heavy boots. 'Miss Grakowski? Nancy?' Trinh called out.

'In the kitchen.'

Nancy hurriedly hid the notebook in the pantry behind the packets of pasta and tinned tomatoes; the two Constables arrived as she shut the cupboard door. Another older white man with sparse fair hair stood behind them. Straight-backed and smiling broadly, the stranger was as tall as Brouwer, filling the door frame.

Trinh glared as the man pushed past her and handed Nancy a business card. 'I'm Pastor Vanhanen. Nice to meet you, Nancy.' His pale-eyed face seemed ageless, anywhere from a worn-out forty-five to a youthful seventy. 'Brother Brouwer called me here because I may be of some help. I have many years of experience with strange encounters like this.'

'Oh really.' Nancy raised an eyebrow. 'So, what's your theory?'

'There are many possible explanations.' He paused and nodded slowly. 'But I'm more interested in addressing the very root of the matter. The source.' As he stared intently at Nancy, the old man's face blurred and she quickly blinked the now-familiar floaters away. 'A cleansing is the only way to nip the darkness in the bud.'

Nancy handed him back his business card. 'I'm fine.'

'Think it over. Please.'

'Don't be a fool, woman!' Brouwer stepped forward.

Nancy's nostrils flared and Trinh held out her hands to separate them.

'It's been a long night. I need to take your statement, Miss Grakowski. And meanwhile Constable Brouwer will escort his friend to his car.'

'But—' Brouwer spluttered.

'Get him out of my house,' Nancy said coldly.

He quirked an eyebrow and Brouwer led him away. 'Call me anytime. Day or night. I'm more than happy to help,' he called back over his shoulder.

Nancy chucked the business card towards the rubbish bin. She missed. The men clumped away, whispering to one another and Nancy sighed at the white card lying on the scuffed linoleum floor.

Trinh faked a little laugh. 'This is becoming a regular occurrence. Maybe we should set up a permanent station here.'

Looking down at the floor, Nancy raked her fingers through her hair and wished Trinh would leave. She needed to think. Make sense of all the craziness of the past few days. Alone.

Trinh gestured to the vinyl kitchen chair opposite her and Nancy warily sat down. She lifted her glasses and pinched the bridge of her nose. 'Let's get this over and done with.'

The policewoman leaned in. 'I came to visit you yesterday after the Festival but you were out,' she said in a low voice. 'Did you report the bones you showed me? I had a look around in the back yard just now but I couldn't see the holes. Did you cover them up again?'

Lifting her chin, Nancy studied the young cop's face. The gleam in Trinh's dark eyes made Nancy's skin crawl, she was just like the men.

Nancy crossed her arms and raised her eyebrows. 'What bones?'

The cop's face crumpled. 'The holes dug up by the dog?

You asked me to look at them yesterday?'

'I don't know what you're talking about.'

It was Nancy's turn to spin a few half-truths.

Sunday dawned grey and gloomy, and there was no milk left in the fridge. And there was no way Nancy could face the mess downstairs without tea. She showered, pulled on her Blundstones and slipped on a raincoat. Her Sunday agenda was set; shop, clean and then redeem Agnes's name.

'Come for a walk, Wolfie?'

From its hiding place under the kitchen table, the big black dog lifted its head from its paws and shook itself upright, the medallion jangling at its throat. The sound a reminder, Nancy dialled Wolfie's owner again but the call went straight to voicemail.

'Hi, this is Nancy again. Your dog is still with me. Please give me a call.' After leaving her details, Nancy turned back to the dog. 'A bit early on a Sunday, I guess. Come on then.'

When they reached the foot of the stairs, Nancy winced at the river of muddy footprints on the floor. Through the doorway, she glimpsed the bakery kitchen with its ransacked cupboards and globs of glue splattered over every surface.

Last night's events still baffled her. Why had so many children descended on her house at once? Mass hysteria? Hypnosis? Video games?

Opening the door, she stepped out into the weak drizzle and gave a half-hearted wave to two unfamiliar uniformed cops. One had a camera and was recording the scratched weatherboards, churned up dirt and trampled grass from every angle, while another was scraping dried blood off the windows into a ziplock bag. Surprisingly, Nancy was unfazed by the police presence in her backyard. She guessed from Trinh's comments last night that the police were as confused as she was by what happened, and so far they seemed unsure whether a crime had actually been committed.

'We should be out of your hair soon,' said the fresh-faced

female cop with the bulky camera.

'Then I can clean up?'

'Yeah, go for it.'

Leaving them to their work, she set out through the side gate. Halfway down the alley, she slipped on the cobbles and almost lost her balance. As she cursed under her breath, she noticed a clump of wet straw stuck to the sole of her boot. She pried it off. The knotted straw was woven into the shape of a small crude doll. It must have belonged to one of the kids. Kicking it aside, she continued on with Wolfie in tow and turned the corner onto Station Street. A bright red plastic shopping bag was propped up against the bakery door.

Wolfie trotted ahead to sniff the bag.

'Careful,' she said. 'It's probably a bomb.'

The dog wagged its tail in reply and promptly ignored her. The package was book-shaped. Another present from Miles?

Her stomach churned as she peeked inside. The book, *A Curious History of Hopetoun* by J.V. Egloff, had the same black and white 1920s photograph of Station Street on the olive-green cover, superimposed with images of a bonfire and a woven doll.

It must be from Miles.

'Maybe I have more than one friend,' she said with a tiny smile. Her comment was directed at Wolfie but the dog was already charging down Station Street in search of more interesting smells. She dropped the gift into her carrier bag and pushed on in the direction of Freshworx for some overpriced milk.

The lights were on at Station Street Books and Miles, dressed in a blue cabled cardigan, was pushing a trolley of bargain books towards the front door. She gulped. This was the first time she'd seen Miles since the night he told her what they were all saying about Agnes. Child-killer.

He unlocked the door, beaming. 'Bright and early for a Sunday?'

'This is afternoon for me. Thanks for the book by the way. You didn't have to.'

'Another satisfied customer.' He lowered his voice. 'I was hoping to run into you today. I hear you had a few unexpected visitors last night?'

Nancy puffed out her cheeks. 'Who told you?'

'There's a local Facebook group. Although I'd advise you don't look at it today.' He bared his teeth.

She could imagine what they were saying.

'However I'm keen to hear your side,' he continued. 'Are you free tonight? The Railway does an excellent Sunday roast.'

There was something about Miles's grin she didn't like. Though he was the only person who'd been honest with her so far, and over dinner, she would have plenty of time to question him about the Sheridan girls.

'If there's gravy, I'm sold.'

'Lashings of it. Say six o'clock? Nice and early for you, Cinderella.'

'Perfect.'

She shook the carrier bag. 'Thanks again for the book. Maybe it'll answer some of my questions.'

Miles opened his mouth to reply.

'Excuse me, mate,' interrupted a tanned balding man. 'I was wondering whether you had a copy of a book. It's got a blue cover...'

'Later.'

Nancy waved goodbye and continued down Station Street. She'd only travelled a few steps when she heard her name.

'Nancy?'

She flinched and whirled around. It was Stella with her violet streaked hair and serpentine grin, standing in the doorway of Morning & Mocha.

'Perfect timing. What are you doing right now? I'm meeting Dajana for a coffee. Join us. Please.'

Nancy stuttered. If Miles already knew about last night, Stella would definitely know, and the last thing Nancy wanted was to be the centre of attention. She needed to be the one asking questions.

'I wouldn't want to intrude.'

Stella waved her hand dismissively.

'I would but I've got Wolfie with me.' Nancy turned back but Wolfie was already happily settled on a dry spot on the footpath.

'Come on.' Stella held open the door.

Out of excuses, Nancy sucked in a breath. This was another chance to find out about Agnes, she told herself. If she was clever and turned the conversation her way. She stepped through the door behind Stella and her glasses immediately fogged up.

The cafe, sitting on the corner of Station and Salisbury Streets, was a white box with large plate glass windows on either side. Through her misted-up glasses, the room was a noisy blur. Conversations battled with the coffee machine, hissing and rumbling in the background. The air thick with spiced raisin toast, warm milk and the reek of rain-soaked clothes.

'You've got a nerve.' A petite woman with blood-red hair blocked Nancy's path inside. 'You should be locked up.'

'It wasn't me,' Nancy said with a gulp, slipping her glasses back on. The woman wasn't familiar but the house had been so busy. 'I don't know what happened.'

'Liar,' she spat.

'Steady on.' Stella stroked the air. 'Caroline, isn't it? I'm sure Nancy can explain.'

'I can't believe you are friends with this…person,' Caroline growled. 'After what she's done.'

'You're talking as if she murdered someone,' Stella scoffed. Nancy swallowed hard.

'If I was you I'd pack up and go. No one wants you here,' Caroline said, then turned on her heel and stormed away.

'Maybe I *should* leave,' Nancy said.

'Don't be silly,' Stella replied and waved over at Dajana sitting by the big windows. As they snaked their way between the busy tables towards her, another couple glared at Nancy and pulled their toddler closer to them. Nancy averted her eyes.

'What a nice surprise.' Dajana, dressed in a black puffer

vest, rose from her seat and leaned across the table, kissing Nancy on the cheek. Nancy instantly stiffened, then followed her lead with an air kiss. Why was Dajana so friendly all of a sudden? The other night, she wouldn't even meet her eyes.

They sat down and Dajana gestured to the angry redhead woman across the room. 'What's her problem?'

'Haven't you seen Facebook?' Stella said.

'I don't really want to talk about it,' Nancy muttered and luckily a tattooed waitress in trainers and a floral dress appeared, delivering Dajana's green smoothie, then taking Nancy and Stella's orders.

'I'm on a digital detox,' Dajana replied with a toss of her ponytail. 'Everyone seems to be on edge today. All my clients were extra grumpy this morning. Whinged the whole time. I made them do even more burpees just to shut them up.'

'I know what you mean.' Stella smiled painfully.

'Something's off,' Dajana said. Yet no matter what she said, her smooth forehead barely moved. Nancy peered closer, with morbid curiosity, searching for Dajana's real face under the cosmetic fillers.

She continued. 'Did you see the police down by the railway lines? All blocked off with tape and people in those white suits. Like CSI.' She shuddered.

Stella nodded. 'Trouble is brewing. Mum's already blaming the Festival. It's going be a bad harvest for us all.'

Nancy narrowed her eyes. 'Harvest? Aren't you a consultant or something?'

'Of sorts.' Stella smiled slyly. 'Give me your hands.'

Reluctantly, Nancy did as she asked. Stella turned her hands over and interlaced their fingers, pressing their palms together. She closed her eyes and a dull cold throb transferred from Stella's hands into hers. Nancy tensed, the pulse biting through her skin and into the bones of her wrists.

'I can feel stress,' Stella said. 'Anxiety. A low buzz of unease vibrating through your entire body. But that's not surprising.'

Drawing her hands away sharply, Nancy laughed and

pushed up her glasses. 'It's been a strange few days.'

'But there's more. Something dark.'

'Sorry for the wait.' The waitress interrupted and placed Stella's black coffee and a stark white tea-set onto the table.

'It's called bio-field therapy,' Stella said. 'Or energy work. For many years it was pooh-poohed by the mainstream medical fraternity. But these days, science is catching up to what we've known for millennia.'

'Interesting.' Nancy tried to hide her scepticism with a sip of tea and burnt her tongue instead. 'But you mentioned a harvest?'

'The Traders Association dates back to the first European settlement. Back when the success of a harvest was crucial in people's lives,' Stella said. 'Like a wise old woman, the Association has seen it all before, and she shares her knowledge. We Association members know when something isn't right. When the balance of the world is off.'

'And how to fix it.' Dajana nodded firmly.

'We have to act soon.' Stella leaned in. 'You look confused, Nancy? I understand this might sound a bit odd to a newcomer but we don't ignore the past around here.' She smiled a hard smile and Nancy fidgeted in her seat. What did Danny say about the Association again?

'We'd love you to join us. Properly. As part of the Association. Tomorrow night, we're having a Festival debrief to brainstorm a few ideas for next year.' Stella broke off and waved out the window to Fred and Neha, walking past in matching blue raincoats.

'Those two give me the creeps.' Dajana shuddered but waved and smiled back anyway. 'Do you think they're swingers?'

'Jana!' Stella spluttered.

'Come on. She's so intense and he's got those shifty eyes. They've probably got a dungeon in their house. Where they host little parties with Russell. He's another weird one. But I suspect I'm far too old for his tastes.'

Stella slapped her on the arm and they collapsed into

giggles.

More neighbourhood gossip was the last thing Nancy needed. She necked her tea like a shot of tequila and placed her tea-cup back into its saucer with a clang. It was time to take charge of the conversation. 'Sorry. I have to go. Sunday is my day for visiting my Aunt Agnes.'

Something flickered across the women's faces. Was it disgust? Or fear?

Stella quickly resumed her poise. 'How is she doing?' She asked with a soothing tone.

'Not great. She's incoherent and agitated. I wouldn't wish dementia on my worst enemy.'

Stella and Dajana both knocked loudly on the wooden table.

Nancy continued. 'I just wish I could help her. But I'm really in the dark. My family knows nothing. Do you know anything about her? From her life before she got sick?'

The women exchanged wary glances.

'Anything is helpful. Please,' Nancy pressed.

'I don't know her.' Dajana shrugged. 'I've only heard the rumours. Everyone did. Back then.'

Nancy turned to Stella.

'Didn't Mum explain everything yesterday?'

'Not really. I want to hear your side.'

Stella sighed. 'I know they were friends once, but Mum never explained why they fell out. We just always avoided her shop.'

Why had Agnes and Mafalda fallen out? The mystery niggled at her, it had to be important. But then again, friends fall out all the time. Why had all of Nancy's friends faded away, one by one? By the time Grant died she had no one left to call.

'Your mum mentioned a run of bad luck. What happened, if you don't mind me asking?'

Stella cleared her throat. 'We lost my Papa to a sudden heart attack and my sister, Maria, in a car crash within two weeks of each other. Mum was devastated. We all were.'

Nancy winced. 'I'm sorry.'

'Mum buried herself in work. Day and night in the

ristorante. Never sitting down for a single moment.'

Nancy nodded. Then she leaned forward, placing her elbows on the table. She lowered her voice. 'Your mother mentioned black magic.'

Dajana whispered. 'So, it's true.'

Stella folded her arms.

'I guess your mum is a little superstitious,' Nancy said. 'It sounded like nonsense to me.'

'How do you know?' Stella said. 'You said yourself, you barely know anything about Agnes.'

Nancy's stomach cartwheeled as she locked eyes with Stella. Her stare was relentless and Nancy eventually had to look away.

'Me personally,' Dajana interjected. 'I can completely understand black magic and all that stuff. I'd be willing to try anything to get rid of these crow's feet. Lead the way to the blood sacrifices, I say.'

Stella laughed. Nancy joined in but the sound was hollow.

'So, a trip to see Agnes?' Stella said. 'And then what? What's on for the rest of the day?'

'Dinner at the Railway.' Nancy blushed despite herself. 'With Miles.'

'Ooh,' cooed Dajana. 'Someone moves fast. Don't worry, Miles is a big teddy bear.'

'No other skeletons in the closet? Anything else I need to know about? He's not married, is he?'

'Once bitten?' Stella asked.

Nancy shrugged. 'It'd be pretty weird to get to our age without a few horror stories.'

'Ain't that the truth.' Dajana laughed. 'It would be a different story if you said you were going out with Danny.'

Nancy didn't ask her to explain. She stood up. With her cup empty and the conversation having moved on from Agnes, she didn't have the time, or the desire, to listen to more Hopetoun scuttlebutt. 'I really have to go.'

'Promise you'll come along tomorrow? I've got an idea about how you could help us,' Stella said.

'I'll let you know.'

Nancy waved goodbye and ducked her head as she navigated through the busy cafe, feeling the hot angry daggers from the other patrons. 'Witch,' someone hissed and Nancy kept her head down until she pushed open the door into the cool air.

Wolfie scrambled upright to meet her and she ruffled her fingers through the dog's thick fur. She glanced back through the window at Stella and Dajana huddled together.

'I don't know, doggie. I just don't know.'

Nancy turned the corner up Salisbury Street and Wolfie raced ahead on long legs up the hill. The dog stopped in front of a shop, wagged its tail furiously and pawed at a door. Lagging behind, Nancy watched as the door opened and Wolfie disappeared inside.

A minute later, she found the big black dog inside a shop— *Hopetoun Optical*—lovingly licking the face of a woman with short grey hair and a peacock-blue polar fleece and matching glasses. Nancy grimaced, the shop-owner looked familiar and she steeled herself for another angry tirade.

Once Wolfie stopped its kisses, the woman looked up at her through the window and waved. Lively hazel eyes gleamed behind her rectangular blue specs as she unlocked the door. 'I hope my boy Shuck has been looking after you,' she said. 'Come in.'

Nancy stepped inside the shop. Spectacles of all different shapes and colours neatly lined the walls, from conservative black and steel, to quirky geometric frames in hot pink and fluorescent yellow. The air smelled of lemon spray cleaner: fresh, clean and trustworthy.

'He's been good company,' she said and her heart clenched as she stroked his back. She should've known Wolfie wasn't hers to keep.

'The Traders Association meeting on Friday? We didn't get a chance to talk.' Of course, the only woman who smiled at her at the Festival meeting in the Railway. And the optometrist business card she'd found in her bag later on.

Nancy chuckled with relief. 'Sorry, so many new faces.'

The woman eyed her up and down. 'You really do look like her, you know.'

'You know Agnes?'

'I know more than people realise.' the woman nodded. 'I know exactly what's going on right now. Do you like Hopetoun?'

Nancy hesitated as she tried to keep up. 'It's interesting.'

'It is an absolutely fascinating place. But you'd know that. Did you like my book?' She leaned forward with wide expectant eyes.

'Sorry?'

'Did the plastic bag keep the rain off?'

'That was you?' Nancy blinked. 'I haven't had a chance to—'

'My masterpiece, you may say. The result of many years of hard work and research. Then I couldn't find a publisher brave enough to print it. Bunch of piss weaks.' The woman checked over both shoulders before continuing, although they seemed to be all alone in the darkened shop. 'But it's not all their fault. They're not allowed to print the truth.'

'Allowed?'

'The powers-that-be won't let them. They don't want us sheep knowing what's going on. But yes, Hopetoun is very significant. It lies in a very particular and specific place. It's no accident. You know about ley lines?' She raised her eyebrows.

'Not really.'

The woman grinned. 'There are lines of energy running around the globe. All the important centres of the world are joined by ley lines. Stonehenge, Alexandria, Mecca, Bethlehem, Atlantis and Hopetoun. Hopetoun is a power centre. You'd never think it but the ley lines pass right under our feet.' The woman stamped on the floor. 'As part of my research I was lucky enough to speak with some of the elders of the original mob. They told me some incredible things. But

I can't breathe a word of it.' She zipped her lips. 'But I will say two words. Ancient aliens.'

Nancy had no idea what the woman was on about but she nodded anyway.

'It all makes sense, you see. Hopetoun has always attracted the strange. We were all drawn here. Agnes. You. Me. It's destiny.' She threw her hands flamboyantly in the air. As her arms dropped back by her sides, Nancy spied a series of dark blue lines on Janet's neck. She squinted to get a better look but Janet's clothes quickly shifted back into place, covering the tattoo again. 'That's why I wanted you to be one of the first to read it. Synchronicity. You arriving just as I've gone to print. It's perfect.' She clapped.

'Janet, isn't it?'

'Of course. How rude of me, Janet Egloff. Optometrist and independent occult researcher.' She held out an age-spotted hand and shook Nancy's own with a feisty grip.

'Pleased to meet—'

'You might find Chapter 7 particularly interesting. It covers the history of the Traders Association and I've explained all their rituals. The bonfires, the salt perimeters, the initiation. You know.'

Nancy recoiled. 'Sorry?'

Janet smiled and patted Nancy's hand. 'Oh you poor innocent. That's why I sent my Shuck boy to look after you.'

The big black dog's ears pricked up.

'You must have Agnes's blood in those veins. Don't tell me you can't see what's really going on here? Open your eyes, my dear. Trust me, I'm an optometrist.' She winked.

Nancy stood open-mouthed. Ley lines and rituals?

This is what Danny meant about the Traders Association. What Stella meant when she talked about redressing the balance. Perhaps she and the others weren't the honest everyday shopkeepers they made out to be. And Agnes had been one of them too.

Her mouth ran dry. Hold on a second. What was she thinking. Magic? The occult? Here in inner city Melbourne in

2018? In one way, it could explain everything, the children last night, the man with the salt by the train tracks but spells and magic weren't real. Were they? Was Janet the local kook or was she the closest Nancy had come to the truth so far?

'Eyes,' Nancy murmured as she snapped out of her whirring thoughts and instinctively rubbed at her lower lashes.

'Forty years in the biz.'

'I've been seeing…smudges. It only started a few days ago. I thought my lenses were scratched at first. Now I'm worried I've got some horrible disease.'

'I see. Ha. Ha. No, seriously. I've got a few minutes before an emergency appointment. Pop in here and I'll take a quick look.'

Janet bustled her by the shoulders into a dimly lit room adjoining the shop. Taking off her glasses, Nancy sat down in an office chair and Janet swung the creaking metal arm in front of her face. 'Lean forward. Put your forehead there.'

Nancy rested her chin on the padded bar. They sat close enough for Nancy to smell the mint toothpaste on Janet's breath and sorbolene cream on her skin.

'Can you see the blurriness now?'

'No.'

'Let's see if there's a simple medical explanation.' Janet shimmied the apparatus closer and adjusted the dials. 'But aside from the usual allopathic diagnoses, there are plenty of alternative theories about the sources of eye problems. Grief. Dark futures. Inability to forgive. Inner torment manifesting as physical problems. Fascinating stuff.'

Bright light flooded in. Her eyeballs turned into glowing orbs, her optical veins casting spidery shadows on the curved white walls. Dark futures. Grief. Her eyes moistened and she blinked away a tear.

'Was Agnes one of your clients?'

'Unfortunately not. Are you wondering if it's hereditary?'

'I don't know,' Nancy mumbled. This was true about so many things.

With a tut of her tongue, Janet pushed herself back from the

112

equipment on her wheeled office chair. 'Perfectly healthy,' she announced. 'But if you're still worried, I can do a more thorough test tomorrow. Although as I said there may be a different, less straight-forward explanation.'

Wolfie started to bark and Janet leapt up from her chair. 'Sorry, my patient must be here.'

'I'd like to know more,' Nancy said as she replaced her glasses and scrambled up to her feet.

Janet was already halfway out the door. 'OK, let me check my appointment book.'

'About everything.'

Janet turned with a mischievous grin. 'I knew you would. What are you doing tonight?'

'Are you free around five?'

'Five-thirty? I have a *kau chin* meet-up in Box Hill after this appointment. Sometimes those divination sessions can drag on.' Janet bustled back into the shop.

Nancy followed. 'The Railway?'

'Perfect. Mine's a Guinness by the way.'

An Asian woman and young boy with an eye patch were waiting on the street as Janet opened the glass door. Close behind her, Nancy held her breath, a new reflex whenever she saw a child, but the mother and son didn't give her a second glance as they crossed paths and Nancy headed outside.

She walked to the kerb to cross the street and waited for the traffic to clear, shaking her head with a chuckle as she tried to decipher half of what Janet told her.

'Take Shuck with you,' Janet shouted after her through the open door. 'You need him more than I do.'

The dog trotted over to her and Nancy threaded her hands under his collar, her fingers intertwined with his warm fur. 'Your owner is a bit of a character, isn't she?'

She was positive that the dog smiled back at her.

Finally Nancy bought her milk and an outrageously overpriced avocado then turned home for a big mug of tea and to start the big clean-up downstairs. Pulling up her hood, she hid her face, she'd had more than enough social interaction for one Sunday morning.

As she passed Station Street Books again, a new wave of panic churned in her belly. Was it a date? What was she going to wear? Her throat felt thick as Grant's laugh rumbled inside her head. It was only a meal with a new friend, she told herself. It didn't mean anything. She wasn't being disloyal. She squeezed her eyes shut and swallowed hard.

With a concerted exhale, her panic eased and Nancy opened her eyes again. Then she saw it. In big black letters, two foot tall on her shop front window.

'WITCH.'

1977 – AGNES

Hopetoun. Agnes chose her new home purely on its name. Hopetoun sounded like the perfect place for a fresh start.

After escaping Braidwood, she hid away in Brisbane for four years, discarding her flowing dresses for the anonymous white cap and sensible shoes of a baker's apprentice. Once her training was complete, she said goodbye to muggy Queensland and headed south with her savings and the money from her inheritance. In an inner city Melbourne suburb called Hopetoun, she found a neglected Victorian-era shop with a flat upstairs. Within a month, she purchased a used baker's oven and Bittesby Bakery was open for business. Perhaps she should have changed her name.

Hopetoun sat alongside the cattle sale yards and if the wind was westerly, the stink of manure and blood seeped through the windows and soiled the damp washing on the line. Wool and wheat warehouses bordered the railway tracks and the flour mill and trucks rumbled around the clock. This was before Hopetoun's gentrification, when coffee was instant, windows had bars to keep out the junkies and the streets stank of Chiko rolls.

In Hopetoun Agnes found a new quiet happiness. She baked her bread and chatted to her customers but kept to herself. She tried not to think of the past. And most of the time, she succeeded.

It was a late afternoon in March when a heavily pregnant elfin woman stepped cautiously through the shop door.

'Can I help you?' Agnes smiled and wiped her hands on her apron. The woman's eyes darted from cornice to cornice, a little boy beside her, their hands tightly intertwined. 'Sorry, I don't have much left today.'

'Busy day? Business is good? You are lucky,' the woman said, a tinge of Italian heritage in her voice. Her little boy pulled free from her hands and squatted on the black and white linoleum floor, playing with a toy car. The woman clutched her

115

hands tightly over her round belly. 'Not everyone starts off so well.'

'I do make a pretty good lamington,' Agnes said with a grin.

The woman chuckled, the sound was throaty but brittle. 'I should have introduced myself. I'm Mafalda Caruso.'

Agnes recognised the unusual name from the Italian restaurant on Linlithgow Street, with its red and white tablecloths and winking candles in Chianti bottles.

'Sorry for being a stranger,' she added. 'It has taken me far too long to come and say hello. Welcome you to our little community.'

'Mafalda herself? What a pleasure. Don't apologise, love. With your own restaurant and this little one, you wouldn't have a moment to yourself.' Agnes turned to the boy. 'Would you like a biscuit, sweetie?'

The boy, three or four years old, rushed over and held out his hand shyly. His eyes were brown and wary like his mother's. Agnes handed him a golden biscuit dotted with red, blue and yellow Smarties.

'Say thank you, Alessandro,' her mother said.

He mumbled a reply, then plucked the Smarties out one by one.

'How about you, Mafalda? Something for afternoon tea?'

'I haven't come for bread.' Mafalda held out a petite hand. 'I came for another reason. Has anyone spoken to you about the Hopetoun Traders Association?'

Agnes shook her head.

'All of the business owners in the area meet once a month. It's a chance for us to talk shop with people who understand our strange ways.' She chuckled again. 'Anyway, our next meeting is tomorrow night at the Railway Hotel on the corner. You are most welcome to come along and join.'

Mafalda stared at her with a gaze so intense, it forced Agnes to look away. She glanced at the floor and pinched at her bottom lip.

Her first thought was to make excuses, but suddenly Agnes ached for life and people and parties. The idea of another night upstairs with the telly and a tumbler of sherry seemed depressing and empty. Perhaps it was time to come out of her seclusion.

'I'd like that.'

'Good,' Mafalda said breathily. 'The community needs to stick together. And you'll be a perfect addition.'

Agnes's chest swelled. It would be nice to belong again.

After fleeing Lorna and the farm house on that night five years ago, Agnes locked her magic away. The thrall of the left hand book was too seductive, too corrupting. The change in Lorna had been a cautionary tale and *Shekinah's Delight* had been her last spell. The power frightened her. A strong hand was needed to maintain the balance, and Agnes chose instead to run and hide. Again.

The bread she baked for Hopetoun was ordinary and free from enchantment. But as soon as she put away her books— she couldn't bring herself to destroy them—her dreams dried up, replaced by a single recurring nightmare, a fear which bled into the daylight. The books would not be silenced so easily.

Sometimes she'd see a blond man in the distance. At the end of the street, standing by the roadside or at the far end of the train carriage. But Walter was always just far enough away for her to question her vision. Every now and then, it was a voice whispering in her ears. It was only a word or two and at first she blamed the wind. The whispers were so sporadic that she easily forgot all about them. Until it reappeared and she was cast back into the world she'd thought she'd left behind.

Try as she might, the magic inside her wouldn't stay dormant. Unsaid spells weighed heavy on her tongue, the knowledge scratched underneath her skin like a dog at the door. With a clench of her jaw, she'd shove the feelings aside and focus. On the next vanilla slice, the next scone, the next loaf. In Hopetoun she made normal bread for a normal life.

It was quarter to seven when Agnes entered the lively Ladies Lounge of the Railway Hotel. Her face blossomed as she smoothed down her new flowing dress. How she missed the bustle of parties, and at first she thought the tingle under her skin was excitement. It was clear, she wasn't cut out to be a hermit. But as she crossed the patterned carpet, the tingle began to sting, and Agnes glanced over her shoulder, half-expecting to see a tall blond man looming behind her.

'You came!'

Mafalda, dressed in a pale-blue pussy-bow shirt, grabbed Agnes by the hand. She pulled her into a circle of two men and a woman, while behind them, a handful of groups of two or three stood and chatted, sipping Moselle or beer.

'Let me introduce you to the rest of the Five.'

A buck-toothed man thrust out a hand with only half a middle finger. Agnes shook his hand feebly.

'Farrugia is the local butcher. And this is Valjoy.'

The tall and matronly Valjoy, with a lacquered helmet of white hair, grinned. 'Pleased to meet you. You do a wonderful finger bun, darl. Oh that pink icing with those little sprinkles. I run the hair salon on Station Street, by the way. *Classy Coiffure.*'

'And this…' Mafalda turned to the final man in the group. '… is Fabian from the travel agents.'

'Delighted,' said the open-shirted Fabian with a toss of his golden head.

'And where's Russell?' Mafalda scouted around. 'There he is. Come here and meet Agnes.'

Agnes clenched as she glimpsed a tall fair-haired man in a suit pushing through the crowd toward them.

It was him. He was here.

'Russell is the local solicitor.'

He stepped into full view, handsome-faced and gap-toothed. 'Welcome.'

Agnes exhaled. It wasn't him but the resemblance was strong. He studied her playfully and Agnes immediately blushed.

She composed herself and cleared her throat. 'How lovely to meet you all. Do you get together like this often? Are you all old friends? How long have you lived here?' Questions poured from Agnes's mouth as she freed years of banked-up conversation. 'It's really a lovely place. I especially like the trees.'

The Five eyed her curiously but kindly and someone handed her a glass of wine. Yet as she spoke, a familiar cold dread returned and gnawed at her belly. Like a bad memory, wiped from her mind, remembered somewhere deep inside her body.

The white-haired Valjoy interrupted and clunked her chunky gold ring against her wineglass. 'Can I have your attention?' She hollered in a voice loud enough to stop traffic.

The chit-chat hushed in the room as the Traders Association members and Agnes circled around her.

'Let's begin. First of all—thanks for coming along. What a ripper turnout. And great to see some new faces.'

Valjoy beamed in Agnes's direction, then the rest of the room turned and stared. Agnes plastered on a smile.

'Alright, the first item on our list. No surprises. It's the thing we've all been talking about...the closure of the sale yards.'

The crowd murmured and grumbled.

'I know. I know. But those buggers at the council reckon they're serious about closing it this time. They're saying it's a health hazard and want the cattle sales moved out of the city.'

'Yes, hazardous to our health!' shouted a man. Agnes recognised his luxurious moustache from behind the counter at the Salisbury Street fish and chip shop. 'We'll starve to death. We'll have no bloody customers.'

'Right, Costa. That's why this year's Autumn Festival has to be our best yet,' Valjoy said with a serious tone. 'There are too many strangers in Hopetoun these days. They're the ones complaining to the council. We need to welcome them in. Bring them into the fold and help them understand us.'

Fabian nodded. 'Hear. Hear.'

'We need to do more,' Russell interjected with clipped English consonants. 'The boundaries need to be refreshed weekly.'

A gaunt man groaned. 'Those sacks are bloody heavy.'

'We have to be diligent,' Russell continued. 'Someone or something is breaching the perimeter. I can feel the gaps. That's how they're getting in.'

Apprehension trickled down Agnes's legs and into her hands. This conversation had a familiar strain.

'We need something new,' said Valjoy.

'A new ritual,' said Fabian.

Agnes gulped. Ritual. She glanced for the door.

'The corn dollies aren't much chop,' Valjoy agreed. 'We need something stronger.'

Mafalda raised her small hand. 'Can I introduce a newcomer to the Association? Agnes Bittesby from the new bakery on Station Street.'

Agnes smiled weakly as all eyes turned to her again.

'She also has the knowledge we need.'

'Excuse me?' Agnes stuttered.

'We know who you are.' Valjoy said with a knowing nod.

Agnes's stomach hardened.

'We can't risk another bad harvest. We need to stop the government wiping out our livelihood,' Russell said. His tone was serious but there was a coy twinkle in his eye. 'We need your help.'

'I think you have me confused with someone else.'

'She's modest.' Mafalda placed a hand on Agnes's shoulder. Agnes flinched.

'Poor love. She probably thinks we're a bunch of loonies,' laughed Fabian. 'Honey, we're only looking to protect ourselves and our prosperity. Nothing nasty.'

'I don't know what you're talking about.'

'I saw you,' Farrugia the butcher said matter-of-factly. 'We all did.'

Agnes recoiled with a blink. 'What do you mean?'

'With that Lorna Gaskill woman.'

Her belly lurched. 'Who?'

'There was a photo in the Herald,' the butcher continued.

'With her obituary. You were in the background.'

'She's dead?' Agnes darted to cover her mouth. Was it true? Was Lorna really gone?

'I saw it and said to my girls,' Valjoy said. ''That's the woman from the new bakery.' We're so pleased you're here with us. It's a sign.'

The other members nodded.

'You must help us,' said Russell. 'We need someone of your talents. How long did you study under her?'

Her heart thumping, Agnes scouted all around the Ladies Lounge, looking for the closest exit. Everyone seemed to step forward, encircling her.

'Please help us, Agnes. Our rituals haven't worked,' Mafalda said with her hands clasped. 'You are one of us now. Show us how. Share your power with us. Please.'

Agnes's mind raced as she swivelled in all directions until she found a weak spot in the circle. She clenched her fists.

'Sorry,' she said and lunged towards an elderly man with a cane. She elbowed him aside and broke free, dashing for the door, ignoring them calling her name.

A familiar sound rang in her ears.

A laugh.

She had been a fool.

Of course, they would never let her get away so easily.

1923 – THE STRANGER

Sweat slid down William Pinckney's backbone as he tossed another shovel-full of sun-baked manure out of the pen. The wind blew a cloud of dust into his damp face, his skin now brown with a sheen of dirt. It was only October but like a school yard bully, Summer had shoved Spring roughly aside and jumped the queue.

'Haven't you heard?' said the scrawny and sly-eyed Coonan. But he wasn't talking to William. No one talked to William if they could help it. 'They're calling it The Ghoul of Hopetoun. A monster roaming the streets, peering into people's houses. Scaring the women-folk half to death.'

'Dirty beggar,' spat the gnome-faced Bowen.

William scraped his shovel along the rock-hard ground, hiding his face as he always did, and said nothing. Bowen and Coonan quickly switched topic to the chances of a horse named *Maid in the Mist* and the rumours of a police strike. They never paid any attention to him anyway.

When the sun went down and the working day was over, William returned to his tiny rented room in Mrs Moriarty's house on Hardiman Street and waited.

Five weeks he'd been in Hopetoun, three years drifting from place to place. When his boat returned from the Front to all the welcoming crowds at the wharf, he turned right instead of left and kept going. His father and mother wouldn't want him back and neither would Mary. Not in the state he was in now. No one could possibly want him.

The nights were getting shorter and tonight William had to wait longer. He lay on his rickety bed, smoking on the thin mattress. He didn't even try to sleep, sleep never soothed him anymore and so he walked instead.

When the sky outside was black and the house was quiet, he tip-toed downstairs for the front door.

'Mr Pinckney.'

He jumped as Mrs Moriarty appeared wearing a white mob cap.

'I was about to bolt the door,' she said with her affected

haughty accent. 'Are you going out? Haven't you heard?'

Averting his face, William shook his head.

'The police have gone ahead with their ridiculous strike. It's lawless out there.'

'I'll take my chances,' he muttered at his shoes.

'Well, knock five times when you want to come back in.' She rapped her bony knuckles on the wooden door. 'Then I shall know it's you. I don't want to open the door to any of those young prowling hooligans.'

With a nod, he passed through the door and stepped out into the enveloping darkness. The streets were sparsely lit but the weak yellow gas-light left enough shadows for a scarred man to hide in. He could breathe in the dark, no one stared or whispered or gasped in horror. If only he could hide himself away forever. Perhaps in a cave, but William was a city boy, he would never last in the bush.

Voices surged around the corner, then a mob appeared carrying lanterns. William quickly turned on his heel to duck out of sight.

'It's him,' a woman shrieked. 'Get him.'

Two speedy lads darted to block William's path. One of the boys held a light up to William's face. 'What an ugly blighter!' he exclaimed as the rest of the group encircled them.

'I don't want any trouble,' William spluttered, his throat tightening.

'Tom. George. Grab his arms.'

'I didn't mean to.' William dropped his head.

If people left their curtains wide open, he couldn't help it if he looked inside. Men smoking their pipes by the fire, women darning by their sides, sleepy children in their nightgowns. It was a glimpse into a world William would never know.

'I'll go,' he gulped. 'I'll pack up and leave.'

'What is he on about?' said the woman. 'Is he soft in the head too?'

'Never mind, let's get him to the Green,' ordered a red-bearded man.

The boys hauled William off his feet and tugged him down

the hill. He whined and tried to pull away but they gripped his arms tight. His captors chuckled and elbowed each other as the mob crossed Salisbury Street and the train line. They passed another gang of younger lads, no older than ten, smashing shop windows and no one said a word. Then William remembered. The police strike. Tonight there was no one to keep law and order, and as they headed towards the park, William could smell burning.

He clamped his eyes shut. The roar of the flames sent him reeling back four years. To the heat, the smoke, the screams, some of them his own. As they dragged him further, his breaths swelled, shallow and fast in his chest. He yanked at his bound arms, desperate to touch the skin on his face, prove this was just another dream. His scars were real, war scorched into his face.

'Here he is!' the woman who found him cried and William's eyes sprung open. He was now in front of a crowd and a towering spitting bonfire.

A statuesque woman stepped forward and sized William up and down with a sneer. 'A stranger,' she turned and said to the crowd. 'Does anyone know his name?'

The onlookers shook their heads.

'Please,' William said until a rough hand was clamped over his lips.

'He must be the bringer of bad luck. The cause of the drought. Look at his face. He's cursed.'

The others murmured in agreement.

'He is the one,' she said solemnly. William widened his eyes and tried to scream but no one took a scrap of notice.

The crowd parted. Three men carried a cage towards him and a fourth man followed, brandishing a scythe.

'We must free the community from the curse of the drought,' the woman said. 'Free the bountiful harvest with the offering of this stranger.'

The cage was made of stiff woven straw, rather than steel. The men swung open the door and shoved William inside, then reaching through the gaps, they yanked him up to his feet.

The matronly leader thrust the scythe above her head. The sharp silver blade glistened red in the light of the flames. 'With a stranger's blood, the fertility is returned and with it, our prosperity.'

The blade sliced cleanly through the bars of woven straw and William's throat. The people cheered, and William clutching at the white-hot pain, slid into an enveloping, and eternal, darkness.

2018 – NANCY

Nancy's glass of red disappeared fast. The front bar of the Railway Hotel was quiet, she'd easily found a private table in the corner and was glad to finally sit down after a Sunday of scrubbing away spray paint and gluey flour. The cleaning had taken up the entire day and she hadn't even had a chance to open Janet's book. But all day long, her head buzzed with theories about the children and questions for Janet. Nancy checked her phone again. The strange woman was already ten minutes late. She hoped Miles wasn't the early type.

The door creaked open and Janet marched in. After a hearty wave at Nancy, she headed straight to the bar and ordered a drink.

'Did you read the story of the stranger?' Janet said as she took a seat at the table.

Nancy shook her head, it appeared there was no time for hellos. 'I was a little busy today.'

'Strangers are a regular guest star in folklore. And even today in urban legends. The stranger always brings bad luck to the community. Ill will and misfortune. A lesson to us all to conform and assimilate.'

'Right,' said Nancy.

'But don't be fooled. Don't dismiss the stories. At heart, we're still a bunch of villagers protecting our turf. Despite all this modernity, we're still ignorant peasants.'

The chisel-jawed barman plonked a pint of Guinness down in front of Janet. She nodded in thanks and took a hungry slurp of white froth.

'In Hopetoun,' she continued. 'There's one documented case of the Traders Association acting against a stranger. I wrote about it in Chapter 26. It was after the long drought of 1923. The stranger was a drifter and they took the law into their own hands.'

Nancy frowned. 'What do you mean?'

'Dragged him down Salisbury Street and threw him onto a bonfire over there in the Green. Apparently the bonfire was as tall as an oak tree and the flames blazed all night. He was burned to a crisp until nothing was left.'

'Are you serious?' Nancy blurted.

'It was 1923. Well-timed. They did it during the police strike.'

'They got away with it?'

'No one was charged as far as I know.'

'Sounds like a lynching,' Nancy said. 'Cold-blooded but nothing magical.'

'It's all connected.' Janet leaned in closer and whispered, her hazel eyes glimmered behind her blue-rimmed glasses. 'The Association dates back to the earliest days of European settlement. When they first arrived there was a terrible drought and the newcomers didn't know how to deal with the conditions here. But they brought their beliefs with them, from all around the British Isles. Of course in those days, the Brits were the only ones allowed in the country, except for a handful of Chinese. They all came together with their different folkways here in Hopetoun, combining their customs to start something new.'

Nancy pressed her lips together as she listened.

'But these days.' Janet waved her arm around the pub. 'The Association lacks the power to do anything useful. Not like the old days. They pretend. Tinker around the edges. Like the perimeter of salt. One of their useless defences supposedly to keep the evil out of Hopetoun.'

The man with the sack by the railway tracks. He was part of the Traders Association.

'Weak. I blame the space satellites. They're experimenting on our neural networks, you see. Infantilising us. Someone should blast them out of the sky.'

'Is all this in your book? What the Traders Association is really up to?'

'Of course. I'm no coward. It's a story which needs to be told.'

'But what do they think about it? Stella and the others?'

'Oh, they think I'm a total crank. But I've never cared what other people think of me. Who has the time? There's far too much to do. You can't let all those nuff-nuffs distract you from your work.'

It was Nancy's turn to lean in. 'Is Agnes in your book?'

'Ah, you really didn't have time to read it.' Janet smiled. 'Yes, the whole tale about the missing Sheridan girls. The real truth about what happened.'

'You know what happened?'

Janet nodded. 'The truth weighs heavily on some people. I know all about the book.'

Nancy's eyes widened. Other people knew about Agnes's recipe book? Who else knew? The book was hers and hers alone. No one else was worthy of it. She wanted to sprint out the door and run home to make sure the book was safe. Stroke the navy-blue cover and promise the book, she would always protect it.

She falsely smiled. 'What book?'

The pub door opened and Nancy's stomach jolted as Miles walked inside, five minutes early. She hid her frown. He easily spotted her and mimed a drinking gesture across the bar. One glass was usually her limit but she nodded and held her glass up in the air. This should give her a few minutes longer alone with Janet.

'Sorry,' Nancy said with a wince.

'But time to go?' Janet said. 'I understand.'

'I have so many more questions.'

'Come up to my house later tonight. I'm up on Louis Street. I'll explain everything. I think you'll be quite proud of your aunt. These fools never appreciated her, the average never do. They always mock those things they are too stupid to understand.'

'Tonight.' Nancy nodded.

'I'll be waiting up for you. It's so nice to have someone sensible to talk to. I'll also give you one of my other books on the numerological systems in the world of finance and the hidden messages from the Old Gods within the blockchain algorithms. Here he comes. I'll leave you to it.'

Miles slipped into an empty seat at the table. 'Don't leave

on my account, Janet.'

'No. No. I just popped over to say hello. Nice to see you again, Agnes. Oops, I mean Nancy.'

The grey-haired woman wandered over to the other side of the pub with her half-drunk pint. She pulled up a chair and took out a paperback, a notebook and pen.

'Ah, so you've met our Janet,' Miles said.

'What's her story?'

'A harmless conspiracy nut. She has to be on the spectrum.'

'Do you sell any of her books?'

'God, no. She tried to convince me to stock them once. Unreadable rants.'

'Was it the local history one?'

'No.' Miles tilted his head. 'I didn't know she'd written about Hopetoun. Is it new?'

'Apparently she's written about the Traders Association.' Nancy watched Miles's face closely. 'The dark side.'

He laughed. 'Boring meetings in the pub and getting council approvals to hold a fete?'

'She did mention magic or something.'

'She's a character. Excuse me,' Miles said and placed down his glass of red. 'Nature calls.'

He ambled across the room towards the Gents and Nancy leaned back in her chair, savouring the moment alone. The conversation with Janet circled like seagulls in her mind, and for the first time in days, Nancy breathed deeply. She finally felt a little closer to the truth.

'Turn it up, Travis!' someone yelled.

The small Sunday pub crowd all looked up from their beers and turned to the television in the corner above the bar.

'In tonight's main story. New developments in a twenty-five-year-old mystery,' the doll-faced newsreader announced. 'Police have identified the body found along the Craigieburn train line, close to Hopetoun Station, on Saturday afternoon as Molly Sheridan. Five-year-old Molly and her older sister

Bridget went missing from their home in Hopetoun on sixth March 1992.'

Nancy's mouth dropped open. The Sheridan girls were headlines all over again. Her chest tightened with dread.

'I told you!' yelled a red-faced man with silver stubble as he jabbed his finger at the screen.

'Bloody hell,' Miles whispered in her ear as he reappeared and slipped into the seat alongside her facing the television.

'Forensic examinations are underway to determine the cause of death. A thorough search of the surrounding area has failed to locate the body of her sister, Bridget Sheridan.'

'Did you hear about the hand—?' whispered a woman at the next table, dressed in leopard-print with a plunging neckline.

'There has been an outstanding reward for any information on the Sheridan girls since 1992. At the time of their disappearance, several suspects were identified but discounted, including the children's estranged father and a local man well-known to police.'

'And the witch…' It was the stubbly man at the bar again. 'This time they'll get her for sure.'

'Ssh.' His rail-thin drinking mate elbowed him and they both glanced Nancy's way.

'She's just as bad. Did you hear about the kids?'

The two barflies weren't the only ones glaring in her direction and Nancy slumped under the weight of the accusing eyes. She wanted to yell back, tell them this had nothing to do with her, but all she could do was clench her fists. Twenty-five years ago, she was a thousand kilometres away worrying about the thickness of her thighs, her marks for Maths and whether Gavin Armstrong had looked at her on the bus ride home. But in Agnes's absence, it seemed Nancy was the new scapegoat. She'd not only taken over the shop, but she'd also taken her place as the local embodiment of evil.

'This is good for Agnes. And you.' Miles slipped back into his original seat across from her, facing the wall rather than the dirty looks of the front bar patrons. She wondered if she should ask to swap places. His round face shone as he nodded. 'With all the advancements in forensics since the 1990s, this time the police will be able solve the crime once and for all. Find the real culprit and finally clear your Aunt's name.'

'I hope so.' Nancy chewed on her lip. 'Are you sure you want to be seen with me?'

'Why ever not? You're quite the local celebrity.'

Nancy scoffed. 'They'll be burning my effigy on the Green soon.'

'Everyone loves a scandal.' He charged his glass in the air. 'Let's drink to putting old stories to bed. Cheers.'

They clinked glasses and Nancy took a large slurp. As she swallowed, she stared out the window, out into the dusk, to the flashing red lights of the train boom gate and the pink glow reflected in the puddles. That's where Molly's body had been, out there, not five minutes' walk away from her warm seat in the pub. The poor little creature had lain cold and alone in a hole as trains rushed by, undisturbed and overlooked, for twenty-something years.

'I've had enough of dead bodies and kidnappings,' Miles said. 'Let's talk about other things. Pineapple on pizza? Yay or nay?'

With a chuckle, Nancy mounted an argument about the merits of pineapple until the fresh-faced waitress appeared with two roast dinners in her hands. Suddenly starving, Nancy grabbed her fork, forgot her manners and gobbled down her first green vegetables for days. Although whether peas smothered in rich thick gravy counted as healthy was not the point. After leaving the golden roast potatoes for last, somehow, she found herself talking about Grant.

'Six and half months. We'd been seeing each other in secret for over three years. After he died, no one would believe me. When I tried to tell his wife, she wouldn't listen, she said I was lying. She wouldn't even let me say goodbye. Then I had some trouble at work and lost my job. And then Gran died. In her letter of wishes with her will, she asked me to come and look after Agnes. I had no job, no lover, no family of my own, nothing to lose, so here I am.'

Miles nodded with a pained smile. 'You've had a tough run.'

'Every day is different,' she croaked, then cleared her throat to swallow away the sadness. 'What about you? Any skeletons?' Nancy gasped and covered her mouth with her hand and Miles raised his eyebrows.

'Peter, Peter Pumpkin Eater…'

'…had a wife but couldn't keep her?'

'Left me a few years ago. It was for the best. Well, that's what she told me. Apparently I was too single-minded. Whatever that means. But it was a first edition copy of *The Magic Pudding*! In hindsight, we were probably ill-suited but love is a curious beastie.'

'Books are very important to you?'

'Stories are all we have,' he replied with a sigh. 'Often a story is more palatable than the truth.'

'Did you come to Hopetoun after your divorce?'

'Longer than that. At least ten years. I came for the cheap rent.' Miles chuckled but the sound was hollow. His laugh stopped abruptly and he lowered his voice. 'This might sound a little weird.'

Miles twisted his wineglass stem between his fingers. Nancy pushed her glasses up. The last wedge of potato seemed to stick in her throat.

'There's something unusual about Hopetoun. It all looks normal on the surface, just another inner city suburb, but there has always been a lingering…'

He paused and bit his lip.

'Darkness?' Nancy replied.

'Exactly. I've never told anyone this before. I lived on the other side of town, at uni when the…incident…happened. The rumours drew me here. And I rented a funny little shop in a peculiar suburb. Do you think I'm ghoulish?'

He grinned and Nancy pressed her lips into a line, her eyes not leaving him for a moment.

'What happened to their mother?' she said.

'I thought we weren't going to talk about them?'

132

Nancy shrugged.

'I understand she passed away. Cancer. But Jackie is still here.'

'Jackie?' Nancy spluttered. 'The woman who hangs around the Green?'

'That's her, Jackie Sheridan. She's their sister. She was babysitting them on the night they disappeared.'

'What?'

Miles nodded and Nancy continued in a daze. 'The missing girls are Jackie's sisters?'

'And she worked in Agnes's bakery,' Miles said.

Nancy clutched her chest.

'Apparently she worked in Agnes's shop around the time they disappeared.'

Her phone buzzed in her pocket but she ignored it.

'Didn't you know the connection?' He frowned.

'But Jackie said to me...' Her breaths were tangled and shallow, strangled by the new information. 'No wonder she's so ...'

When she first thumped on the bakery door, Jackie said Agnes was calling to her. But why? And why now? After twenty-five years, what could Agnes possibly have to say to her?

Nancy's phone rang again.

1977 – AGNES

Fleeing the Railway Hotel, Agnes went straight upstairs without turning on the lights or closing the curtains. She poured herself a large sherry and lay on the couch, chain-smoking in the dark.

Someone knocked at the door and a man called out her name. She waited until it was quiet and then went to the window. A blond figure was standing directly across the road, under a street light by the train line. She flinched but when her eyes adjusted, she realised it wasn't Walter. Instead it was the travel agent, Fabian, watching her house.

Stepping back into the shadows, she paced the hallway in her stockinged feet, up and down until her cigarettes were all gone and her sherry glass was empty. Her past was more difficult to escape than she imagined, old mistakes returning like cold sores. Lorna's death would have been front page news in Sydney, and now everyone would know of her connection to Lorna—the Witch of Woollahra.

She sighed. One day she had hoped she'd reconcile with Pamela. In her daydreams her sister would appear on her doorstep, having finally stood up to her bully of a husband, and they'd cry and talk all night. But after this?

Emptying the bottle into her glass, Agnes glanced out the window again. Fabian was gone and this time it was Russell gazing up at her window. A changing of the guard? She scrubbed her forehead and slurped at her sherry. Or had it been Russell standing out there all along? Her thoughts were like scrambled eggs.

She'd always expected she'd feel something when Lorna died, wake-up one morning with a lightness in her chest and she'd know. But she felt nothing, her body was as heavy as ever. Perhaps their bond had been broken a long time ago, maybe even on the day she left the farmhouse. The chains were only in her mind and she'd been free all along. Either way, Lorna was gone and there was nothing left to be afraid of. No one would force her to use her skills for ways she didn't agree with. She had complete control.

She headed into her bedroom and pulled a battered suitcase from the top of the wardrobe. She flicked open the locks and stared inside at two notebooks. Like chancing upon a lost love in the street, excitement fluttered in her belly, and she caressed the cardboard covers. She opened one and started to read, her heart bursting into song as she rediscovered old words, her fingertips gracing the scribbles in the margins. Part of her soul unlocked as she turned page after page and welcomed the magic back again. Agnes Bittesby—hearth witch, healer, helper. That's who she was and who she is. It was time to set herself free.

The perfect recipe would be here.

It would be nice to belong again.

2018 – NANCY

Nancy's phone buzzed again. Jackie. Agnes. The Sheridan sisters. In a daze, she pulled her phone from her pocket.

Speak of the devil. The call was from Willowmere Residential Home.

'What's wrong?' Nancy scurried away from the table and out of Miles's earshot.

'Miss Grakowski. This is Meredith Chung, Centre Manager of Willowmere,' a woman said in an efficient tone. 'I'm afraid I have some bad news.'

'Oh no.' Nancy grabbed the wall. 'Is she gone?'

'She hasn't passed.' The Manager cleared her throat. 'She's missing.'

'What?' Nancy barked.

'Her room was empty when we came to collect her for dinner. We've searched the grounds but we've been unable to find her. The police have been informed but we're sure we'll be able to find her very soon.'

'I'm coming.'

'Leave it with the professionals, Miss Grakowski.'

'Fat lot of good you professionals have done. I'll be there as soon as I can.' Nancy ended the call and scrubbed her hand across her face. 'Shit.'

Back at the table, she downed her remaining wine in a single gulp. Miles stared up at her wide-eyed. 'Agnes is missing. I have to go look for her.'

'Oh, my god. Let me get you a cab. You can't drive now.' He pointed to the empty wine glass in her hand.

'I don't have a car. Anyway I should go home first. I'll need my coat.'

'I'll walk you.'

'You don't have to.'

'I want to.'

Marching through the front bar of the pub, the other patrons all looked up to watch Nancy leave, and this time she ignored their looks of disapproval. Once she was out the door, she set off along the footpath at a brisk pace, with Miles puffing behind her, struggling to keep up. There was a touch of winter in the air and Nancy pictured poor Agnes wandering the streets barefoot, confused and cold.

'It's weird,' she said, more to herself than Miles. 'I don't even really know Agnes but living in her house and taking over her business, now I feel she is part of me.'

'She's family,' Miles wheezed from a few steps behind. 'You share the same blood.'

The boom gates clanged again. A train rumbled into the station and squealed to a stop. The doors bleeped open and a trickle of people passed through the open barriers and joined the dog walkers and night joggers on the footpath.

'Was that Dajana?' Nancy said as a blonde woman in black jogged away into the night.

'I don't think so.'

Nancy studied each face she passed but there was no sign of an elderly woman with long grey hair.

'Only last week Mum told me that I'm named after her. My gran insisted but Mum thought Agnes was too old-fashioned.'

'You've always had a connection,' Miles said. 'It's understandable.'

'But I never got a chance to know her. Maybe I should have tried harder.'

They passed the terrace houses and unoccupied shops but as her own shop came into view, Nancy gasped. A sense of dread dropped over her like a kidnapper's hood.

'What is it?' Miles said.

Nancy ignored him and headed straight for the shop door, her keys rattling in her shaking hands.

'Is there something wrong?' Miles called out when she finally managed to open the door, but Nancy was already whisking through the swinging door and clumping upstairs.

All seemed quiet and normal but as soon as she set foot in the lounge room, she knew it was gone. Her knees went to jelly. The coffee table was empty. She should have hidden it away safely before she left to meet Janet.

Fool.

Agnes's book was gone.

Maybe she was wrong. She rushed into the room like a cyclone. Couch cushions, discarded clothes, books and letters were pushed aside and tossed into the air. But it was pointless, in her gut she knew it was gone.

Who would do this? Who even knew the book existed? Janet?

'Are you alright?' said Miles, cowering in the doorway.

She stopped in the middle of the lounge room and scraped her fingers through her hair. 'Fine,' she said.

Who had a key? Agnes? Is that why she escaped from the home tonight? Who else would want an old woman's recipes? The book didn't even contain Agnes's award-winning bread recipe.

The thought of the book being lost forever made her double over. It was a disembowelling pain she knew well. Grief.

Wolfie started to bark from the back yard. Downstairs, a heavy knock banged on the door. Miles jumped and Nancy glanced up.

'Police.' A voice called.

With a sigh, Nancy peeked outside through the lounge room window. 'Great.'

Four people were standing on her doorstep downstairs; Trinh and the bald one in uniform with a man and a woman, both in business suits. The bald one, Brouwer, glanced up and spotted her, his eyes narrowed to slits.

She trudged downstairs and opened the door to four serious faces, her hands on her hips. 'Is this about Agnes?'

A middle aged woman in a grey suit and wavy brown hair stepped forward. 'Detective Lennart. North Melbourne CID.' Her plain masculine suit was brightened by a hot pink shirt. 'I have a warrant here to search the premises.'

'What?' Nancy recoiled. 'Why?'

'In the matter of the Sheridan case.'

'But that was...'

'Please remain here, Miss Grakowski.' Lennart turned back to the others. 'Brouwer, start here in the shop. Trinh, go upstairs.'

'Ma'am, there are a few sheds outside,' Trinh said and Nancy avoided meeting her eyes. 'They might be a good place to start?'

'Just secure the place, Trinh. The bobcat digger will be here later.'

Nancy stepped back with her hands up in surrender and allowed the two Constables to come inside. 'I can't deal with this right now. I have to go and look for Agnes. Detective, my great aunt is missing.'

Lennart nodded. 'We've already got a team helping with the search. It's best if you remain here for now. Have you had any contact with her?'

'She's got dementia. She's not exactly big on Facebook.'

'It's important you contact us if you hear from her or see her. I realise she's family but she's important to our enquiries.'

'You can't question her,' Nancy snapped. 'She's ill.'

'We want to ensure she is safe first.'

Nancy pushed past Lennart out through the front door. Her cheeks were red-hot and she clutched at her forehead. She shouldn't have had that second glass of wine.

'Where are you going?' the Detective demanded.

'For some air.' Nancy marched out onto the footpath.

Light beamed from every window as the police searched both floors. With the two police cars parked out front, and after the evening news, it would be obvious to any onlooker what was happening. Blame had come to Bittesby Bakery again, and thanks to social media, the whole neighbourhood and the whole world would likely already know.

'This is rather exciting.' Miles sidled up to her, rubbing his hands. 'Although you should get a lawyer. Do you want me to call someone? I know people.'

'You should go. You don't have to hang around here.'

'I'm happy to stay,' he said. 'For you.'

'I don't want to drag you into this.'

'Are you sure?' he said but he'd already half-turned away, the relief plain on his face. 'If you need anything, just call.'

She waved him off and he disappeared into the night. She pressed the heels of her palms against her eye sockets. 'Focus,' she muttered to herself.

Someone cleared their throat and the other suited man was standing in front of her, expressionless. 'I'm Detective Caruso.' He was built like a bantamweight boxer with thinning black hair. 'Sorry to hear about your aunt. But if you could help us out, we'll be out of your hair as soon as we can.'

Nancy grunted.

'I understand you've only been here a few months and you've been cleaning out the place?'

'My aunt wasn't well.'

'When you were tidying up, did you come across anything unusual?'

'I'm not sure what you mean. It's an old shop filled with old woman's things. Papers, dust and clothes. Nothing *weird*. No murder weapons. No lead pipe in the billiard room.'

The police could search as much as they liked, the only real treasure was gone.

The detective with the unreadable face said nothing in reply.

'Caruso. In here,' Lennart yelled from the doorway.

He lifted a dark eyebrow at Nancy. 'Don't go anywhere.'

Ignoring him, Nancy followed the stocky detective inside. Lennart and Trinh were huddled together in the bakery kitchen. The large dusty pickle jar was sitting on the bench, the one Nancy found in the shed with the book. Trinh was craning her neck and angling her torch in all directions to get a better view of the contents inside. Nancy wondered whether she should explain how she found it but she stood back and didn't say a word.

'Is that…?' Lennart peered through the crusted glass.

'Looks like it to me,' Trinh said.

'What?' Caruso came closer.

Trinh pointed inside. 'See. There. Phalanxes. Human finger bones.'

'What?' Nancy cried. 'It can't be…they're just…'

Lennart rubbed her chin. 'Small enough to be a child.'

140

'A witch bottle, eh?' Brouwer whispered from the doorway. 'Finally gotcha, you old hag.'

Chapter Six
ANTICIPATION

1977 – AGNES

Agnes laid everything out on the bench top. A saucepan of blackberry and apple stewed with cinnamon, allspice and clove, a pot of golden honey and a hill of flaked almonds alongside a bowl of puffy dough. She tipped the dough onto the bench and carefully removed the one cent piece. The bronze coin had to sit inside the proving dough for exactly seven minutes. Seven was the number for prosperity.

Closing her eyes, she plunged her hands into the white dough. She squeezed it through her fingers and concentrated hard, conjuring up a vision of the future. Wealth and prosperity billowed out from every window and door in her shop until every house in Hopetoun was wrapped in a warm embrace of good fortune. Droves of customers poured through her door and all left smiling, their arms loaded with bags. Her bread, whether as sandwiches or jaffles or toast, in school lunchboxes or picnics or midnight snacks, blessed all who consumed it. And at the end of each day, when she locked the door, her wire shelves were bare and her till was full.

Her hands tingled as she dreamed and kneaded, and the dough glowed with a violet light. She blinked away the glow, and rolled the white mixture into flat narrow sheets. Then she spooned a stripe of purple blackberry and apple out along the pastry. The stewed fruit was topped with another white layer, and tucked up like a child at bedtime. The log was sliced into segments, then moulded into crescents and finally each horseshoe was brushed with honey and melted butter, taking care to cut the butter from only one end of the pat, and garnished with flaked almonds.

It was daylight by the time Agnes finished her batch. She opened the door and let the welcoming smell of baking pastry flow out into Station Street and into the quiet cool Hopetoun morning.

With coloured chalk, she drew lucky horseshoes and arrows on the footpath, and advertised a special price of 25c. Then Agnes wiped her hands, stepped back and grinned. She was all prepared to participate in the Autumn Festival.

Later that day, a queue of people stretched out of her bakery door, exactly as Agnes had pictured. Happy little faces, young and old, left the bakery with purple stained smiles. Flakes of golden pastry stuck to their upper lips or beards.

Mafalda came by, as did all the Five, one by one. She bought five horseshoes and nodded approvingly. 'This is perfect. I can sense the change already.'

'I can only hope,' Agnes replied.

'We are lucky to have you here.'

Agnes smiled. 'I'm the lucky one.'

After closing the bakery for the day, Agnes headed to the Green to join the rest of the festivities, arriving just in time to catch the last of the three-legged and egg and spoon races. Night fell, bringing an autumnal chill. A towering bonfire blazed in the centre of the Green and the first fireworks were launched into the dark sky. Wood smoke intermingled with gunpowder, melting marshmallows and hot chips. Families gathered to ooh and aah at the fluttering flames and explosions, snuggled up in winter coats for the first time that year. Boys and feisty girls ran wild, launching rockets from their hands while the young and timid clutched sparklers, luminous ephemeral shapes dancing through the air with a wave of their hand.

Agnes hugged herself as her new community made merry on the Green. It had been a mistake to hide away her true nature. Her contribution may have been small, only a single batch of horseshoes, but she could already see good fortune blossoming in the faces of the people around her. This time, she was part of a greater good. A grinning child handed her a sparkler and Agnes sealed her good wishes for Hopetoun, writing sacred symbols in the air with the glowing stick.

Within the week, the government announced the sale yards would remain open for another five years. The Traders Association celebrated the news at the Railway and Agnes joined them, drinking a few too many sherries with Mafalda and her newfound friends. Her till was full and her shelves were bare at the end of every day, exactly as she imagined. She even had enough money leftover to buy herself a new colour television set and two new dresses.

But in the early hours on the thirteenth of April, it all began to change.

Already awake and baking, Agnes heard the sirens herself. Earlier she'd smelled smoke but assumed the old Greek man a few houses down had fired up his incinerator again. But as the sirens drew closer and louder, dread knotted in her stomach.

Eventually, curiosity got the better of her and she abandoned her bread and stepped out into the backyard. She gasped. An ominous yellow glow filled the sky, the source was further up the hill, beyond her back fence.

She grabbed a coat and scarf from the rack, wrapped her face and headed out the gate, following the grey plumes of smoke and the flickering firetruck lights up the bluestone laneway.

On Brough Street she caught her first glimpse of the angry fire. The spitting flames leapt hungrily from one weatherboard cottage to another, eating up the whole street. Helmeted firemen in yellow jumpsuits ran from truck to house. White hoses gusted jets of water. Dazed families clustered together, blankets and coats over their pyjamas, their faces blackened with smoke and dirty with tears. Agnes joined the onlookers and they all watched impotently as one window after another shattered in the heat.

'Get back,' a fireman yelled as a weakening roof beam groaned. Milliseconds later, the whole house toppled, white dust and red sparks showering the fire men and squealing onlookers.

Feeling useless in the crowd, Agnes did the only thing she could do to help, she went back home and baked. When she opened the shop a few hours later, she put up a sign offering free bread to anyone affected by the fire.

When the flames were finally out, five homes had burned to the ground and one cat was feared dead. Her own house was coated with ash and the stink of smoke lingered for weeks. And yet Agnes thought nothing of her own role in the fire until she remembered other bad news from the suburbs adjoining Hopetoun. A week earlier, a drunk driver crashed into a train at nearby Willowmere Station killing two people and a severe case of measles struck whole classes of a primary school in Flemington. Maybe because the incidents had happened outside Hopetoun, she hadn't made the connection at first.

Strange noises started again. Mean-spirited laughter echoed in her ears. Sometimes it was vague, only living on the edges of the wind but one night, the whispers turned to shouts. Familiar voices tore Agnes from her sleep, one roughened with nicotine, the other with a Middle-European accent.

'Fool.'

'Liar.'

The wardrobe door slammed shut. Her bedroom was dark, unusually dark. Was the door closed? Why? She never closed the door. Her heart racing, she blinked into the pitch black.

'You never listened,' Lorna hissed into Agnes's left ear. The sound so close, Lorna could have been lying in bed beside her. 'If you'd listened, this never would have happened.'

'We only ever wanted to help you,' Walter said in his condescending way. His voice on her right, the couple berating her in stereo.

'Go away. This is a dream. You're not here. You're dead.'

'You're not as powerful as you think,' Lorna said with a smirk in her voice. 'Look at all the damage you've caused.'

'I don't understand,' Agnes said with a gulp.

'How many deaths now? Can't you feel it on your conscience? I never thought you, of all people, would turn out to be a cold blooded killer.'

'I haven't,' Agnes whimpered. 'I didn't.'

Smash.

Something delicate hit the floor. Probably the milkmaid figurine from the mantelpiece.

'I was doing good,' she protested.

Lorna laughed. 'Idiot child.'

The fire. The crash. The measles.

'We know about the books,' Walter added.

'The books are dangerous in your hands. Hand them over to us,' Lorna said.

'We know what to do with them,' Walter said.

'I don't know what you are talking about. Leave me alone.' She covered her ears.

The quilt lifted up on either side of her and the mattress shifted. Two shapes shimmered towards the doorway, laughing as they disappeared into the darkness.

She waited with fists clenched until she was sure they were gone. Her pulse slowed and the flat was quiet again. She slipped out of bed and checked the suitcase above the wardrobe. Her books were safely inside but Agnes did not sleep again that night.

The next day dragged. Nothing seemed to distract Agnes away from her thoughts. As the minutes ticked down to closing time, she stood behind the counter picking at her cuticles until they bled. She was rubbing her gritty eyes and wishing she had a time machine when the pregnant Mafalda waddled through the door.

'Business is good, yes?' She smiled and pointed to the one lonely loaf of bread left on the rack. 'Me too. I'm booked out again tonight. Thanks to you. We should do it again. Strengthen our good luck.'

'No.'

Mafalda's sunny smile disappeared. 'What do you mean?'

'No. I won't do it again,' Agnes said, firmly yet quietly.

146

'You can't let us down.' Mafalda scowled. 'Not now.'

'The fire was all my fault,' Agnes blurted and rested her head in her hands.

'Don't be ridiculous. Some idiot fell asleep with a cigarette.'

'I meddled with the balance. I forgot how it all worked. I should never have gone back to the books. The crash. The measles outbreak. Those poor people.'

'Tragedies happen,' Mafalda scoffed. 'You look tired. Have you been sleeping?' She leaned over the counter to pat Agnes's hand but Agnes tore her hand away first.

'We stole our good fortune from other people. From our neighbours. Don't you get it?'

'Who cares about strangers. We are still doing well,' Mafalda said with a shrug. 'You can't abandon us now. Your new friends. We need you. Look what you're capable of.'

'Exactly! People have died because of me. I'm never going to bake from my books again. And no one will convince me otherwise. Not you. Not anyone.'

'You're making a big mistake.'

Agnes crossed her arms and lifted her chin. 'I've made up my mind.'

'Well, you're a fool.' Mafalda stormed off, slamming the shop door behind her.

'You could be right,' Agnes said to the empty shop. She slumped onto the bench and sounds of familiar laughter started to ring in her ears.

2018 – NANCY

It was past midnight. Nancy leaned on the shop counter and yawned. She rested her head in her hands while a woman in a white hazmat suit scraped residue off the walls into ziplock bags. 'I don't know why you're bothering. I repainted two months ago.'

But like the others, the white suit ignored her. The whole house was crawling with cops and no one had explained what was going on, treating Nancy like a ghost in her own home.

The backyard was bright with blinding floodlights. An excavator roared and thumped as it churned up the back garden and men yelled instructions. She yawned again. Sleep would be impossible with all this, and anyway, why should she bother going to bed? It would be pointless to open the shop tomorrow. Only the oblivious or the morbid would want to buy anything from Bittesby Bread now. She whistled out a long low sigh.

Maybe Miles was right and they'd find nothing, and Agnes's name would finally be cleared. But even if they declared her innocent, people believed what they wanted to believe. A shadow would hang over the shop forever, no matter how hard she tried. Tears prickled under her eyelids. This all seemed too familiar. Her life in tatters all over again.

Plucking her phone from her pocket, she made a call to the Willowmere Home. 'Any news?'

'Unfortunately not,' said the receptionist. 'The police are still out looking.'

Nancy grimaced. The police had two reasons to find Agnes now. 'What was she wearing?'

'A pale blue dressing gown and floral slippers.'

'Call me straight away if there is any news. Anything at all. No matter what time.'

Nancy shoved the phone back in her pocket and sneaked over to the coat rack, grabbing her coat and beanie. She scribbled on a sheet of paper and taped a handwritten sign on the door frame. *Closed due to family issues.* As if he read her mind, Wolfie appeared from nowhere and they slipped out the front door without a word to the police.

A light rain fell as Nancy trudged along the empty streets of Hopetoun, Wolfie trotting alongside her. Raindrops slapped against her glasses and her boots squelched through the mess of fallen leaves. She shivered under her coat and forced herself to walk faster. Agnes was out here somewhere in the rain in only her dressing gown.

Phone torch in hand, she peered into bushes, behind bins and down laneways. The minutes turned into hours without any sign of Agnes and nothing to drown out her thoughts. The missing book. The twenty-five-year-old corpse. Her first intruder, Lorraine. The sleepwalking children. The rumours, the connections, the accusations. Lies and truth. Past and present. Her new life had turned into a fever dream.

Salisbury Street continued up the hill. This was the most direct route between the shop and the care home. Would Agnes find her own way home like a lost pet? Maybe Nancy should've waited in the house. Where else would the old woman go?

She sniffed away a tear and Wolfie licked her hand with his warm rough tongue. She chuckled, choking back the lump in her throat. If only the dog could help her piece together all these half-truths. Nancy didn't know where to start.

The bluestone St Bart's church stood at the crest of the Salisbury Street hill, and as they passed under the elm trees and by the spiked iron gates of the graveyard, a single word rang in Nancy's ears.

Who?

Who killed Molly Sheridan?

Who took the notebook?

And who wanted to blame Agnes for everything?

She trudged down the other side of the hill, her chest aching as she pined for her stolen book and her missing aunt. And if that wasn't enough, crops of blisters were blossoming on the balls of her feet.

They'd reached the wealthier part of Hopetoun with its manicured hedges, tasteful restorations and luxury cars and

Wolfie began to whimper. He broke away from her and veered down a side street. Louis Street to be precise.

'I completely forgot! Janet! You want to go home?' Nancy grimaced. 'It's too late now, Wolfie. We'll come back tomorrow. I have lots of questions for your mum but we have to find Agnes first.'

The renovated houses dwindled away, replaced by brick warehouses, anonymous industrial parks and in the distance, the mammoth concrete pylons of the elevated freeway above Willowmere train station.

The buildings disappeared completely, turning into vacant land with chainmail fences. Nancy continued and crossed the bridge over the rain-swollen Moonee Ponds Creek.

The murky water churned with fallen leaves, cigarette butts and fast food wrappers. She stopped and leaned against the railing, watching the swift current toss a black garbage bag. She imagined the bin bag was Agnes, confused and scared, gulping for air as her head dipped below the surface. Maybe it wasn't Agnes at all. Maybe she was only thinking about herself.

Why was Nancy here? Searching the streets for an old lady she didn't even know? She could jump on a plane and be back home in Sydney before breakfast. No one would care. The only disappointed person would be her mum but after thirty-six years, she was used to being disappointed by Nancy. The police would find Agnes on their own. What was the use in fighting? They'd already decided she was guilty. It would be easier to walk away from all the strangeness of Hopetoun and pretend it never happened.

Or was it pointless to run? Would Nancy's shadows follow her wherever she went? Did she and Agnes share more than just a name?

She stared into the cloudy enticing water. A whisper of wind sneaked underneath her hood, caressing her neck like a lover's breath. Nancy flinched and glanced over her shoulder. She squinted into the dark but she was alone with Wolfie on the bridge. A truck roared on the freeway overhead and there was movement in the gloom around the train station underneath.

Agnes?

'Get him,' a male voice echoed under the concrete pylons and three figures came running across the bridge towards her. One shadow being chased down by two faster ones. A low growl grumbled in Wolfie's throat. She stroked his coat, his muscles were tensed.

The two attackers in hoodies quickly caught up to their victim and hurled the young Asian man to the ground by his backpack straps.

'Leave me alone,' he screamed before his face hit the bitumen.

The others, nothing more than man-sized boys—one white and one black—laughed and kicked at him.

'Hey! Hey!' Nancy yelled, her hand gripped around Wolfie's collar.

The white boy stopped and looked up with a smirk. He laughed again.

Holding out her phone, Nancy marched towards them. On cue, Wolfie lunged and tugged at her hand with a fierce snarl.

'I'm filming you. And my dog is really hungry.'

'Go on then. Make me a YouTube star.' The white boy strutted and posed for the phone camera.

'Nah, fuck this,' the black one said and stopped. With a glare at Nancy, the white boy spat on the pavement and grabbed the man's backpack, then they both ran back towards the station with mean high-pitch laughter.

Nancy hurried over to the man, curled up in the gutter. 'You alright?'

'Fuck off,' he grumbled and then coughed.

'I can call the cops?'

'Don't you fucking dare. I don't want your help.'

Stumbling up to his feet, blood was streaming down his face from a cut on his forehead, his pale-grey hoodie stained red. Nancy reached out and grabbed hold of his shoulder as he swayed.

'I said leave me alone,' he snapped and shoved her hand away.

'Alright,' she said, her hands in surrender.

'Fucking do-gooders,' he muttered and limped away into the night.

She sighed as she watched him disappear.

'Come on,' she said to Wolfie. 'Forget it. Let's go find her.'

She plodded on into the night, her arms and legs like concrete, peering into the shadows. It was the only useful thing she could do.

MARCH 1992 – AGNES

Agnes knocked on the door tentatively. A bunch of pink and white carnations clutched close to her chest and a plate of Mafalda's favourite jam tarts in the other hand. Hopefully Mafalda still liked raspberry after all these years.

At the cemetery a week ago, Agnes had stayed back on the footpath, out of sight, watching through the iron fence. On Wednesday, when they held the second funeral, she did the same. Both times Mafalda stood by the open grave, all in black, her face pinched and grey. As placid as stone while her sisters-in-law and cousins wailed like Italian banshees. Agnes paid her respects from a distance in silence. She presumed no one noticed her until two days later, when an invitation was slipped under her door. Strange how death often reunites the living.

'Come in.' Mafalda opened the screen door, dressed from head to toe in widow's black and Agnes stepped into the familiar kitchen.

Unlike the two women, nothing in the room had changed. The wooden louvre cupboard doors and orange laminex were now out of style but still scrubbed as clean as a hospital. The former friends were drifting into middle-age, their hair streaked with silver and their skin etched with new lines. How had fifteen years slipped by so quickly?

'Coffee?'

'Please.' Agnes handed over the carnations and the plate. 'I am so sorry. I wish there was another word. Sorry isn't big enough.'

Mafalda nodded and a big golden cross swung from her thin neck. 'I wonder what I have done to deserve this.'

'Don't blame yourself, my dear.'

But Mafalda busied herself and didn't reply. She tore the plastic wrap from the plate and filled the stove-pot espresso maker. Sweet raspberry jam and strong coffee floated across the room.

How quiet the house must feel. Years of laughter, tears and arguments now deathly silent. Three white lilies sat in a glass vase in the centre of the kitchen table, an unnecessary reminder.

Once the coffee was poured, they sat in awkward silence, cups in hands. There was so much to say but their mouths were cobwebbed over after so many years apart.

Mafalda was the first to speak. She placed her cup down and stared directly at Agnes. The years had not weakened her gaze.

'I know we've had our differences. I can be a stubborn old woman.' She sighed. 'But I need your help.'

A familiar dread thickened in Agnes's belly. She responded with a nervous smile.

Mafalda reached across the table. 'I need you to help me bring them back.'

2018 – NANCY

After returning home wet, cold and empty-handed—then sneaking upstairs to avoid the cop left on duty—somehow Nancy slept that night.

She dreamed of a beautiful blue morning. Golden sunlight pressed softly against the window, a glow peeking around the edges of the curtains. Nancy stretched her limbs with a satisfied moan and someone handed her a cup of tea. She wasn't scared by a stranger in her bedroom. It was Agnes standing by her bed in a floral housecoat, her flowing white hair piled neatly on her head.

'Come on lazy bones. It's time to learn,' she said and Nancy sipped the tea. It had the right amount of milk, three dashes, and the perfect hint of sweetness from half a teaspoon of sugar. She couldn't have made it better herself.

'I'll see you downstairs. Wash your hands. And tie up that hair. My recipe requires absolute cleanliness.'

'It's a deal,' Nancy said as she emptied her cup. 'But only if you make me more tea.'

'Cheeky.'

Nancy washed the sleep from her face and pinned up her hair, just like Agnes. On the bed she found a matching floral housecoat laid out for her and when she headed downstairs, another steaming cup of tea sat waiting for her on the bakery kitchen bench. But as she tried to step through the doorway, Agnes blocked her path with an outstretched hand.

'Before you enter my kitchen,' Agnes said. 'You need to remove every scrap of doubt from your mind. Every fear, every frustration, every worry. To make the perfect bread, your mind must be calm. The yeast knows. The yeast is a living creature like you and I. It has intelligence and it can read your intentions.'

'Easier said than done.'

'It's not so hard to expel the pollution from your body. You only need to breathe out the emotions you don't need. Watch.'

Nancy looked on bewildered as coils of black smoke drifted from Agnes's nostrils.

'Your turn.'

Nancy closed her mouth and gathered up all her worries, all her problems old and new. The list was long but Nancy mashed all her troubles into a messy ball and followed Agnes's instructions.

She exhaled and like Agnes, smoke began to pour from her nose like a car with a dodgy exhaust.

'Good. Good.' Agnes nodded. 'But I'm sure that's not all.'

Nancy sucked in another breath and this time, she exhaled through an open mouth. Dirty smog wafted out of her throat and soared past her eyes towards the ceiling, until eventually her lungs were empty and the fog dwindled away to nothing.

'Now you're ready to replace the dark with light. It's time to flush your soul with purity and hope. Think of the excitement of childhood Christmases and birthdays. The anticipation of summer holidays. Champagne. Laughter. Languid love-making. Everything that is good and delicious in our world.'

Waves of pleasant memories lapped over Nancy. An easy smile came to her lips and her whole body lightened.

'Good.' Agnes said, matching Nancy's grin. 'Now you can come in.'

The ingredients were laid out on the kitchen bench; flour, yeast, water and salt. Nothing unusual, everything required to bake bread. Agnes deftly measured the dry ingredients into a large metal bowl then added water and mixed until she had a smooth white lump of dough.

'One last ingredient.' Her eyes twinkled. 'Something special.'

She grabbed Nancy's wrist, and with a small penknife, she swiftly pricked the tip of Nancy's finger. Nancy gasped but Agnes gripped her hand tight. 'This is your commitment to the bread. We must all make sacrifices.'

A single drop of Nancy's blood dripped into the bowl, bright red against the white mixture. Agnes stirred seven times clockwise, and three times the opposite way, before tipping the dough onto the floured bench top. Nancy watched, sucking her finger.

Agnes pulled her floral apron up over her head and folded it on the bench. Then she unzipped her dress, unhooked her bra and slipped out of her underwear until the old woman stood naked.

Nancy stifled a giggle. 'That's your secret?'

'The purity of skin.' Agnes grinned and muscles rippled under her sagging arms as she kneaded the dough, forward and back. Nancy sipped her tea and looked out the window into the sun-dappled backyard, chuckling to herself. If only the judges at the Royal Show knew the real reason Agnes's bread was so special.

Nancy woke up on the floor of the bakery kitchen, stark naked. She pulled herself up to her feet and yawned. The room was warm, the oven was on and she could smell freshly baking bread. She turned her hand and checked her finger. It was almost invisible but she spotted the tiniest of nicks in the flesh of her index finger. She raised an eyebrow and grabbed an apron from the hook behind the door to cover her nakedness. It was the same orange and yellow floral housecoat she'd worn in her dream, a housecoat she'd never seen before. She saw movement outside the window and gasped. The police were still out there, rummaging through her backyard. She giggled to herself, wondering what they'd seen and wrapped her apron tighter.

Inside the oven sat six perfect white loaves. She pulled out the rack and knocked on the golden crust, the hollow sound meant the bread was ready. With a beaming smile, she lay the loaves out on the bench to cool, then scrambled upstairs to find a pen and paper before the dream completely faded away.

2018 – NANCY

It was ten o'clock and there had been no news from Willowmere, not even a single text.

'This isn't good enough,' Nancy said when she called.

'Our apologies,' the receptionist said calmly.

'I need regular updates. At least every two hours. Whether you have news or not.'

'Of course. I'll pass on your concerns to Mrs Chung.'

'But there's no news?'

'Sorry. No. But be assured we are searching thoroughly.'

With a harrumph, Nancy ended the call and stared at her phone. Should she call her Mum? She could already hear the disappointment in her mother's voice, as though the whole situation was somehow Nancy's fault. Would the discovery of Molly Sheridan make news in the Northern Territory? And how could she possibly explain everything in a five-minute conversation? Nancy decided to put off the call until later.

She'd tidied-up the lounge room, yet there was still no sign of the notebook. She'd even asked the jump-suited crime scene investigators, still fossicking around in the backyard, if they'd seen it. They hadn't. For some reason she was not surprised, she knew the book was gone but not forever, a tugging sensation told her it was still close. 'I will find you,' she said to the air. 'Both of you.'

She made a plan. With the shop closed, she would devote all her energies to the unanswered questions.

She avoided the cops in her churned-up backyard and left through the shop door. The rain had gone and the daylight glistened in last night's puddles. For a moment she paused in the sun and closed her eyes, enjoying the rosy red light through her eyelids.

Her first stop was Station Street Books.

She found Miles at the front counter, hunched over a keyboard with a half-eaten almond croissant at his side. Nancy wondered where he'd bought it from.

'I was going to call you,' he said, wiping pastry flecks from his whiskers. 'Any news?'

158

'Nope,' she said with a sigh.

'And the police?'

'Most of them are gone now. They took something away last night.' Nancy said with a dismissive wave. 'I need your help.'

He straightened his posture with a smirk. 'Anything.'

'Where is your occult section?'

Back home, an hour later, with a big mug of Irish Breakfast, a crispy bacon dream bread sandwich and slow jazz on the radio, Nancy cracked the spine on the *Encyclopaedia of the Occult*.

She went straight to the index.

> A witch bottle is defined in two ways. As either a protection against witches, often hidden inside the walls of a house to keep them away or as a device for casting spells. A witch bottle can contain needles, nails, urine or menstrual blood, bone, wood, glass or hair. A witch bottle is effective as long as it is hidden.

A black and white picture of a jar sat beside the definition, a jar very similar to the one she'd found in the walls of the shed.

Nancy sagged back into the couch and scrubbed her face. Had everyone got it wrong? Was Agnes in fact protecting herself against witchcraft? And by moving the bottle, had Nancy broken the protection spell? Was it all her fault?

She turned the page to a dark Renaissance painting of a naked woman with long grey hair, huddled over a book with a circle of candles and a strange symbol drawn at her feet. She gulped and pushed away her bacon sandwich.

Voices wafted in through the open window from the street below. Nancy peered out. Four unfamiliar people were standing at the shop door. She frowned but at least it wasn't the police this time.

'Devo'd,' said a green-haired girl reading the sign on the door. 'I so wanted to buy something from here.' She pulled a sad face and snapped a selfie against the door. She began to sing. 'Chew. Chew. Where are you? Bones, teeth. Sister stew.'

'Come on. I know where the body was found,' said a lanky guy with a quiff. 'Down this way.'

Nancy slumped against the wall. The bakery had already turned into a gruesome tourist attraction. She'd never be able to reopen the shop now.

Her phone beeped. Nancy's stomach leapt but it was only Stella, with a reminder about tonight's Festival debrief. Nancy chewed her lip. She would probably end up being the centre of attention again. But maybe someone would say something useful. She sighed and texted back.

'See you at the pub.'

Stella responded immediately. 'No. My consulting rooms above Mum's ristorante.'

'OK.'

She closed the *Encyclopaedia* and reached for the next book—Janet's *A Curious History of Hopetoun*. She flicked through the pile of books on the coffee table but couldn't see the olive green cover anywhere. Thinking back, she didn't recall seeing the book during her mad search last night or her tidy-up this morning. Yet, she was sure she'd left it here. Standing in the middle of the room, she tapped her fist against her lips.

Ten minutes later she was outside *Hopetoun Optical* with a loaf of dream bread under her arm, an apology for jilting Janet last night. The shop security grill was down. Mail, rubbish and fallen leaves were piled up in the doorway. According to the sign, Janet's business should be open from 10-5 on a Monday. Nancy pulled out her phone but her call went straight to voicemail. With a scowl, Nancy dashed off a quick text. 'Sorry about last night. Will you be at the debrief later? I need to talk to you.'

'Nancy!'

Dajana bounded down the hill, dressed in lycra and trainers with her blonde ponytail swinging. A pair of boxing gloves swinging around her neck. 'How'd your date with Miles go?' She smirked.

'It wasn't really a date.' Nancy half-shrugged. 'Did I see you out jogging last night?'

Dajana frowned but as usual her tanned forehead stayed smooth. 'Boring night at home for me, I'm sorry. So what did you talk about? Did he tell you about his wife? Eek, I mean *ex*-wife.'

'A bit. He said she left him because he was too obsessed with his work.'

'Hmm.' Dajana pursed her lips. Underneath the fake tan and thick foundation, a few fine lines splintered around her mouth. 'I don't want to gossip.'

Nancy waited for the *but*. She didn't have to wait long.

'Don't tell Stella I told you.' Dajana leaned in. 'But that's only half the story.'

'There's always two sides.'

'I heard he ripped off her family.'

Nancy blinked.

'There was a big fuss about some old book which belonged to the family. He sold it for a huge sum and shafted his in-laws on the deal. It got really messy and ended up in court. Miles got his fancy lawyer brother onto it.' Her phone bleeped in her hand. 'Whoops. I have to go. You're coming tonight right? I'll see you there. Bye.'

Dajana jogged off with a finger wave, leaving Nancy with her mouth open. Miles swindled his own wife's family? Out of the corner of her eye, someone was waving to her from the pizza shop across the road.

It was Danny. She shuddered and remembered Stella's warning about him. Should she trust anything these people told her?

After a cursory wave back at Danny, she stared down at the footpath and made her way home.

'Whoa there,' said a man's voice.

Nancy skidded to a stop and lifted her head to see a tall man's suited chest. It was the friend of the bald policeman, the pastor.

'Why hello, Miss Grakowski. A pleasure to run into you.'

161

He chuckled and her skin crawled.

'Hi,' she muttered.

'I was hoping I'd hear from you.' He smoothed his thin colourless hair across his forehead. 'Especially after last night's news. One is lost and another is found.'

'We're all worried.'

'You know I can be of help in your current...situation.'

She averted her eyes. 'Thanks for the offer but—'

'Don't be so hasty. I might know more than you realise.'

'Sorry. Things to do.' Nancy dropped her chin again and skirted around him, continuing along the footpath. Suddenly Hopetoun seemed very claustrophobic.

'Have you found the books?' he called after her.

Nancy didn't look back. She shaded her face with her hands and strode away, pretending not to hear him.

But she heard exactly what he said.

Books? Plural.

She needed to find Janet right away.

1992 – AGNES

Agnes gulped again.

'You have the power,' Mafalda pleaded. 'You must help me. My family has been cursed.'

'You know what happened last time, love,' Agnes replied quietly. 'The fire?'

'This is different,' she spat. 'We both know you have the powers.'

'I'm only a kitchen witch, I wouldn't even know where to start to resurrect the dead,' she lied.

'You forget. I know you.' Mafalda squinted. 'Better than you think I do. I know all about your studies. Your long hours in that witch's house studying every book under the sun. You know exactly how to make it happen. You could do it right now. But you don't want to do this for me.'

Agnes shuffled in her chair. 'But how would you explain it?'

'I don't care. We'd run away. Out to the country where no one knows us, where we can live as a family all together again. No one else needs to know.'

Mafalda's eyes were dark and direct, and dry.

Looking away, Agnes stirred sugar into her coffee. The clang of the spoon against the porcelain was the only sound in the house. 'What about the others? Can't the Five help?'

'Pah. They couldn't even make grass grow. You're the only one who can bring back the dead.'

'I'm not as powerful as you think.' Agnes's hands shook as she lifted the cup to her lips.

'If I must choose one of the two, bring back my Maria. She was only sixteen. Her whole life ahead of her.'

Agnes sniffed back a tear. Smart-mouthed Maria had been as small and fierce as her mother, with a broad Australian accent and a spiral perm.

'She missed out on the chance to marry and have a family of her own. Buried in a box in the ground before she got to live.' Mafalda thumped her fist against her heart.

She sighed. 'Vincenzo. My great love. At least he lived a

163

full life. We had many years together.' She stopped and chuckled, her face brightened briefly before it turned gloomy again. 'But Maria. My Maria. She had nothing. She doesn't deserve to be dust.'

With a gentle nod, Agnes reached across the lace table cloth and patted Mafalda's arm. Mafalda flipped her hand around and gripped Agnes's forearm. Her strong fingers bit deep into the skin and Agnes inhaled sharply through her teeth.

'Unless it was you,' Mafalda growled. 'Was it you?'

'What? No. I would never—.'

'Is this your way of getting back at me? All of us? We were upset when you wouldn't help us.'

Agnes glanced for the door, her throat thickening. She'd lost count of the number of times when one of the Five crossed the road to avoid her.

Mafalda's grip was relentless. 'We are more alike than you think. I understand you. You hold grudges.'

Agnes yanked her arm away. 'You don't know anything about me.'

'Don't you remember? At one time, you were happy to tell me everything. The drink loosened your tongue you know. You told me all about how Lorna used you and your nightmares about the man you called the Alsatian. You're not so pure. You're filled with hate and regret. You have the evil eye.'

Agnes shoved her chair away from the table. The chair leg screeched along the linoleum.

'If it was you…' Mafalda jabbed her finger at Agnes across the table. 'I want you to lift the curse from my family. Right now!'

'I had nothing to do with it,' she stammered.

'I'll go to the police. There are still laws about practicing witchcraft, I checked. You'll go to jail.'

'This is the 1990s.' Agnes tried to laugh and pulled at the chafing collar of her shirt.

'You must help me. Please. Money? You want money?' Mafalda leaned even further forward, her neck ropey with strain.

164

'No!' Agnes recoiled.

'There's Vincenzo's life insurance money. You can have it all, every cent if you bring them back.'

'I can't,' Agnes whispered then turned away. 'How can you forget Brough Street? And the train and the measles. People died because of us.'

'You don't want to help me. You don't think I deserve it. You want me to be unhappy.'

'No. Never. Please.' Agnes's chin quivered.

'I won't beg. If you won't help me, I'll go to the others and together we'll grind you into the ground. Magic is not the only power in the world. You'll regret saying no to me.'

With trembling knees, Agnes scrambled up to her feet. 'I know you're in pain. I can only imagine your suffering but I can't do what you ask. There are repercussions if you meddle with life and death.'

'But you know how?' Mafalda's eyes gleamed and Agnes swallowed hard. 'This is different. Last time, we asked for good fortune. This time we are reversing bad fortune. Wouldn't that bring more good fortune?'

'I don't think it works that way. I don't know. It could be worse. Much worse.'

Picking up the plate of tarts, Mafalda catapulted them across the room. Agnes cowered as her plate smashed against the cupboard doors and red jam splattered over the floor. 'Enough of your lies. Get out. I should've known you'd never help me. But I'll find a way. You know me. I won't give up so easily.'

'I'm sorry,' Agnes spluttered. She grabbed her handbag and rushed out of the screen door.

Out in the street, she stopped and lit a cigarette with shaking hands.

She couldn't, could she?

2018 – NANCY

Nancy tore up the stairs, the pastor's words still ringing in her ears. Her eyes were aching and raw, her brain like porridge. Books. How did the pastor know about Janet's book? What was his connection to all of this? Someone must have stolen both books from her house last night. Her instincts about Janet were right, she must have skated too close to the truth about Agnes. If only she'd had a chance to read the chapter herself. But who? This was the question. The question on top of the pile. Who had the most to gain by framing Agnes?

Nancy flopped down on the couch and every ounce of remaining energy drained from of her body. Before she could stop herself, she'd kicked off her shoes. No, she told herself. She needed to get out there and find Janet. Her body argued back. Three nights in a row of broken sleep. Just rest for a minute or two.

Worries swirled in her head and she shaded her eyes with her hand. What on earth was going on in Hopetoun? Why was this happening to her? A thought slithered into her mind, sucking and growing like a leech until she bolted up from the cushions. Was Agnes's book even real? Or had Nancy imagined it all? Was Agnes even truly missing? They'd accused Nancy of lying before. Of being delusional. Were they right?

She slumped down again. Her eyelids like concrete. Just a few moments. A respite from the madness.

When her eyes flickered open, it was dim in the room. Shadows stretched over the carpet.

'Crap,' she said and scrambled upright to check the time on her phone. It was ten minutes before the debrief session was due to start. She grumbled again and yanked on her shoes, desperately hoping Janet would be there too. Otherwise, Nancy had wasted the whole afternoon sleeping.

The sign read 'Fundamental Energy Therapy' with an image of glowing hands, and Nancy presumed she was in the right place.

Pushing through the door, she headed up the carpeted stairs to the first floor. From halfway up, she heard voices. She grimaced and regretted coming empty-handed. People would expect a baker to bake, but it was too late now. She continued to the top of the stairs with an apology ready on her tongue.

The stairs opened up to a small waiting room with white walls, armchairs and spider plants in pots. Stella, Mafalda, Danny, Miles, Dajana, Russell, Neha and Fred were already there. Their chatter stopped dead. They all stood up from their seats, their faces stony.

The heating unit grumbled in the background as Nancy stepped into the waiting room. Her belly clenched and she squinted. The grey smudges were back. Their faces were all enveloped in fog.

'Evening, everyone. Am I late?' she chirped while her heart raced underneath her skin. She shot a little grin at Miles but he stared back at her blankly.

'We're glad you could come, Nancy,' Stella said, her voice as clinical as the white walls around them.

'No probs,' Nancy replied with a casual shrug.

'Let's begin.' Stella nodded at the others and they stepped forward, forming a circle around Nancy.

'Where's everyone else?' Nancy surveyed the room. 'Where's Janet?'

'We're all here,' Russell said.

'No one else is coming,' Miles added, his usual grin was nowhere to be seen.

'I thought this was a debrief about the Festival?' Nancy laughed nervously. 'What is this? An intervention?'

'We need to talk to you,' said Dajana, her face as expressionless as a mannequin.

'Well, here I am,' Nancy said in a breezy tone.

Neha leaned forward with a penetrating glare. 'We know what you've done.'

'We all know,' Fred hissed. 'And we want it to stop.'

Nancy guffawed. She gestured at Fred and Neha with her thumb and looked to the others in the circle. 'What're they on

167

about?'

'The spells,' Stella said matter-of-factly.

'We should've known her curse would come back.' Mafalda pulled her lips tight. 'She said she destroyed it but we should never have trusted her.'

'Curse?' Nancy echoed. 'What *are* you talking about?'

'I should've known the first day you arrived here and reopened that shop,' Russell said, his nostrils flaring. 'I tried to convince myself it would be different this time. But history repeats, it's always the stranger.'

Dajana nodded. 'The stranger upsets the balance and brings trouble to our community. The stranger must be dealt with.'

Nancy held up her hands. 'Wait a sec.'

'We're not unreasonable people. We're giving you a chance to fix this whole situation,' Stella said calmly. 'Bring the book to us and we'll get rid of it. Once and for all and end the cycle.'

'Book?' Nancy shrugged but her cheeks flushed with heat. What did they know about the book?

'Agnes's book,' Stella said. 'We know you have it.'

'Do you mean Agnes's recipes? You've got it all wrong. I don't have them. I wish I did.'

'They're not recipes. They're spells,' Mafalda spat. 'You've been foolishly playing with black magic.'

Bile rushed up Nancy's throat. She bunched her hands into fists. Spells? No. The instructions were just a little unusual. She gulped.

'It's your fault that the Festival was a disaster. You and your family brought misfortune to us. Again.' The old woman jabbed her finger at Nancy. 'Or did you do it on purpose?'

Nancy's legs lurched. She looked for something to grab on to. All of a sudden, the last few days began to make a type of perverse sense, Lorraine and the muffins, the children at the back door. Had she been so blind? Had she naively caused it all? Never mind the rumours and accusations, had the real proof, the evidence that Agnes was a witch, been right under her nose the whole time?

She glanced over at Miles. He met her gaze steadily,

vacantly. Only last night, they'd shared wine and secrets, she'd confided to him about Grant, and now Miles was standing before her with his arms folded in disgust. Dajana, Russell, Stella, Mafalda, Danny, Neha and Fred were all the same, their masks had dropped.

At least, now she knew who wanted the book.

And why.

Now Nancy knew where she stood.

They were lying, all of them. The book wasn't evil. They were jealous, they knew the book didn't want them. This must be why she was drawn here to Hopetoun, the book needed her protection. If only she knew where it was.

Sucking in a breath, Nancy pulled herself up to her full height and lifted her chin to meet their stares.

'Are you all mad?' she snapped. 'I don't know what you're talking about. I don't have your stupid book.'

Dajana sneered. 'Liar.'

Nancy glared back. 'Come search the shop. Top to bottom. The police already have. There's no book there.'

'The sleep walking spell? The chocolate muffins? It had to be the book,' Mafalda said. 'You must have found it.'

Nancy shrugged.

'You have twenty-four hours to bring us the book,' Stella declared.

'Or what?' Nancy folded her arms.

'You have one day.' Stella continued without blinking. 'Or face the consequences.'

'You're all crazy. I've had enough of this.' Nancy turned and set off down the stairs, forcing herself to walk nonchalantly and not run away. But as soon as she was out of their sight, her eyes brimmed with angry tears. She shoved the door open and exhaled as she stepped into the coolness of the street.

Footsteps came after her down the stairs and a firm grip grabbed her by the arm.

'Nancy. Stop,' Danny said, his brow furrowed.

'Don't touch me.' She tore his fingers from her arm and wiped away her tears.

169

'You've got the book, don't you?'

'How many times do I have to say no?'

'If you don't have it? Then who does?'

'How should I know? This is all your crazy idea—nothing to do with me.'

'You have to find the book. You don't realise what they're capable of.'

'Those bunch of shopkeepers don't scare me.'

'Well, they should. I've tried but they're convinced that you're responsible. They'll do anything to protect their livelihood. Especially Stella.'

'I'm a big girl, thanks. I can look after myself.'

'Just bring them the book and it will be all over. Please. Believe me it's for the best.'

'Why do you care? What's in it for you?'

'I don't care about books and balance. I just want this strange shit to end.'

'You and me both.'

Nancy strode away and left him standing open-mouthed in front of Mafalda's restaurant.

1992 – MAGGIE

With her eyes covered, Jackie called out to her sisters. 'One hundred. Ready or not. Here I come!'

She dropped her hands, pushed aside the empty pizza box and heaved herself up from the couch. Once she was on her feet, she froze and listened hard. She bent down and peeked under the armchairs. No Molly. No Bridget. They were probably too big to hide under the seats now anyway.

Jackie headed down the carpeted hallway. The house was quiet. She frowned. Little girl giggles usually gave them away. Her sisters were getting better at this game.

'I'm coming for you,' she said and her voice echoed around the tiled kitchen. She checked behind the kitchen bench and inside the pantry.

With another scowl, Jackie closed the linen cupboard door and continued her sweep through the house. Next was their shared bedroom, decked out in pastel pink and yellow. There was no sign of the girls under the bunk beds or inside the built-in wardrobe.

'You better not be in Mum's room!' she called. 'You know that's out of bounds.' She checked anyway and nothing seemed out of place in her mum's frilly bedroom.

The laundry was the only place left, she even tried inside the washing machine. It was empty. Had they snuck out the back door when she was counting out loud?

Grabbing the torch, she switched on the outdoor light and stepped outside. Her bare feet squelched into the damp grass as she headed for the most obvious hiding place, their weatherboard playhouse.

She stuck her head inside the open door with a grin. 'Found you!'

All she found was Molly's baby doll Sunshine and the pink teddy, Strawberry Bear, sitting at the table in the single wooden room, patiently waiting for someone to pour their tea.

Where were they?

Jackie chewed her lip and did a circuit of the big lemon tree. The swing set was empty. The corrugated iron shed was padlocked shut. She rattled the door to double check. She beamed the torch through the scrappy bushes along the fence.

Then her heart stopped.

The broken-down chest freezer.

Uncle Dave was supposed to take it to the tip in his van but last time Jackie looked it was still there. A waist-high white rectangle big enough to hide the both of them. They wouldn't be that stupid. Would they?

How long had she been searching?

How much air would be inside?

Jackie gulped and raced towards the freezer.

2018 – NANCY

Hot tears of frustration spilled onto Nancy's cheeks as she stomped up the Salisbury Street hill. Was it true? Had she conjured up something evil with the muffins and Imps? Had family loyalty blinded her just as Mafalda warned? She buried her hands deep into her pockets. Someone else was responsible. Perhaps it was the Traders Association themselves. And the witch bottle was supposed to protect Agnes from them.

Whoever was responsible, she would never hand over the book to them. Wherever it was, the book was somewhere close, waiting for her to rescue it. The feeling was faint, a happy hum inside her bones, the book hadn't abandoned her. But if the Traders Association didn't have it, then who did?

Nancy didn't slow her pace until she was half-way up the Salisbury Street hill. It was peak hour and the road was a sea of red tail-lights. An angry commuter beeped his horn and Nancy glanced up briefly as a cyclist sped past with her middle finger outstretched.

She tightened her fists. Tomorrow, she'd open the bakery to spite them. The jotted notes from her dream were pinned to the fridge. With Agnes's help, tomorrow's batch of bread would be her best yet.

Her phone buzzed with a text from Willowmere. '*No update. Search continues.*' She snorted and shoved her phone away. By now the police should have put out a public call for help to find her, Agnes's face should be all over the evening news. There'd been nothing further from the detectives after their dig in her backyard. Guilty or not, it seemed Agnes was subject to a different set of rules.

St Bart's sat on the crest of the hill, floodlit and glowing like a beacon. The heavy oak doors of the bluestone church were wide open and a choir of worshipping voices rolled out into the street. A graveyard stood behind the church, bordered by elm trees and a six foot spiked iron fence.

Through the fence, Nancy glimpsed a pale blue blur on the other side of the graveyard. The same blue as Agnes's dressing gown. She grabbed hold of the railings and pressed her cheek against the cold iron, squinting over the headstones and marble angels. The blue figure was gone. She dashed around the perimeter, holding back from calling Agnes's name. She didn't want to spook her. There were countless stories of children lost in the bush, confused and frightened, who hid from the unfamiliar rescuers, and Agnes was more like a child these days.

Nancy sprinted around the corner, searching for a way inside. She almost tripped on a retractable dog leash, invisible in the dark. She grumbled at the woman dog-owner and her yappy poodle but kept running.

On the other side, the main gates were secured with thick chains and three enormous padlocks. She gripped the railings again and scoured the graveyard. Nothing moved, only stone and grass. She buckled over to catch her breath. Her eyes were playing tricks on her again. Why would Agnes come here anyway?

'Where are you, Aunty Agnes?' she mumbled to herself as she looked all around her. 'Help me find you. Please.'

No one answered.

1992 – AGNES

Later that night, Agnes sat on her couch with her two books laid out in front of her; the good and the bad, the black and the white, the left hand and the right hand. On first inspection, the books, the same type of exercise book used by school children, seemed innocent but inside the text was woven from a millennia of esoteric wisdom. With a cigarette in hand, Agnes studied one recipe very closely, the one which could deliver Mafalda what she wanted, and most of the ingredients were already sitting in the pantry downstairs. She slammed the book shut. This was madness.

The clock said eleven. She rubbed her eyes but she would never sleep with all these wrestling thoughts inside her head. Even before Mafalda and her demands, sleep had become slippery for Agnes. Long stretches of insomnia seemed to follow middle age like a shadow.

There was a knock at the front door, the sound travelling up the quiet stairs from the shop. Agnes sighed and slid on her slippers. She scuffed downstairs and peeked through the blind on the shop window. It was Mafalda on the doorstep dressed all in black. She sighed and her hand hesitated over the lock but Mafalda caught sight of her through the gap. Her old friend waved and Agnes sighed again.

She swung open the door and Mafalda stepped inside. Then a second unfamiliar hand grabbed hold of the doorjamb. Agnes flinched as out of the night, Mafalda's children appeared, and Alessandro and Stella followed their mother into the shop.

Nineteen year old Alessandro was short but built like a bull terrier while Stella on the other hand, now fifteen, was tall and as lithe as an Italian greyhound with sharp cheekbones and her mother's cold dark eyes.

'What do you want?' Agnes gulped as Stella closed the door behind them.

'We have come to ask you to reconsider,' Mafalda said calmly.

Agnes pulled her cardigan tight across her chest. 'It's late, Mafalda. I'm not going to change my mind. You should go home.'

She'd never been much of a fighter before, running had always been the easiest option, yet tonight she found her feet were stuck defiantly to the floor.

'Look at them.' Mafalda gestured to Alessandro and Stella. 'My children, my two remaining children.'

Agnes glanced from face to face. Mafalda and Stella glared back, cold and dark, while Alessandro's face was reserved and unreadable.

'I've lost half my family. And you could bring us back together. But you are standing here and telling us 'no'.'

Agnes pressed her hand against her breastbone. 'I'm so sorry for your losses. Truly I am. But I can't do what you ask.'

'Can't? Or won't?'

'I don't know the damage it might cause. Remember the fire.'

'Coward!'

'There's nothing else to say.' Agnes reached for the door handle. 'Please leave.'

'You're not a mother. Or a wife. You could never begin to understand my heartache. A lonely spinster like you.'

Her words were like a knife to the ribs. Agnes bit down hard on her lip.

'Enough,' Mafalda said. 'Trova il libro.'

Before Agnes could reply, Stella pushed past her deeper into the shop and then through the swinging door.

'No,' Agnes cried and lunged after her.

Alessandro grabbed her by the shoulders and shoved her against the wall.

'Just do what she says,' he said in a low rumble. His grip was firm but not cruel and there was conflict in his voice. 'I don't want to hurt you.'

Drawers rattled and cupboard doors slammed inside the bakery kitchen through the door.

'Leave me alone. Get out. Get out of here now. You don't know what you're doing.'

'It's upstairs!' Mafalda yelled to Stella. 'In the flat.'

Agnes jerked forward again. This time the young man slammed her against the wall hard. She squealed. Her spine smacked against the plaster.

'Co-operate. It'll be easier this way,' he said sadly.

Agnes choked on a sob as Stella's footsteps thumped across the ceiling overhead. The books were in the lounge room, sitting on the coffee table on full display. Only a blind person would fail to find them.

She had to save them.

She steadied her breath and charged, jabbing a bony knuckle into Alessandro's throat. The boy spluttered and recoiled in surprise.

'You leave my children alone!' Mafalda ordered but Agnes was already through the swinging door and running up the stairs.

When Agnes reached the lounge room, Stella was nowhere to be seen. Sounds of scraping coat hangers drifted down the hall from her bedroom and Mafalda was only steps behind. Agnes bolted into the room and shoved the coffee table up on its end. Newspapers, mail, cigarette butts and the crystal ashtray scattered across the room, and the notebooks slid to safety under the couch.

Mafalda stopped in the doorway and scrunched up her nose at the mess. 'Stella! In here.'

Stella rushed in, followed by her brother. 'Have you got it?'

Agnes lunged for the telephone on the side table.

'Hold her back,' Mafalda said. 'We don't want another curse on us.'

Alessandro grabbed her wrists. 'Don't be stupid,' he said. He crossed her arms like a straitjacket in front of her chest, while Mafalda shuffled through the papers on the floor and Stella checked inside every book on the shelf.

She clenched her jaw and her fists as she helplessly watched them search. The corner of one of the notebooks was poking out from beneath the couch. It was only a matter of time until they saw the navy blue cover too.

Ignoring Alessandro's grip, she closed her eyes and focused

on her breath. In. Out. In. Out. When her mind was still, she began her own search, sifting through all the old knowledge hidden inside her brain. More than twenty years had passed since she'd last performed a veiling spell and she was as rusty as an old gate.

Once her spirit and body were serene and clear, she gathered her intentions and formed a ball of energy in her mind. The transparent ball slowly spun and glistened like a bubble. She opened her eyes and the orb was still there. It hovered in the air in front of Alessandro, the glimmering curves distorting his face. He stood still, completely oblivious as Agnes sent the veiling ball towards the couch.

The orb drifted through the air like dandelion fluff on the wind and floated over the edge of the notebook. She suppressed a smile as she exhaled. They would not defeat her. She had powers they could only imagine.

'There!' Stella called out and Agnes's mouth dropped open as the girl reached through the bubble and grabbed the notebook.

Her spell didn't work.

'No!' she cried as Stella handed the book to her mother.

Mafalda lifted an eyebrow. 'You won't help us so we'll help ourselves. You underestimated us. We Carusos are as tough as nails and we don't need anyone else.' She opened the book and ran her fingers down the page. She nodded. 'This is exactly what we need. Let her go.'

Alessandro released his grip and Agnes slumped against the wall. 'Stolen spells never work,' she croaked.

'And you're so pure? Didn't you steal them to begin with?' Mafalda secured the book under her arm. 'We're done. Let's go home.'

The family of three walked out of the room and clumped down the stairs. The front door slammed and the building was quiet.

Agnes collapsed onto the couch. She pressed her face deep into the cushions and screamed until her throat was hoarse. She rolled over and pulled her knees to her chest, and wished the couch would swallow her up forever.

When her angry tears eventually subsided, she felt a tiny glimmer of hope. Mafalda had dabbled with a few simple rituals as part of the Traders Association but in the end she was an amateur. The book was written by Agnes for her own reference, she'd never intended for anyone else to use it, and there was a good chance the spells would fail in a novice's hands. But her relief was short-lived. They had taken the left hand book, the dark book. What would manifest if Mafalda performed the incantation incorrectly? There were sinister entities out there, waiting to take advantage of foolish amateurs like her.

Perhaps she should've agreed to help them bring back their dead. But she hadn't. The risk was too great, and if her failed veiling spell was any indication, her powers had also grown stale. She'd made her decision. Now she must sit alone with her regrets, and wait.

2018 – NANCY

The iron gate of Number 26 squealed. Wolfie pushed past Nancy and bolted down the front path. Like all the others on Louis Street, the Edwardian-era house was double-fronted but its wild overgrown cottage-style garden was in contrast with its manicured neighbours. The car space on the street in front was empty. Maybe Janet was out. Maybe not. There was a bike chained to the front verandah post and she suspected Janet might be the cycling type.

She rapped on the heavy brass knocker. The curtains in the front windows were closed. Instead, she peered through the opaque glass sidings in the old wooden door. Weak light gleamed from the back of the house and Nancy made out the silhouette of a hallway stand and a long corridor. No one came to answer the door.

'Janet?' Nancy called and knocked again. 'It's me. Nancy from the Bakery.' She stepped back and spotted a surveillance camera in the eaves. She waved with a smile, but again, there was no reply and nothing seemed to move inside the house.

Wolfie came crashing from out of an overgrown daisy bush. She stroked his wiry fur as he butted her leg with his head. 'Where's your mum, boy?'

Wolfie replied with a thin mournful whine. She frowned and tried knocking one more time.

Nothing.

She rang Janet's number again. It went to voicemail and Nancy rummaged in her bag for a slip of paper to write a note. Wolfie pawed at her leggings, his overgrown claws hooking into the black fabric.

'Oi.' Nancy went to shove Wolfie away but he jumped down and disappeared around the side of the house with another heart-breaking howl.

Grimacing, Nancy followed him.

A concrete path ran between the house and the side fence, and Wolfie sat clawing at a gate, whining. The six-foot high corrugated-iron gate was scored with scratches. Nancy sighed. 'You don't have a key?'

She glanced around, looking for another alternative, but eventually with a big breath in, she grabbed hold of the top of the gate. She planted her right foot on the first rung of the wooden fence running between the two properties. This was the easy part; the first ledge was only a few inches off the ground. The real effort was next.

Nancy secured her left foot on the rippled face of the corrugated iron gate and heaved herself up. She shifted and kicked up her right leg, aiming for the shoulder-height second rung. Thirty years had passed since her last ballet class and she had never been very good to begin with.

Her left shoe slipped and she spilled forward. She scraped her shin against the gate and was back where she started.

'If I'd known I was going to be breaking and entering, I would have worn different shoes,' she grumbled and rubbed her sore leg.

She bunched her fists and tried again.

This time, her sole stuck to the gate and her opposite foot easily found the top ledge. She hoisted herself up and over successfully. But at the top, she found herself caught in a precarious place, legs dangling on either side of the fence, her arms holding her an inch above the top of the gate. Her fingers began to ache and her arms quivered under the strain.

With gritted teeth, she leaned her weight forward, and with all the grace of a sack of potatoes, she toppled onto the path with a thud and a shriek on the other side of the fence.

Her hands were grazed and bloody, and her elbow was sore but nothing was broken, and for the first time ever she was grateful for her layers of padding. She groaned up to standing, picked up her glasses and unlatched the gate. Wolfie almost pushed her off her feet as he bounded past her to the back of the house.

Following him, Nancy stopped at a second window. She cupped her hands on the glass and peered inside through the sheer curtain. With the help of a light somewhere in the house, she made out a bed and a lump under the covers. Nancy knocked on the window but the shape didn't move.

181

'Janet? Wake up.'

She knocked again and her belly turned as hard as concrete. Nothing.

Wolfie howled from the backyard and Nancy hurried around the corner. Underneath a pergola, the dog stood up on his hind legs, seven feet tall, and bayed at a glass sliding door.

She wrenched the handle and the door slid open.

Both Wolfie and Nancy dashed into the tiled kitchen and she followed the dog down the hall.

From four steps away, Nancy could smell something terrible. Like raw meat in a bin on a hot summer's day. She stopped and gulped, and after gathering her courage, she covered her nose with her shirt and stepped through the doorway.

It was the room she'd peered into. The lump lying in the bed was Janet. She was wrapped in a white sheet, stiff and stained with dried brown blood. Wolfie had his paws up on the bed and was licking Janet's grey face lovingly with his long tongue. Nancy retched at the sickly stench of rusty blood, thicker and more pungent than her heaviest period.

'Who did this to you?' she whispered to the dead woman she barely knew.

Nancy stepped carefully around the room, she knew from experience not to get too close. She tugged the whining Wolfie off the bed and cuddled the big black dog on the floor.

Shadows passed by the window and Nancy swallowed hard. Wolfie scrambled to his feet and bolted out of the room, his claws scraping along the wooden floors. The sliding door squeaked as it opened, and Wolfie growled and barked.

'Whoa, boy,' cried out a male voice.

Boots clumped up the hallway. Nancy frantically scoured the room for a place to hide.

Two uniformed police officers appeared in the doorway. Two unfamiliar faces, a tall slim man with oval-shaped glasses and a solid blonde woman with a gap between her two front teeth.

'Police. Thank fuck.' Nancy breathed and clutched at her

chest. 'Who called you?'

'Step away from the body.' The female gap-toothed cop held out her gun.

'What?' Nancy replied.

'Hands up.'

'OK. OK.' Nancy lifted her hands in the air and backed away towards the wardrobe. 'I just found her. I've been here two seconds.'

The woman approached the bed and the man in the glasses turned to Nancy. 'Why are you here?'

'She invited me.'

'How did you get inside?'

'Her dog led me around the back. The door was open.'

'Your name?'

'Nancy Grakowski.'

The female Constable took a pen from her top pocket and gently lifted up the sheet. The man lunged forward to block Nancy's view but he was too late.

Nancy gasped. Underneath the sheet, Janet's throat was slashed from left to right, the wound like a red scarf draped across her shoulders. Two large tattoos sat in the hollows of Janet's clavicles, the two Egyptian eyes now wept tears of crusted blood. A second bloody slit started at the base of her throat and snaked down her body, a jagged line cleaving her floral nightgown and her skin in two.

As bile rushed up Nancy's throat, the man grabbed his radio from his belt. 'Constable Herron at 26 Louis Street, Hopetoun. Deceased female, suspected murder.'

The woman lifted the sheet a little higher. She blinked rapidly, then dropped the sheet and swung around to face Nancy. 'We need you to come down the station with us.'

'The blood is all dried! I had nothing to do with…'

The woman looked back with a dead-eyed stare.

Nancy's body slumped, and this time, she decided to keep her mouth closed.

'Come this way, please.'

1992 – AGNES

The buzz of her alarm clock snaked down the hallway into the lounge room from her bedroom. Waking up on the couch, Agnes prised open her sore eyes. She moaned and stretched out the crick in her neck. Then she remembered why the carpet all around her was strewn with papers.

With limbs as heavy as stone, she forced herself up onto her feet and into the shower. The hot water washed the sleep from her face but her regrets didn't budge. She'd failed again. She should've destroyed the books years ago. In her heart, she knew how dangerous the recipes could be in the wrong hands. Even her own.

She couldn't call the police and report them. She suspected Mafalda was right about witchcraft still being a crime in Victoria.

All Agnes could do was wait and bake.

Down in the dark bakery kitchen, she switched on the lights, slipped on an apron and checked on last night's proving dough. The dough under the tea towel was soft and smooth and her worries began to fade as she tipped the dough onto the floured bench top. As she kneaded, she did her best to focus her mind and infuse lightness and joy into her hands, but as an incantation began to form on her lips, she stopped short, reminding herself that these days she was only a baker. She had left the hearth-witch part of her behind long ago.

She slid the bread tins into the oven and set to work on the coffee scrolls, yet Mafalda's flashing eyes kept reappearing in her mind. The dark forces would know immediately what Mafalda wanted from them. She'd attract them like sharks to blood. Agnes chewed her lip as she coiled up the raisin-dotted buns ready for the oven. Perhaps she wasn't so powerless.

It was only 4 o'clock, there was still time to bake something new. She dusted off her hands and headed upstairs. They'd only taken one of her books, she still had the good book, the book of the right hand side. It contained all the recipes she used to delight Lorna and the others at the farmhouse, bringing joy and luck into their lives. She needed a sea wall against the high tide,

185

a ritual to hold back the unleashed darkness. The balance must be maintained.

As she skipped upstairs, she remembered a recipe for black and white cookies, iced in a yin-yang symbol, designed to restore the balance. It was the first recipe in the book and it was perfect. By the time, she reached her ransacked lounge room Agnes was smiling again. She stacked up the letters, folded up the newspapers and groped under the couch for the book of light. She pulled it out and opened to the first page.

She started to read. 'What?'

The first recipe was *Chocolate Fou* or Chocolate Madness, a spell for driving your lover mad with passion and obsession. A spell from the left hand.

Mafalda had taken the wrong book.

Shaking her head, Agnes pressed the dark book against her chest.

The balance was safe.

For now.

But how long would it be before they realised their mistake? And then what would they do?

2018 – NANCY

Nancy shuffled into the room, clutching a plastic cup of lukewarm tea. The room was windowless, the brick walls painted white, the only furniture was a table and four hard chairs. This was not going to be a cosy chat like she'd had with the police a few days earlier.

'Sit down, please,' said the gruff uniformed male officer. His polite request more like a threat than good manners.

The chair legs screeched across the linoleum floor as Nancy sat under a strip of harsh fluorescent lights. The air conditioning whistled in the corner. She sipped and grimaced at the overly sweet, chalky tea. The officer silently took a chair by the door, and again she waited.

There was nothing to do but think. Once more, Janet's butchered body flashed through her mind. The brown blood, the slashed skin. She shuddered in the warm room. They'd only met a few times but somehow Janet felt like the closest thing she had to a friend in Hopetoun. Now she was gone.

Nancy refused to believe in coincidences. It had to be a random attack, a serial killer, violent ex-husband or a stalker, then again, who knew what strange circles Janet mixed in. And yet, Nancy's lungs were thick with dread.

Two suits breezed into the room. Familiar faces: Detectives Lennart and Caruso. Nancy straightened her posture and put on a friendly smile. Not too friendly, someone had been murdered after all. She rolled back her shoulders, this was just a misunderstanding, an overzealous rookie's mistake. She'd answer a few questions and be out of here in no time.

'Detectives. We meet again,' Nancy said casually. 'Any news on the search for my aunt?'

'We're here to talk about the murder of Janet Egloff,' Lennart replied flatly as she sat down. Nancy closed her mouth like a scolded child.

The stocky male detective with thinning slicked-back hair pressed a series of buttons on the recording equipment. 'Detective Caruso and Detective Lennart in attendance.'

'Do you usually have this much contact with the police?'

Lennart said, wearing a blindingly yellow shirt under her suit.

'A run of bad luck?' smirked Caruso.

'I've had better weeks, yeah,' Nancy replied, keeping her voice light. 'Although to be fair, none of it's been my fault.'

The detectives stared back with faces as blank as the walls.

'Why were you at 26 Louis Street at 7 o'clock today?' Lennart said.

'As I said to the Constables.' Nancy cleared her throat. 'Janet invited me to visit her on Sunday night but with Agnes going missing and then you know, the police searching my house, it slipped my mind. I went to apologise to her today but her shop was closed so I tried her at home.'

'What did you want to talk to her about?'

Nancy pushed her tongue into her cheek. How much should she explain? They already knew about the witch bottle and the accusations against Agnes. Should she tell them about the missing notebook and the threats from the Traders Association? It all sounded ridiculous enough inside her own head. Would anyone possibly believe it was true?

'She said she knew the truth about Agnes,' she replied.

Lennart raised a dark eyebrow and tilted her head. 'What did she tell you?'

'We didn't get a chance to talk properly on Sunday. She's also written a book about Hopetoun where she explains what happened. She gave me a copy to read but I can't find it now. I looked everywhere. I'm sure I left it on the coffee table.' Nancy stopped to collect herself. She took another sip of the lousy tea and the two detectives watched her patiently. 'I wanted to find out what she knew. I wanted to clear Agnes's name.'

'So you went to visit Janet Egloff at her home a day later than agreed?' Lennart said.

'Yes.'

'Who let you inside?'

'No one answered the door. Then I called her and she didn't pick up. The dog seemed anxious and I was worried.'

'You were found inside the house. How did you get in?'

'The door was open,' Nancy said sheepishly.

'The front door?'

'No. The sliding door at the back.' Nancy crumpled the plastic cup in her hand.

'Did you regularly visit Ms Egloff? Did you often let yourself inside her house unannounced?'

'No,' she mumbled.

'How well *did* you know Janet Egloff?'

'We only met once or twice. Through the Traders Association.'

'You were seen together in the Railway Hotel earlier on Sunday evening.'

'That's when we made the arrangements to meet later.'

'She was found in bed. Were you lovers?'

Nancy blinked in disbelief. 'What? No.'

Lennart leaned back and steepled her fingers against her lips. Nancy tried not to wriggle in her seat as the detective scrutinised her.

Silent seconds ticked by.

'I've been a detective a long time,' Lennart said eventually. 'I've seen the same scenarios play out time and time again. Means, motive and opportunity. Same reasons. Same excuses.' She gave Nancy another once-over, tapping her finger against her lip. 'Not a crime of passion and I don't think money is involved.'

Nancy frowned.

'Perhaps you were covering up another crime?'

'You're barking up the wrong tree. I had nothing to do with this.'

'Or was it revenge?' said the male detective, breaking his silence.

'Janet Egloff was known for being out-spoken,' Lennart added.

'I hardly knew her.'

'What was she saying about Agnes? What did she write in this book of hers? Did you go to her house to silence her?'

'It can't have been me,' Nancy said with an unintended squeak. 'She was dead when I got there. I don't know anything about blood and forensics but she has to have been dead for a while.'

'About eighteen hours. Where were you between midnight and 2 A.M. Monday morning? We know you left your house. We were there.'

'Searching for my aunt. Like you bastards should've been doing.'

'Where were you precisely?'

'Walking up and down Salisbury Street towards Willowmere.'

'Near Louis Street.'

'No. Yes. I guess,' she gulped.

'Did anyone see you? Can anyone verify your whereabouts?'

'No. Except for my dog,' she said. 'Well, he's actually Janet's dog.'

'I thought you said you didn't know her very well? But you've got her dog?' The male detective said smugly.

Nancy met his gaze. She paused and squinted. His dark eyes were familiar. Very familiar. 'What's your name again?' she said slowly as her stomach knotted.

'This is Detective Caruso,' said Lennart.

'Caruso?' She gasped. 'You're one of them! They put you up to this, didn't they?'

He blinked and matched her glare, his face expressionless.

Nancy jumped to her feet. Heat spread up her neck as she jabbed her finger at him. 'You know I had nothing to do with this. Let me out of here. Right now.'

'Sit down, Nancy,' Lennart said while Caruso leaned back in his chair and folded his arms.

She ignored Lennart and continued to jab her finger at Caruso. 'You're just fucking with me because your mum told you to. They won't find the book. No matter what you do.'

Caruso shrugged at his partner.

'Nancy, please.' Lennart thumped her palm on the table top. 'Sit down.'

Nancy glared at Mafalda's son as she obediently slumped

190

back into her seat. Her heart thumped slowly in her chest as she watched him. Is this how it would end? They couldn't get Agnes or her book and so they'd get the next best thing?

'Let's continue,' Lennart said. 'Can anyone verify your whereabouts between midnight and 2 am on Monday?'

'No,' Nancy grumbled.

On Monday morning when Nancy returned home, there was one remaining policeman on guard in her backyard. Sick of explaining herself, she'd snuck in through the front door and tip-toed upstairs without him seeing her. At the time she didn't know she'd need an alibi.

'This is what we do know. Luckily we were on site,' Lennart said. 'When I came to tell you we were leaving the property, just after midnight, you were nowhere to be found. The Constable on duty patrolled the house at 2 A.M. and again, reported you were not in the building.'

'I came home soon after.'

'When?'

'I don't know the exact time. Maybe a neighbour saw me.'

Lennart referred to her notebook. 'Constable Spiteri reported that you returned to the house at 3.11 A.M. Once again, can anyone confirm your whereabouts during this time?'

Placing her elbows onto the table, Nancy rested her head in her hands, blocking out the harsh light and Lennart's scrutiny.

'Is that blood on your jacket?'

'What?' Nancy jerked up and inspected her cuffs. There was a dark stain on her left forearm. 'The guy! The guy at the station. I helped him get up, he got mugged by these two other boys. There must be CCTV from Macaulay Station.'

Caruso leaned forward. 'Are you sure the blood didn't come from Janet?'

'Course not. Check the footage from the station.'

'What did you do with the hand?' He eyed her closely.

'What do you mean? Hand?' She spluttered.

'The body is missing its left hand. Sound familiar?'

Bile scorched the back of Nancy's throat. Molly Sheridan.

'Don't play innocent, Nancy,' he continued. 'We know all

about you. Your past.'

Nancy gulped. Her heartbeat quickened. 'I don't know what you're talking about.'

'We've had a very interesting conversation with Western Sydney CID,' Caruso said and Lennart nodded.

The room was suddenly as hot as February. Caruso jiggled his leg under the table and the fluorescent tube above them buzzed like a fly.

'This isn't your first,' he said. 'Is it?'

'I want a lawyer,' Nancy mumbled.

'I thought you might,' Caruso said.

'The charges were dropped, you know.'

'Interview suspended at 12.43 A.M.,' Lennart said. The detectives collected their papers and stood up without another word.

'I didn't kill him!' Nancy yelled as they walked out the door. Her shrill voice echoed out the open door and down the corridor. 'I didn't kill Grant!'

Chapter Seven
POSSESSION

1992 – AGNES

Agnes knocked at the screen door, her breaths shallow in her chest.

Since she'd discovered she still had the dark book, her mind had tossed like a feather in the wind. She pictured Mafalda's grief-stricken face and the tears of her fatherless children. She'd hear the roaring flames from Brough Street, then Lorna's cackles, reminding her she was nothing without her.

Mafalda opened the kitchen door. 'You.' She raised her eyebrows yet waved Agnes inside.

The air in the kitchen was warm and fragrant with fried garlic and onion. Stella and Alessandro sat at the table eating macaroni in bright red sauce from bowls while Mafalda wiped her hands on her apron. It was idyllic, a perfect portrait of family life, except for two unoccupied chairs. The two empty seats at the table were like a black hole, draining the light and the life from the room.

'Hungry?'

Agnes shook her head.

'Sit down.'

She glanced again at the empty seats and shrugged. 'I'm fine.'

Mafalda and Agnes stood in thorny silence. The children ate at the table and scraped their forks against their white pasta bowls. The women stared at each other interchangeably, each dropping her gaze the very moment their eyes locked. Back and forth like a see-saw, the moments turned into minutes and the tension swelled. The door was only a few steps away, there was still time to change her mind. Again.

Eventually Agnes cleared her throat and spoke. 'You probably know by now; you stole the wrong book.'

Mafalda shuffled her feet.

'I've been thinking about what you said.' Agnes stopped

and sighed. 'If you give me back my book, I'll help you.'

Mafalda's face brightened.

'But you must promise not to tell anyone,' Agnes added. 'Not a single word ever. Promise?'

'On my children's lives.' Mafalda nodded heartily. 'Should we start now?'

'I need you to bring me a handful of dirt from their graves, gathered at exactly three o'clock in the morning. Right on the dot. Then bring the dirt to me and I'll bake a small batch of rolls for you to eat. All three of you.'

'And then what?'

'We wait.'

'How long?'

'As I said before, there are no guarantees. I don't know what will happen. It might not work at all. Are you ready for that?'

'They'll come back to us,' Mafalda said firmly. 'I know they will.'

'And then you'll leave Hopetoun?'

'Right away. I'll pack up the car and we'll drive far away from here. And never come back.'

'Leave?' whined Stella.

'Yes. No one must know about this. Or us. It must be a secret.' Stella's skinny shoulders slumped and Mafalda patted her arm. 'You want your Papa back and Maria.'

'Sure but start a new school? All my friends are here.'

Agnes stifled a smirk. The seriousness of life and death was nothing when compared to a teenager's social life.

Mafalda grabbed her hand. 'Thank you.' The words choked in her throat and tears spilled down her shining face.

Agnes averted her eyes. Her body felt as hollow as a husk. She would never know first-hand the depth and ferocity of a mother's love for her child.

'You're going to bring Papa back?' Stella said with a hopeful smile, and blinking back her regrets, Agnes nodded. But within seconds, the feeling of benevolent warmth was gone and the cold dread in her belly was back.

Alessandro knocked at her door soon after three o'clock. She was awake, of course, chain-smoking and pacing the linoleum. He said nothing as he handed over the paper bag, and neither did she. She peered inside and the earthy scent of soil coiled up out of the bag.

'I'll come to your house in an hour,' she said and got straight to work.

The oven was red hot and the dough was ready, awaiting the final ingredient. She sifted the dirt into the bowl and stirred, the grave soil turning the mixture from white to ash-grey.

Her hands worked deftly, automatically, without reference to the recipe, guided by something or someone else. Later, Agnes would barely recall how she made the *Fantasma de pa*.

She tipped the grey dough out on the bench and rolled the mixture into a long thin tube. She cut it into thirds and shaped each piece into a snail. The three breads were basted with butter, then dusted with poppy seeds, then slid into the oven.

As the rolls baked, savoury scents of fenugreek and dill drifted across the kitchen but there was something dark and unearthly underneath the aroma. The oven would need to be scrubbed thoroughly with salt and rosemary before she baked again. She'd have to close the shop tomorrow. It would probably take her all day to cleanse the kitchen and she made a mental note to call Jackie and tell her to stay home.

When the timer pinged, she placed the *Fantasma de pa,* the Bread of the Undead, upside-down to cool for a few minutes before she slipped the three rolls into a paper bag and left for the Caruso house.

Her nerves were too jangled to drive and so she walked. But every step through the deserted streets was a chore, the small bag felt as heavy as stones in her hand. It was done. She had to finish the task. She'd promised. With a grimace, she silenced her second thoughts and kept walking.

All the lights were on when she arrived and the kitchen door opened immediately when she knocked.

No one spoke as Agnes tore open the bag on the kitchen table and laid out the three snail pastries.

'Eat.' Mafalda handed them to her children and Agnes held her breath as they took their first bites. Would thunder boom and the sky fall in? Or worse, would nothing happen at all?

Stella gagged and Mafalda coughed as they chewed. Agnes poured them each a glass of milk. 'Every last bite,' she said.

'You hear, Stella? No excuses.'

Stella nodded and swallowed stoically while tears leaked down her cheeks. On the other hand, Alessandro wolfed his roll down without missing a beat.

'When will they come back?' Mafalda asked as she wiped the last crumbs from her upper lip.

'I don't know. Magic doesn't play by our rules.'

'We'll be ready.' She turned to her children. 'Now, we must behave as normal. No one must know about this. Right Stella? Right Alessandro?'

Stella scoffed. 'As if I'd tell anyone about this?'

Alessandro nodded.

All they could do now was wait.

2018 – NANCY

Inside the cell, there was nothing to distract Nancy from the memories. She should have known she couldn't outrun her past.

When her tears were dry, she started to think about lawyers. There was Nicola Donegal, her no-nonsense Sydney lawyer, but she was hesitant to call her. Being suspected of murder twice in a year might make her look like a serial killer.

Miles had offered to help with a lawyer before but there was no way she'd trust him after the Traders Association ultimatum. Danny, a self-described escapee from the law, was another option. Not him either. She chewed on her lip. She'd have to take her chances with an over-worked and under-paid Legal Aid solicitor.

Then a long-forgotten name popped up, Donna Zhou, and Nancy called for the duty sergeant.

Her old house mate Donna, from the cockroach-infested house on Hercules Street, seemed unperturbed by the random early morning call and request for help after twenty years. It probably happened to lawyers all the time, no one called their lawyer when they were having a good day. Donna promised to send over one of her colleagues as soon as possible.

Back in the cell, Nancy closed her eyes, and despite the thin mattress on the hard concrete platform, she drifted off.

An hour or two later, the lock in the door clunked. 'Get up. Your brief's here,' said the ruddy-faced duty sergeant.

Nancy smirked. Donna didn't mess about.

The sergeant led her into another small anonymous room and a Sophia Loren lookalike got up to her feet. Nancy smoothed back her wayward hair, suddenly feeling shabby next to the lawyer with her perfect red lipstick.

'I'm Aysen Demir.' She held out a hand with long red nails and shook with a grip like a rugby player. This was a woman Nancy was glad to have on her side.

'Thank you so much for coming,' she said as they sat.

'No trouble. Donna and I go way back. I owed her one. Now, tell me what happened.'

197

Nancy sighed and then explained the meeting with Janet, her foolish decision to jump the fence and her missing aunt. But she left out some of the story—she didn't want to appear unhinged by mentioning witches and black magic. Demir watched her attentively, scribbling notes before she folded her arms across her ample cleavage and nodded.

'Don't worry, Nancy. I'll have you out of here in no time. This sounds completely ridiculous and totally circumstantial.'

'Maybe I should mention. I've been charged with murder before.'

Demir's eyelashes briefly flickered before she uncapped her fountain pen again. 'It shouldn't be a problem but tell me everything.'

She cleared her throat and then began to tell the story.

It was a Thursday night in early September and Nancy was in her cubicle. She was pretending to work late to meet an urgent deadline, but in truth, she was waiting for the last of her colleagues to go home.

'See ya tomorrow, Nance,' John the marathon-running actuary said with a wave. Nancy's stomach flipped as he lugged his sports bag over his shoulder and disappeared around the corner.

As soon as she heard the security door close, she smoothed back her hair. There'd been no cancellation text today, no family emergencies or school pick-ups. Tonight was their time, and she had to make the most of it. She squirted herself with his favourite perfume and got up from her desk.

The walls of his office were glass but frosted white for privacy. They'd only been interrupted once, and that was a mistake the red-faced cleaner never made again.

Nancy rapped sharply on the closed door but didn't wait for a response. She knew from experience that there wasn't enough time to be bashful. She thrust open the door and stepped inside with a cheeky grin.

But his chair was empty.

Her shoulders dropped.

Where was he?

Fifteen minutes ago he'd sent a dirty text, he couldn't wait to see her. Had he gone home without saying goodbye? She'd worn her new red lacy knickers especially.

Sighing, she turned back to walk away. But in the corner of her eye, she saw a big pale blue shape on the floor alongside the desk.

Grant.

Sprawled on the ground. Face first into the carpet. His chair tipped over beside him.

The next part was a blur.

One minute she was standing in his ordinary beige office, confused. Why was Grant lying down there? Then her whole world was sucked into a dark tunnel. Loud static hissed in her ears. People ran into the room and someone was tugging at her arms. She fell to her knees and they tried to drag her away from him but she scratched like a feral animal as they yelled into her face. Didn't they understand? Her chest had been ripped open, her heart gouged out and stamped into the carpet. He was gone and she was nothing.

They said she had strangled him: the cleaner, the security guard and the police. She couldn't explain why they found her with her fingers gripped around his throat. The police cuffed her and she vomited onto the carpet next to her dead lover before they pulled her away.

Three long hazy days she spent in custody. At first their forensics were inconclusive and no one believed her story. After the autopsy, his aneurysm was confirmed and the charges were dropped. She left the station, numb and hollow.

She went back to work, back to her same desk halfway down the floor, and over her shoulder, Grant's old office remained dark. Her workmates smiled in her face but they whispered behind their hands and openly glared when they thought she wasn't looking. Anonymous notes appeared on her desk and she never looked at her Facebook again. Their affair now public, everyone claimed it was her fault, she was the cause of his stress. No matter what the police said, she killed him. There were no offers of condolence for Nancy. No one cared about her pain.

A week later, she was summoned to the Managing Director's office. Cuts needed to be made and her position was now redundant. Although it appeared she was the only one in the entire company to go.

No Grant. No job. No life.

She hadn't even been allowed to say goodbye. When she turned up to the funeral home uninvited, Grant's wife Melanie slapped her across the face and shoved her out into the street, screaming. Apparently a widow was justified in throwing a tantrum but Nancy had to bottle up her tears and pretend nothing had happened.

Why wasn't she allowed to grieve?

She loved him too.

Demir nodded sympathetically. She assured her that, once again, the forensics would put Nancy in the clear. At least this time, she hadn't touched the body. Then the curvaceous Demir left the interview room and the guard escorted Nancy back to her brick box.

If Demir was as good as she suspected, soon Nancy would have to go back out there to real life.

To her house. The demands of Mafalda and the others. Agnes. The notebook. The Sheridan girls. And the murder. If she didn't kill Janet, then who did?

She scrubbed her forehead.

In the corner of her mind, there was a hum, like a plane high up in the sky. Not only a sound, a vibration too. It was the book calling to her. Reminding her she and the book were one.

The feeling was familiar, like the early hungry days with Grant when they snatched spare moments alone in the stairwell or in the cleaner's cupboard. When her eyes were bright with secrecy and excitement, and she ached to touch him again.

Somehow Nancy knew the book would come back to her. They would not be separated for much longer. Had Agnes heard the call as well? Is this why she'd wandered from the care home? It was hard to tell, yet Nancy couldn't shake the feeling that Agnes was nearby too.

She pressed back against the wall. There was nothing to do in the small room but think and plan her next steps. Soon the book would be back in her hands and everything would be right. With the book, she would fix it all.

1992 – MAFALDA

Mafalda worked all day. She packed suitcases and boxes, and scrubbed the house to hospital standards. When the sky was completely black, she finally sat down. She sat and waited, wringing her hands at the kitchen table, listening hard until fingernails began to scratch at the back door.

She dashed to her feet and flung open the door. Her hand flew to her mouth. Two people stood on her doorstop.

Mafalda clutched the door frame as the world spun and her bones turned to jelly. It was them, her one true love and her first child. They were home.

Stefano stood in his black suit, his white shirt smeared with dirt. Beside him, Maria was dressed in her torn pink party dress, drool spilling onto her taffeta chest from her slightly open mouth.

Despite her joy, Mafalda shivered. Their fingernails were blackened and their skin was mottled like rotting apples.

'My love,' he croaked and walked through the door like he'd done a thousand times before, but his eyes were clouded like an old fish. Maria followed him inside and a sickening stench of decay blew into the room.

Mafalda ran into his arms, her cheeks wet with tears. Her heart was like a flooded river bank, brimming over with love as he pulled her close to his chest. She pressed her face into the familiar place where her nose met his shoulder and breathed. But rather than the musky scent of the man she loved, her nostrils were invaded by compost and dust, and his body was ice-cold.

'They're here!' she yelled as she pulled away from his embrace. From deep within the house, she heard Stella and Alessandro drop whatever they were doing and come running.

'What is going on, wife?' Stefano grumbled. 'Why am I dressed like this? Why was I in the cemetery?'

'Did anyone see you?' Mafalda said and her husband shook his head, his face creased with angry confusion.

The kids skidded to a halt in the doorway. Their mouths dropped open and Alessandro put a protective arm around his taller but younger sister. Their father and Maria ignored their arrival, instead they blinked around the room like strangers, inspecting every corner.

'Is it really them?' Stella hissed. 'It looks like them. Kind of.'

'Your papa and sister are home.' Mafalda nodded, faking a smile and hiding her own misgivings.

'Mama.' Maria's voice was as rough as sandpaper. 'What happened?' The staples on her face were still visible through the thick mortician's make-up. Over twenty tiny metal stitches were used to reconstruct her face for the open casket viewing.

Mafalda embraced her daughter and stroked her hair like she'd done since she was little. Her fingers got quickly stuck in Maria's matted curls.

'They're creepy,' Stella whispered.

'Quiet,' Mafalda barked as she yanked her hand from Maria's hair.

'She's right, Ma. It's not natural.' Alessandro shuddered. 'They're…weird.'

'Your father and sister are home. This is all that matters,' Mafalda said. 'Go and get the suitcases and load up the car. We're leaving. Now. Before anyone else sees them.'

'I don't want to get in the car with them, Ma,' Stella whined.

'Enough. Do as you're told. We have to be miles away from Melbourne by the time the sun comes up.'

'I'm not going anywhere,' her husband roared, his voice like a slap. 'You explain what happened to me. Now!'

Mafalda tugged the cross around her neck. 'Are you hungry?'

With a growl, Stefano picked up a chair and threw it across the room. The chair slammed against the kitchen cupboards and one of the legs snapped in two. The piece of jagged metal ricocheted and thwacked Alessandro in the head.

'Answer me!' Stefano bellowed and Alessandro clutched at his bleeding temple.

Mafalda blinked back tears. 'I think you should sit down, my love.'

2018 – NANCY

With a sigh, Nancy slammed the shop door behind her. Demir had been true to her word, the evidence was flimsy at best and she was out within two hours. It had been a shame Caruso hadn't been there; Nancy would have loved to smirk in his face as she strolled out the door, but as she left the station, Lennart warned her not to plan any interstate trips.

With Agnes missing and everything else on her plate, a holiday was the last thing on Nancy's mind. All she wanted right now was a hot shower and a nap. As she put her keys away, something moved inside the darkened shop. She flinched. Someone was standing by the front counter.

'Who the hell are you?' she yelled and lunged for the light switch.

The fluorescent tubes sputtered before blasting the room with light. It was Jackie, in a torn blue puffer jacket with white stuffing spewing from the sides. She looked straight through Nancy like a window.

'How did you get in?' Nancy grumbled. 'If you've broken a window.'

'I still have a key,' she replied lifelessly. Her big eyes were blank as she held up a bronze key between her fingers. 'For twenty-five years I've kept my key to this shop. I don't know why but I have.'

Nancy sighed. 'I've had a rough few days, Jackie.' She opened the front door wide and continued in the most persuasive voice she could muster. 'Please just leave. I don't want any trouble.'

The last thing Nancy wanted to do was call the police again.

Jackie didn't move. 'I came to see Agnes but she's gone.'

'We're all out looking for her.'

'It's too late. Dead and gone.'

'She's not dead.' Nancy frowned. 'She's just lost. Missing. She's out there somewhere.'

'Good riddance,' Jackie spat.

'I don't know what happened between you and Agnes but please, have a little respect. She's an old sick woman now.'

'Respect!' Jackie snapped. 'After what she did to me? What she did to my sisters?'

'Your sisters?' Nancy blinked and pushed her glasses up. 'Do you know what happened?'

Jackie caved in on herself and nodded with a whisper. 'Yes.'

This one word washed all of Nancy's tiredness away. She closed the front door and stared at Jackie intently. 'Tell me.'

Jackie grumbled and turned her face away.

'I know it's hard after all these years.'

'It wasn't my fault.'

'Of course not.' Nancy grabbed two chairs down from the cafe table. She gestured to an empty seat. 'I need to know the real story. Please tell me what happened.'

Fear flashed over Jackie's face.

'Everyone deserves to know the truth, don't you think? Isn't it time?'

'You won't believe me.'

'I will I promise. No matter what you say about Agnes. Please.'

Jackie eased herself down gingerly on the edge of a chair and Nancy joined her.

'Everything was so blurry. For years,' Jackie said, her hair covering her face. 'But now she's dead I can suddenly remember it all. Clear as a bell. As if it happened yesterday.'

Nancy leaned forward. 'Go on.'

'I saw her.'

Remembering her promise, Nancy bit her tongue and listened.

'I remember now. I saw her do it.' The faraway look disappeared from Jackie's face, her hands were still, her voice clear and sharp. 'It's a shame she's dead, there should have been a court case.'

Why was Jackie so convinced Agnes was dead?

'Then everyone would know the truth. They'd know it wasn't me. That none of it was my fault and she'd get locked up forever.'

Nancy smiled painfully. Whatever the truth, Agnes was

already locked up. Inside her head, inside the home.

Jackie tapped her temple. 'She did something to my mind. Some kind of spell to make me forget. But it didn't work, not one hundred percent. There were nightmares and horrible visions. And the truth was always there, on the tip of my tongue. And in the corner of my eye, teasing me, no matter how hard I tried I couldn't grab hold of it.'

She clenched her fists.

'That old bitch stole my memory and left me with all the guilt. All this time I thought I was to blame. If only I hadn't suggested we play hide and seek maybe they'd still be here.'

'Hide and seek?' Nancy spluttered.

'I can picture her perfectly now. With the bodies in her wheelbarrow.' She pointed at the swinging door. 'Out there in the backyard.'

Nancy swallowed hard. Hadn't she seen a wheelbarrow out there somewhere?

'She kept saying it went wrong. She said she told them.'

'Who?'

Jackie swatted away the question, her eyes misting with old pain again. 'It was her. She did it. She let me blame myself.'

Jackie dropped her chin and began to sob. 'Molly. Bridget. My sisters gone. Now she's dead. I'm never going to get my justice.'

'Why do you keep saying she's dead?' The knot tightened in Nancy's stomach. 'Do you know where she is? Tell me.'

'You're the only one left.' Jackie jerked up and thumped her fist on the table. 'You. Your family. Your fault.' She jumped to her feet, knocking her chair to the floor. 'I'm going to the police. I will never forget anything again.'

'Stay. I need to know more.'

Jackie was already striding for the front door. She threw the key on the ground and spat. 'I remember now. I remember everything. But it's too late. I've remembered too late.'

Flinging open the door, Jackie stormed off down Station Street, yelling to herself. A mother with a pram looked up with alarm and crossed to the other side of the street.

With shaking hands, Nancy dead-bolted the shop door and raced towards the backyard. Wheelbarrow.

The first shed, the one where she'd found the notebook, was crammed with dusty junk of all descriptions. She pushed through the mouldy boxes and past the broken chairs but there was no sign of a wheelbarrow.

Wiping the filth from her hands, she moved on to the next shed, the disused dunny. The hinges on the old outhouse door creaked as she yanked it open. The first thing she saw was a cobwebbed rusty wheelbarrow leaning against the toilet bowl.

Her heart sank.

This wasn't conclusive proof. Lots of people had wheelbarrows. If she wanted certainty, she'd need the help of the police. She bit her lip.

As she debated calling Lennart, a whisper tickled at her ears. A joyful playful song, it grew louder, thrilling her skin and waking the blood in her veins. Then she glimpsed it, in the rafters above the stained cistern. She shoved aside the wheelbarrow, the dried up paint cans and a box of mouse-nibbled Christmas decorations and climbed up onto the old toilet seat.

'How did you get up there?' Her fingers tingled as she graced the corner of the cover. She eased the notebook free from its hiding place and clutched the dust-covered book to her chest. 'I knew you'd come back.'

After a long scalding hot shower, she sat down at her kitchen table in her dressing gown and fluffy socks. A slice of dream bread slathered with butter and blackberry jam beside her. Wolfie had reappeared, scratching at the backdoor, and now with a belly full of chops, he dozed at her feet.

Clean and fed, Nancy got back to the task she'd started in the police cell. With a pen in hand and a clean sheet of paper, she tried to document and sort all her jumbled thoughts.

The Sheridan girls. One body found. Other unknown bones in the backyard. It had only been two days since the police dug up the yard but it felt like a month. How long did it take to get back forensic test results?

Hand bones in the jar. Even if the witch bottle was planted for protection, that didn't forgive the gruesome fact that there were human bones inside. And whose were they?

Then there was Jackie with her wheelbarrow story— although it'd be hard to find a more unreliable witness.

Agnes missing. Nancy circled her name several times. Was her disappearance somehow connected?

The page was almost full and she was as lost as ever. She scrubbed her hand across her forehead. At least she had her book back. The book sat on the table alongside her jam sandwich and Nancy reached across to stroke the navy-blue cover. Yet in spite of her relief, uncertainty still gnawed at her. Was the book full of innocent recipes as she thought or were they spells? Who was the bigger fool? Her or them?

She flipped open the cover. The first recipe was for *Horseshoes*. Nancy stopped and frowned. Wasn't *Chocolate Fou* the first recipe in the book? She could have sworn she'd never seen the recipe for *Horseshoes* before. She ran her finger along the middle fold. All the pages seemed to be intact. Nothing had been removed.

Frantically, she rifled through the rest of the pages, past unfamiliar recipes for *Baby Babas*, *Pax Cakes* and more. On the very last page, she found a recipe for *Bread of Light* and she grinned with recognition. This was the dream bread, the recipe Agnes taught her with the special ingredient. This must be a second volume. Someone had mentioned books. Plural. Who was it?

Now the lingering emptiness made sense. There were two books and like twins, they needed to be together. The original book was filled with recipes called *Fat Rascals* and *Cold Dogs* and other darker names, she'd even seen a recipe for a *Bread of the Dead*. While in this book, all the recipe names were hopeful and positive. This must be the book of light in her hands while the other, the missing book, was the book of dark.

Dread hardened in Nancy's stomach. The others were right and they'd been right all along. Here was the real proof of Agnes's affiliation with the occult. Nancy slumped. She felt dirty. What part had she unwittingly played in bringing the book back to life. Her thoughts spiralled downwards, deeper and darker into shame, until the now familiar comforting hum sang in her bones again. The dark book was calling to her, consoling her, reminding her. The book wasn't bad. It was them, they didn't understand. As the rightful owner of the book, Nancy must protect it from Stella and the others. It was close, it was safe, she could sense it. But who had it in their hands?

She tapped her fingers on the table top. One name kept reappearing no matter how she turned the puzzle pieces. Means, motive and opportunity. It had to be her. It all made sense but how had she done it? And why was she lying to the others?

Nancy picked up her phone and as she unlocked the screen, a scribble in the margin of the notebook leapt out at her. She pulled the book closer. It was the doodling of a name. Lorna.

She searched again for the photograph of Lorna and Agnes outside the courthouse.

Then she saw it.

Another familiar face on the courthouse steps, standing alongside them.

'How could I be so stupid?'

1992 – MAFALDA

Mafalda cowered into the corner of the kitchen.

'You brought me back from the dead?' Her husband snarled.

'I did it because I love you. I missed you,' Mafalda pleaded. 'I did it for you.'

'Strega! What have you done? You put a curse on me?' He punched the cupboard door above her head with a roar. 'You soiled me. Took away my entry into heaven.'

On the other side of the room, Maria was sweeping all the mugs, plates and glasses out of the cupboards and laughing as they smashed onto the tiles. She picked up a shard of glass and scraped the jagged edge along her blotchy forearm. Her skin unfolded, opening like a zipper. The wound was dry and not a drop of blood oozed out. Maria stared curiously at her arm then with the glass shard in her hand, smiled at Stella.

'Why couldn't you leave me in peace? My time was up.' He clutched the greying hair at his temples. 'Why did you interfere?'

'You were taken too young. I love you, tesoro. I didn't want to be without you.'

'I was on my way. There was light. It was warm. Now you bring me back here.' He held out his dirt blackened fingers. 'In this.'

'Mama,' Stella whimpered as she darted away from Maria, her sister was giggling and brandishing the shard of glass.

Mafalda slumped into a chair and dropped her head in her hands. 'I thought I was doing the right thing.'

Stefano slammed his fist on the table. 'Take us back. Now!'

Chapter Eight
RESTORATION

1992 – AGNES

The phone rang and Agnes jumped. She scurried over to grab it and almost knocked the handset off the side table.

'Mafalda?' she blurted.

'Sorry?' said a familiar voice.

'Oh, Jackie, darl. I was expecting someone else. What's wrong?'

'I need your help,' Jackie implored. 'I'm sorry. Are you busy? You're probably busy.'

Agnes frowned. 'What's going on, sweetie?'

'They're gone and Mum's going to go troppo.' Her voice trembled.

'Who?'

'I'm supposed to be looking after them. Mum's out on a date. She'll probably think I did it deliberately.'

'Take a deep breath. Your sisters? Your sisters are missing?'

'We were playing hide and seek but I can't find them anywhere. What if someone has taken them? It's all my fault. Mum'll kill me. I didn't know who else to call. Can you come with your car? Will you help me look for them? Please.'

Agnes sucked in a breath and looked at the clock. Didn't they say no news is good news? The Caruso family must be on the road, half-way to their new lives by now. They didn't need her or her help any more. Unlike Jackie.

'I'll come right away.'

Agnes dropped the phone. There was a clenching in her chest but she didn't know why. She batted it away and went for her keys.

The phone rang again but she didn't hear it as she closed the back door.

2018 – NANCY

Nancy rifled unsuccessfully through her handbag. She tidied up the ransacked lounge room, replacing the cushions and neatly stacking the books and papers but she still couldn't find it.

She harrumphed and threw her hands in the air. Her memory blurred by all the craziness of the past few days. Where had she seen it last? She rushed into the kitchen and there it was on the scuffed linoleum, hiding halfway under the fridge. She picked up the business card, pressed her lips together and searched the address on her phone.

Outside the sky was steel grey and Nancy bundled up in a coat and beanie. As she headed down the stairs, Wolfie scuttled to her side.

'I don't think so.' Nancy shook her head and he whined in reply. 'I have to find her myself.'

He looked up with his big chocolate-brown eyes, and, for once, Nancy said no to chocolate.

She closed the door on Wolfie and set off down Station Street, her hood pulled up and her shoulders hunched to hide her face. Her chest tightened as she approached Station Street Books, recalling Miles and his cold betrayal the last time they met.

The bookshop door flew open and the bald Constable came rushing out into the street. She froze but Brouwer was too busy to notice her, a childish grin on his middle-aged face as he strode to the patrol car, his phone clutched firmly to his ear. As he hurtled past, Nancy's fingers began to oddly burn. She inspected her hands but could see nothing out of order, the pain subsiding as quickly as it appeared. Brouwer drove away. Nancy readjusted her hood and kept going, hurrying past the large bookshop windows.

She crossed over Salisbury Street and headed up the hill, past the Foodworx but when she reached the corner of Birch Street, she paused. In a split second, she changed her plan and took a detour down Birch Street.

Her belly curdled as she passed Jackie's house. Wheelbarrow. The more she mulled over the evidence, the

213

more it pointed at Agnes, a child-killer and witch. Yet when she said the words inside her head, she still wasn't convinced. She needed to find Agnes and the truth would follow.

At the end of Birch Street, she left the path and ducked under the narrow timber overpass and onto the gravel beside the deserted train line. Soon peak-hour would start and trains would rattle past every few minutes in both directions. The white salt line was still there running alongside the tracks, but the once solid trail, their useless defence against evil, was now faint and broken.

She crunched through the stones towards North Melbourne until she spied the blue and white police tape flapping in the breeze. She gulped as she drew nearer. This was the spot. The place where little Molly Sheridan had been dumped and forgotten, where, for twenty-five years, trains full of people had rushed past without knowing she was there. Nancy stopped, still and solemn. She wanted to look, yet at the same time, she wanted to run. Eventually she kneeled down and placed her palms flat on the earth.

'I'll find out what happened,' she whispered into the hole. 'One way or the other.'

With a heavy chest, she left the site of the shallow grave. She wandered alongside the tracks, hoping for answers, finding only gravel, rubbish and leaves.

'Agnes. Agnes.' Without knowing why, she started to call out her name. 'It's me, Nancy. Pamela's granddaughter. Come out. You're safe.'

Her voice bounced off the retaining walls and fences bordering the railway line.

'Agnes,' she lamented one last time, her voice hoarse and shrill.

Did she really expect Agnes to come running out from behind the bushes? She slumped and swallowed away the lump in her throat.

Her phone buzzed with a text. Her heart leapt. Perhaps it was news about her aunt, somehow she'd heard her calling. But the text was from Stella. 'An hour until the deadline.'

Nancy scoffed and shoved the phone back in her coat pocket, then took the next path leading away from the tracks and down a narrow laneway between two old sandstone warehouses. One building was deserted with smashed windows and a rusted roof, the other side was scrubbed clean and rumbled with manufacturing. She followed the laneway to the end and emerged on Quigley Street. Her original destination.

The afternoon sun had started to dip in the west and the meat-scented breeze wafted down from the Pendleton Brothers Pie Factory down the hill. She continued down Quigley Street, past a whirring refrigerated truck idled at the kerb and an abandoned import-export office before she found was she was looking for. The City Church of Light.

'Finally,' said a voice behind her. 'We've been waiting for you.'

Nancy swivelled around as a firm hand landed on her shoulder.

'Come in.'

His grip tightened. She tried to shake him off but he had strong fingers for an old man. She winced.

'I have something to show you.' His smile was constant despite his heavy grip. 'But you already knew that. Didn't you?'

Nancy nodded. But it was a lie. The puzzle piece had only just slid into place.

'Where is she, pastor?' She said. 'Or can I call you Walter?'

1992 – AGNES

Agnes pressed herself right up against the steering wheel and squinted into the dark as her custard-coloured Volvo crawled down Leishman Street.

'Where are they?' Jackie drummed on the dashboard as she swivelled from side to side, her window smeared with fingerprints and greasy face marks. But after two hours of trawling the streets of Hopetoun, there was no sign of either Molly or Bridget.

'They'll turn up,' Agnes said, trying to reassure herself as much as Jackie. As each fruitless minute passed, her chest tightened another notch.

'They're only little. They can't have got far. What if one of those perves got them? You know the guy with the red parka and the dog, the one who hangs around near the school?'

'Let's go home, sweetie. We need to raise the alarm. Get the police.'

With a nod, Jackie collapsed back into the seat and dissolved into sobbing. Agnes turned the car back toward Birch Street.

When they arrived, the weatherboard house was blazing with light and the front door was wide open. As soon as the car door slammed, Jackie's mum burst out of the house and Jackie trudged towards her like a prisoner to the gallows.

Still dressed in a black taffeta cocktail frock, Jackie's mother's eyes were fiery under her smudged make-up. 'I've been worried sick. Where have you been? It's midnight!' she snapped. 'You're in big trouble, young lady. I just called the police.'

Jackie's mum noticed Agnes trailing behind and softened her tone. 'Hi Agnes. What's going on? Where are the girls? Are they asleep in your car?'

'I'm sorry, Mum,' Jackie whimpered, staring at her shoes. 'I don't know where they are.'

Within the hour, every house on Birch Street was lit up. The police had arrived in five patrol cars and immediately began knocking on doors. The neighbours, all now awake, pulled on their coats and formed yawning search parties, wandering down Birch Street, along the railway line and around the abandoned warehouses.

'Bridget.'

'Molly.'

For two more hours, their voices rang out through the streets of Hopetoun. But the police and the search parties found nothing. The two little girls had vanished.

Eventually the police sent the volunteers home for a few hours' sleep with instructions to begin again at dawn. Agnes tagged along with Jackie back to the house and made herself useful by putting on the kettle. There was no way she would be able to sleep.

'Can't you do something?' Jackie whispered to Agnes in the kitchen.

Her mother was out of earshot and deep in discussion with the detectives about her ex-husband. Russell from the Traders Association had also appeared and blatantly cold-shouldered Agnes. When she asked, Jackie had explained Russell lived two doors down and was a regular visitor to their house.

'What do you mean, darl?' Agnes lined up the mugs on the counter, a slight tremble in her hands. 'We're all doing the best we can. How does your mum take her coffee?'

'You can do other stuff.' Jackie kicked at the tiles with her toe. 'I know.'

Saying nothing, Agnes turned. She pulled open a drawer in search of spoons while dread wormed inside her belly.

'I've always known there was something different about you,' Jackie said.

Averting her face, Agnes squeezed her eyes shut. She thought she'd been careful.

'Your cakes, your bread,' she continued in a hushed voice. 'There's something, I dunno. Spooky? Magical? Can you use your powers to find them?'

Agnes spun around and grabbed Jackie by the shoulders. 'Have you been eavesdropping?' she hissed.

The teenager shook her head vigorously.

'Have you told anyone else?'

'People talk about you. I'm not the only one who's noticed.'

Agnes winced and let go of her grip. Did everyone in Hopetoun know?

'Please,' Jackie said, her big wide eyes wet with tears. 'For me.'

'I don't know what I can do,' Agnes mumbled and scrubbed her hand across her forehead. Her heart ached as Jackie stared up at her. It was deja vu.

'Try?'

She swallowed away the bile inching up her throat. There couldn't be a connection. It had to be a coincidence.

Agnes nodded wearily.

She left the coffees and got back into her car. A few minutes later when she pulled up, a figure was leaning in her shop doorway. Agnes clutched her keys around her knuckles and approached the door.

She reeled as Alessandro stepped out of the shadows. 'Where have you been?' he said.

'What are you doing here? You should be gone by now.'

'He wants to go back,' Alessandro sighed, sounding more like a boy than a man. 'He's so angry. You have to come.'

Agnes pinched the bridge of her nose. Why had she let Mafalda talk her into this? Then the sickening reality of what she'd done struck her like a bullet to the chest. Her worst fear. She threaded her fingers through her hair and wailed without making a sound.

'Come on,' she croaked and dashed back to the Volvo. Alessandro scrambled inside and Agnes put her foot down. The car burned along Station Street and up the Salisbury Street hill.

'You missed the turn-off.' Alessandro tapped on the window towards Reynolds Street.

Agnes said nothing, she pushed her foot down harder, flying up the hill until they arrived outside the cemetery gates.

218

'Where are you going?' Alessandro said as she jumped out of the car.

The moon was a sliver in the sky as she pushed at the iron gates. A waxing moon was generally used for positivity and growth magic but it could also intensify any power invoked. The gates were locked with a thick chain and only budged slightly.

'Give me a leg up.'

Alessandro cupped his hands and hoisted Agnes up and over the iron spiked gates. She hit the ground on the other side awkwardly, rolling her ankle but she'd made it over without impaling herself. Not bad for a woman nearing her fiftieth birthday. As she dusted herself off, Alessandro hurdled over the fence with ease.

Agnes marched toward the fresh graves, remembering exactly where they were. Long shadows stretched over the gravel path, flanked by looming headstones and mausoleums. The winged angels sprouted sharp teeth and horns in the dim light.

Stefano and Maria Caruso's headstones sat side by side. The dirt on their graves had been disturbed. The smooth mounds had been churned up by someone. Or something.

Agnes queasily dropped to her knees and scooped away the top layer of soil from Stefano's grave. She inhaled sharply and the whole world began to spin. She brushed the earth away with the back of her hand and from underneath the dirt, a little girl's face stared back at her. Her blue eyes open and vacant.

Molly Sheridan.

Agnes tenderly graced the girl's cheek with her fingertips, her skin was as cold as the marble headstone above.

'What?' Alessandro spluttered behind her.

'Get the tarpaulin out of the boot.' She threw Alessandro her keys and without a word, he hurried away.

Agnes darted over to Maria's grave, and quickly unearthed another small corpse. This time it was Bridget with her eyelids serenely closed.

'No,' Agnes moaned. She stumbled back and retched by the

side of the grave.

If only she'd said no. If only she'd been stronger.

Two little girls dead.

The balance had been redressed. Exactly what she'd feared. Two lives taken for the two resurrected.

And it was all her fault.

She collapsed to the ground, the cold grass against her face.

What an arrogant fool she was. The abyss was always waiting for the unwary. The dark power she'd invoked had taken its deadly payment. In a cruel joke, it had hidden the girls in the graves which *she* had emptied with her own spell. Her hands were not the ones which squeezed the life from their throats, but she was just as much to blame.

Hollowed out with shame, she stared at the shallow grave, aching to lie down beside them, wrap herself in dirt and join them in their eternal sleep.

'Another dead kid?' Alessandro cried, dropping a grey plastic sheet. 'Who the hell did this?'

Sucking a shaky breath, Agnes tried to settle her nerves. There had to be a way to fix this. Reverse the spell. Restore the balance. She tightened her fists and dragged herself up to standing.

She pointed at the bodies. 'Help me,' she said without explaining further and Alessandro obeyed.

Luckily, little girls don't weigh very much and Agnes and Alessandro easily carried the bodies down the path and carted them over the fence. But with every step, Agnes glanced furtively left and right, waiting for someone to step out of the shadows and stop them.

Once the two bodies were bundled into the boot of her car, they darted into their seats and headed for Reynolds Street. But as Agnes clenched the steering wheel, her mind was blank. She had no idea how to fix this.

2018 – NANCY

The pastor chuckled and gestured towards the open door. 'This way.'

Nancy pushed her glasses up, straightened her spine and followed him.

'Welcome to my humble little church,' he said as they stepped through the door way. 'As I said, we've been waiting for you.'

They turned right into an open space, the high-ceiling room reminding Nancy of her local Scout Hall, home of her childhood discos. The room was dim, lit only with fading daylight from a row of skylights above, and two fire braziers, one on each side of the low stage at the end of the room.

Rows of empty chairs faced the stage with a wide aisle down the centre. The interior was bare, without stained glass windows or frescos. The only decoration being a banner on the wall, the name of 'The City Church of Light' surrounded by lines, beaming out in all directions like a lighthouse.

A single grey-haired churchgoer sat in the front row, next to the left burning brazier, her head bowed in prayer.

'Agnes?' the pastor called out. 'You have a visitor.'

With a shaky laugh, Nancy raced down the aisle to her Aunt's side. As she approached, breathing freely for the first time in days, Agnes lifted her head with an innocent smile.

Nancy grabbed Agnes's delicate hands. 'I've been so worried. Are you alright?' Agnes appeared clean and well-fed, and with a new brightness in her eyes. A sparkle Nancy had never seen in the nursing home.

'Get your hands off me.' Agnes tore away from Nancy's grasp. 'Who's this, Walter?'

Nancy's heart shrivelled. Had she really expected a big emotional reunion?

'Your great niece, my dear.'

Agnes laughed huskily. 'You were always full of shit, Walter.'

Nancy guffawed.

The pastor continued. 'We've been having a lovely time,

haven't we, Agnes? Old friends together. Reminiscing about the good old days.'

'But it didn't work.' Agnes pointed a bony finger at him. 'You said it would work!'

'You lied, Agnes. You tried to outsmart us,' he replied calmly. 'It backfired and all of this is your fault.'

The old woman crumpled back into the chair. She buried her head in her hands and moaned softly. 'Liars. Liars. We're all liars.'

'How did she get here?' Nancy said. 'Where did you find her?'

'I helped her escape from that horrible home. It was time for a reunion.'

'I think you'll find that's called kidnapping.'

He shrugged, then clapped his hands together. 'Now that everyone is here, I have something to show you both. A surprise.'

Nancy steeled herself.

'Agnes,' the pastor continued. 'You've been hiding something from me for years. You knew the consequences and I told you I'd be watching. But now all is forgiven.'

With a triumphant grin, he thrust the navy blue notebook up into the air.

Agnes yelped. 'No!'

Nancy gasped. Her hands instinctively reached out and the warm song of the dark book returned to her ears. The book was safe. And close by.

'You managed to keep it quiet for so many years,' the pastor said. 'But I always had an inkling that the books were still here. And now it's mine.'

Nancy raised an eyebrow. That's what he thought.

'That's why you kidnapped her,' she said. 'You hoped she'd show you where the books were. But she couldn't tell you. She was sicker than you realised.'

'She's not sick,' he scoffed. 'At first I thought she'd finally worked out how to lift the curse but then I realised I had the wrong person. It wasn't Agnes at all behind the odd little events

222

of the last few days. But Agnes had other uses. She was the perfect bait.'

'So then you broke into my house and stole the book.'

He tossed his head. 'I would never do anything so crass. The book has had quite a journey over the past few days. There are many greedy hands in Hopetoun, but in the end justice prevailed and the book found its way to me.' He lifted the notebook towards the sky. Nancy's lips parted as she followed it with her eyes. 'I have the left hand book, the potent one, and I have the two of you. Everything I need. Finally.'

Agnes glanced up. 'You were always the weak one,' she hissed. 'You lived in her shadow.'

'As you keep reminding me.' He shrugged. 'But she's dead and I am not and after thirty years of waiting, I have the book to do with as I please.'

Agnes turned to Nancy. 'Get the book back from him, Pamela. Don't listen to him or the book. Block your ears or you'll end up like me.'

Nancy leaned away. Didn't Agnes realise the book needed her to protect it? Of all people, the author of the book, she should understand what it needed.

'Only you can take care of this mess. You know what you need to do.'

Then Agnes closed her mouth. She hunched her shoulders, chewed on her nails and rocked gently from side to side.

'Who's Pamela?' the pastor asked.

'It's my grandmother. Her sister,' Nancy blurted, her mind still reeling with Agnes's confusing instructions. What did she mean?

She blinked and focused back on the book, calling out to her from Pastor Vanhanen's hand. She stood up to her full height. 'Looks like your plan isn't going to work. You might have the book but she's in no state to help you.'

'She has her lucid moments, but yes, she's completely unreliable.' He smiled with sharp yellowed incisors. 'But it appears I don't need her. All of Hopetoun has seen what you can do. The zombie children were quite a neat little trick. You don't quite have Agnes's flair, lack of training I gather, but if you follow the recipes to the letter you can produce some adequate results. Familial connections are always the strongest.'

'I'm not going to help you,' Nancy sneered.

'I think you will. As long as I have old Aunty here.'

Glancing around the church hall, Nancy sized up her options. He was an old man but taller than her and he'd proven his grip was still strong. Nancy shoved her hand into her handbag for her phone.

'One thing I don't understand,' Nancy said, buying time as she fumbled through the scraps of paper, sanitary pads and pens in the bottom of her bag. 'How does Janet fit into all of this?'

He tilted his head. 'Who?'

'Janet Egloff? You must remember murdering her?'

'I haven't killed anyone,' he guffawed. 'Do you mean that conspiracy theory nut woman? She's dead? That's a shame. She was a lot more interesting than most people around here. I met her once or twice. We had a great conversation one time about ecstatic religious rituals. She did love her aliens though.'

'Someone killed her and hacked off her hand.'

'Sounds like your handiwork, Agnes?' the pastor chuckled at his own joke.

Agnes mumbled through her fingers. 'Why won't you nosy bastards leave me alone?'

Nancy's mouth fell open. 'Agnes?'

224

1992 – AGNES

Butting out her cigarette, Agnes swallowed hard and stepped inside the eerily quiet house. The kitchen floor was strewn with smashed plates and glasses, the table tipped over on its side. She heard a sniffle and spotted Mafalda and Stella in the corner of the room, huddled together like frightened rabbits.

Out of the shadows, Stefano lunged at her and grabbed her by the throat. She spluttered as he shoved her up against the wall and his dirt-crusted fingers squeezed her windpipe.

'Take me back,' he snarled with death-scented breath.

She choked and nodded feverishly. 'I can fix this.'

'Don't you dare lie to me.'

'Never,' she croaked, her stomach clenching. Did he know she was groping in the dark? Could the dead see better than the living? Could they see right through to your soul?

Releasing his fingers, he stepped back and Agnes rubbed at her bruised throat. Her attention darted around the room, looking for inspiration and answers. This was her domain, the kitchen, the place where her magic lived. The hearth may be long gone from a modern kitchen but the wisdom was still here and it buzzed within her. She licked her lips as an idea surfaced.

She straightened her posture. 'I need a white candle and a bowl of water.'

Mafalda scrambled up to her feet and disappeared down the hallway. Stella began checking the ransacked cupboards.

'You should never have meddled with death,' Stefano grunted as he paced the floor in front of her.

On the opposite side of the room, Maria smirked and leaned against the wall in her torn party dress. 'I like it here, Papa,' she said. 'I don't want to go back.'

'Quiet. Not another word. Do you want to end up in eternal damnation?'

Maria pouted. 'Whatever.'

Mafalda returned out of breath with a thick white candle, yellowed with age. 'This is the candle from our wedding. I light it every year on our anniversary.'

'Perfect,' Agnes said.

Stella handed her a metal bowl filled with water. 'It's the cat's bowl. She smashed all the others.' Stella grimaced at her sister and Maria smirked in reply.

'Thank you. It will do fine.'

Pausing for a moment, she gathered her scattered thoughts and calmed her jittering nerves. Now was not the time to think of failure. She sucked a rasping breath into her diaphragm. Oxygen filled her lungs like balloons and pushed away her doubts.

'Stefano and Maria,' she directed. 'Go and stand by the door.'

Stefano gripped Maria's wrist and tugged his scowling daughter across the room. Then from somewhere within the depths of her memory, Agnes's lips found the right incantation.

'Turn back the clock
Reject the hemlock
Swallow the words
Forget what you heard.'

The two undead visitors stood like statues while Agnes dipped her fingers into the cat's bowl and flicked water across their faces. With his eyes closed, Stefano smiled as the water hit his grey skin. Maria's lips curled in revulsion.

'Go back to your shell
Reverse this bad spell
Untangle the bind
My words please unwind.'

Agnes grabbed the white candle with both hands and broke it across her knee, the snap as loud as a thunder clap. Then an unseen force threw Agnes off her feet, the light bulb exploded overhead and showered the room with shards of glass. The room plunged into darkness and Agnes hit the floor.

Then everything went still.

Agnes's heart battered in her chest as the seconds passed.

226

One. Her breath held as she waited. Ten. Her body clenched. Twenty.

'Did it work?' Mafalda whispered from somewhere in the darkness.

Agnes fumbled back on her feet, slicing her hands on the broken glass and porcelain on the floor and hissing with pain.

A circle of white light appeared in the doorway. 'Where are they?' Alessandro said and swung his torch beam all around the smashed-up kitchen.

Squinting into the shadows, Agnes sighed. 'I think they're gone.'

Alessandro switched on the range hood light, the fluorescent tube twitched like a strobe before lighting up the room.

'I'm so sorry,' Mafalda cried out, standing in the middle of the wreckage. 'I should never have done it. Come here, bambinos.' Stella and Alessandro rushed into their mother's open arms. The petite Mafalda nuzzled into their chests, before leaning back and making a declaration to the sky. 'Lord, I promise I will never again want more than I have. From now on, I will be happy with what you have given me.'

As the family sobbed, Agnes tried to slip away out the open door. She didn't share Mafalda's relief. Not yet.

Mafalda glanced up at the sound of the squealing screen door. 'Agnes,' she said. 'Promise me, you won't tell anyone about this.'

'You don't have to worry about that,' Agnes replied with a half-hearted chuckle.

'I'm serious. We must never speak of this again.'

Agnes pressed her lips and nodded. 'I understand.'

'No.' Mafalda shook her head. 'I don't think you do. This never happened. None of it.' She waved her arms around at the mess. 'I should never have asked you to help me. I don't want you anywhere near me or my family ever again.'

'But...' Agnes's chin began to tremble. Alessandro looked away but Stella shone with spite, a carbon copy of her sinister dead sister.

'Like my first baby girl and my husband, you are dead to

227

me. You are the one who brought the darkness into this house.'

Choking back tears, Agnes raced out the door and back to the car. She never should have opened the suitcase and brought out her books again. They were too unpredictable and dangerous for this world. When she got home, she would lock them away forever.

As she reached the boot, her stomach clenched and she paused with her fingers on the handle.

She lifted the lid and gulped.

Two little lumps wrapped in grey plastic. They were still there. The spell had only half reversed.

Agnes jumped into her car and sped back up the hill to the cemetery. After three attempts, she managed to haul herself up and over the iron railings, and sprinted for the Caruso graves.

The dirt under Stefano and Maria's headstones was smooth and undisturbed. The dead had returned to their rightful graves as though tonight had never happened. So why were the Sheridan girls left behind?

Footsteps crunched along the gravel path behind her. Agnes flinched and spun around as a figure came towards her.

'You silly, silly girl,' said the familiar voice, dressed in tweed.

'What are you doing here?' Agnes spluttered as Lorna shimmered before her. The spicy smell of cigarillo smoke lingering in the air. 'You're dead.'

'You never listen, child,' Lorna tutted. 'Look what you've done this time.'

Agnes withered as Lorna scolded her, until a voice whispered in a corner of her mind, reminding her that Lorna was the charlatan and she was the one with the true power.

'Did I teach you nothing? Did you seriously think everything would go back neatly as it was?' Lorna scoffed. 'You know better than that.'

But how could Lorna be here in the cemetery, if she didn't have some kind of gift? Or was she a figment of Agnes's own guilt-ridden imagination?

'If the dark forces allow you your little mortal wish, they

always take a levy along the way. You're a fool if you didn't expect it. You brought this punishment on yourself.'

Agnes hung her head. She knew perfectly well. She just chose to ignore the consequences. If only she'd listened to her misgivings.

'I was trying to help,' she whimpered.

'But you made it worse. Much worse.'

A tear escaped and dribbled down the curve of Agnes's nose.

'What would you say if the police pulled you over right now?' Lorna said. 'They are still searching everywhere for the girls. I doubt they'd be very understanding if they found their bodies in your car. How would you like prison, Agnes?'

She squeezed her eyes shut and regretted the words before she even said them. 'Please help me.'

Lorna smiled. She grabbed for Agnes's hand. Her touch was like ice, like Stefano. 'Good girl. There is a way but it too has consequences. It won't fix everything and you'll have to live with what you've done. Forever.'

Agnes swallowed and nodded. Then Lorna's cold grip disappeared and so did the familiar smell of tobacco. She fluttered her eyes open, then frowned. There was no one there, Lorna had gone. But someone new was standing at her shoulder. Someone tall and blond.

'Where did she go?' Agnes mumbled.

'First.' Walter continued as if he had been at her side the whole time. 'If I am going to help you, you must hand over the books.'

Give her books to Walter? His demand jolted her awake, sweeping all confusion from her mind. Not while she still had breath in her body. She pursed her lips and met his gaze steadily. 'Too late,' she replied.

Walter folded his arms. 'What happened to them?'

'They're gone.' She shrugged.

'Where?'

'I burned them as part of the ritual,' Agnes said and sighed dramatically. 'You and Lorna were right and I was wrong. I was a fool; I should have never played with the powers. Never tried to document them in the first place. I destroyed the books so it could never happen again.'

'You wouldn't lie to me, would you? Because if you are lying, I'll know.'

'Believe me. They're gone. Please help me fix this.'

'As long as we understand each other.'

Agnes produced a watery smile. Then Walter stepped forward and whispered directions into her ear.

She listened, then gasped in horror.

Chapter Nine
OBLIGATION

2018 – NANCY

Nancy puffed out her cheeks and exhaled, she watched Agnes pick at a loose thread obliviously. Could it be true? Were those dainty age-spotted hands guilty of murder?

A shadow appeared in the doorway of the church, then a dark-haired woman in a blue uniform strode down the aisle towards them.

'Constable Trinh,' the pastor said with a slimy grin. 'What a nice surprise. Welcome.'

'Good timing. You've saved me a call.' Nancy pointed at the pastor. 'Arrest him.'

'Joey!' Constable Brouwer appeared. He chased Trinh down the aisle and grabbed her by the arm. 'Joey. Why do you bring us here?' he hissed, his hairless head flushed red.

Trinh, half his size, shook him off. She lifted her chin and faced him toe-to-toe. 'Your friend has something I want,' she said. 'I know you gave it to him.'

Dread curdled in Nancy's stomach while the smile never left Pastor Vanhanen's face.

Brouwer folded his arms. 'I don't know what you're talking about.'

From the sidelines sitting in the front row, Agnes giggled, then the pastor joined her with a guffaw. Trinh swung around with narrowed eyes as the two pensioners openly chuckled at the bickering police.

'What's she doing here?' Brouwer's face paled as he looked to the older man for fatherly reassurance.

'Is that her?' Trinh said with awe. She inched closer. Agnes had stopped laughing and was fiddling with the loose thread on her sleeve again. 'Agnes Bittesby? She looks so…'

'Frail? What did you expect? She's an old woman,' Nancy said. 'But she didn't go walkabout. Your friend here abducted her from her nursing home.'

'He's not my friend,' Trinh muttered.

'Miss Grakowski is a bit confused.' the pastor shrugged and Nancy pursed her lips tight. 'I can explain, of course. But all that matters is Agnes is safe and well.'

'It's a relief she's been found but that's not why I'm here,' Trinh said and stretched out her hand. 'Where is it?'

Pastor Vanhanen blinked down at her. 'I'm sorry, Constable. I have no idea what you are eluding to. Forgive me, I'm a simple man of God. You'll have to spell it out.'

'The book. I know you have it.'

Nancy's breath snagged in her throat. She glanced at the pastor but he was empty-handed. In the confusion, he must have hidden the book somewhere but she could still sense it was nearby.

'You don't understand, Joey,' Brouwer said.

'It seems clear to me. It's evidence in a murder but you gave it to him.'

Like a protective mother lion, Nancy interjected, her nostrils flaring. 'The book is mine.' She poked her finger into the bald cop's face. 'How did you get it? You stole it from my house, didn't you?'

'It wasn't me.' Again Brouwer looked back to Pastor Vanhanen for help, but the smirking pastor stayed quiet. Brouwer regained his composure and stood to his full height. 'That fat bloke had it.'

'Brouwer took it from the bookshop,' Trinh explained. 'I didn't know what it was at the time but now I know how important it is.'

'Miles?' Nancy blurted.

She raced back through the events of Sunday night, the evening her book disappeared from the coffee table. They'd been together in the pub, so how did it end up in his hands? Did he steal it before he came to meet her? Then she remembered walking past the bookshop on Monday afternoon when Brouwer barrelled past her with a big grin on his face. How her fingers had burned inexplicably as he sped by. Brouwer had the book with him and she never even realised.

'Why do you care, Joey?' Brouwer objected. 'It has nothing to do with you. You laughed in my face when I told you about the witches. And now you want the book for yourself?'

Before Trinh replied, another silhouette darkened the doorway.

'No.' Nancy shook her head, recognising the gait of the newcomer as he strode out of the shadows. 'You idiot.'

His heeled boots stamped along the floor towards them, his chest puffed out like a pigeon. 'Nice work, Constable Trinh,' Detective Caruso said. 'Now, who's going to hand it over?'

'You're working for him?' Brouwer baulked.

'Of course I am. I'm doing my job,' Trinh said tapping her chest. 'Unlike you. Running around like this old man's flunkey. While you've been playing witch hunts, I've been solving a murder. Three murders actually.'

'Where's the book?' Caruso said again.

'My book,' Nancy clarified but no one listened.

'It's here somewhere. Pastor Vanhanen was just about to tell us where.' Trinh glared at the pastor, then turned back to Caruso and looked towards the door. 'Where's Detective Lennart? Should I arrest the old woman?'

'Poor Trinh. Haven't you worked it out? He's one of them.'

'Should I arrest the old woman, sir?' Trinh repeated but this time her voice wavered. 'Sir?'

'Don't you know what it is, Joey?' Brouwer said. 'It's not a notebook, it's a book of black magic. He's not going to put it into evidence. He wants it for himself.' He shook his head. 'You and your bloody career.'

'Shut up, Brouwer,' Trinh said. She looked to Caruso with hope but he said nothing in reply. Instead, he pushed past her and made a beeline for the pastor.

'Pastor Vanhanen,' he said. 'I'm sure you want to help me with my enquiries.'

The pastor replied with an innocent half-shrug, then Caruso spied Agnes in the front row.

'Nice to see you too, Agnes. It's been a long time.' Caruso strolled over to her.

'You?' Agnes barked. 'Back again? Why won't you stay dead?'

He bent down, his hands on his thighs to face her. 'Now, Agnes, you know what happened last time. Isn't it easier if you just tell me where your book is?'

Agnes swatted him away like a fly.

A shiver snaked down Nancy's spine. Then from the corner of her eye, the familiar cover of the navy notebook jumped into view. It was hidden in plain sight, on a lectern on the stage, under a hefty leather-bound Bible. Nancy locked eyes with the pastor, an uncomfortable understanding passed between them, and she kept her mouth closed.

'Pamela,' Agnes screeched and reached out a shaking hand for Nancy. 'I didn't mean it, Pamela.'

Nancy rushed to her side and took her aunt's bony hand. Her head began to pound as the book butted in, whining and demanding her attention like a toddler. Agnes yanked Nancy down to her knees and grabbed her by the chin. The old woman stared hard into Nancy's face and Nancy tumbled into her eyes, disappearing down a long dark tunnel. The church and all the chaos around her was gone as thirty years of cold guilt wormed into her soul.

She and Agnes were now one.

'I thought I was doing the right thing,' Agnes said but the words seemed to reverberate inside Nancy's head like her own thoughts. 'I was trying to help them. I just wanted to belong. For once. Forgive me, Pamela. I should never have started this.'

Nancy shivered and blinked into the darkness.

'You have to stop this. It's happening all over again,' Agnes whispered inside her head. 'Look at what it cost me. I lost everything. My business. My mind. Myself. All because of the left hand book.'

'Where is it, Agnes?' Caruso bellowed, his voice like a hammer on glass and Agnes let go of Nancy's jaw, sending her tumbling onto the ground and back inside her own body.

The murky veil lifted from Nancy's mind as she returned to the church and the reality of Hopetoun. Finally, she understood.

She could see through its promises, past the enchantment to the horror beneath.

She hoisted herself up to her feet and pushed her glasses into place. She nodded slowly at Agnes. 'I know what I need to do,' she said and kissed her aunt's crepey cheek.

Her chest tightened as she turned back to face the others. The police stood in a semi-circle glaring at her, while in the background, the pastor watched with a quirked eyebrow.

'What did she say to you?' Caruso said, his hands on his hips. 'Did she tell you where it was?'

The coals in the brazier shifted with a clunk, sending a spurt of sparks in the air. Nancy glanced over at the lectern just behind the fire and she took a single step towards it.

Voices echoed from the doorway and Nancy's stomach dropped as Stella, Mafalda, Miles and Dajana stepped inside.

'I told you. They're going to use the book themselves,' Brouwer grumbled at Trinh. 'Only Pastor Vanhanen can be trusted to do the right thing.'

'Constable,' Caruso said the word with disdain. 'Do I have to remind you to do your job? Find the fucking book. Now.'

Brouwer's face reddened and tightened but he said nothing.

'Come on in, Mum,' Caruso called. 'You're just in time.'

'Mum?' Trinh repeated incredulously.

1992 – AGNES

Agnes shoved open the side gate. A plastic bag from the hardware store swung by her side. The sun blazed down and the heat bounced back off the concrete, slapping Agnes in the face. The old woman summer had returned for one more day. She winced at the fierce Melbourne sun beating on the tin roof of the shed, imagining the rising temperature inside. She couldn't wait until it grew dark again. Luckily none of the neighbouring house overlooked her backyard and no one could witness what Agnes was about to do.

Dawn had been peeking over the horizon when Agnes finally got home from the cemetery. It had been too late, or too early, to finish the job as Walter instructed. Instead she hid the loaded wheelbarrow inside the shed and paced the floor of her upstairs flat, chain smoking until the hardware store opened at nine.

No matter how hard she scrubbed, her skin still felt filthy. She covered every mirror, disgusted by the sight of her own face, knowing what she'd done and what she still had to do. Twice she even picked up the phone, her fingers hovering over the numbers, ready to confess. But she slammed down the handset again.

There was one precaution she could make inside the house. Taking an old fountain pen and ink, she pricked her finger and mixed the ink with her blood. On the inside of both books, she drew a small symbol and chanted to charge it. This sigil would seal the books forever - from now on, the recipes would fail if used by anyone without her blood. She couldn't bear to destroy them, and so this was the next best thing. At her age, her time for children had passed, so no one could use them now.

Now she had everything she needed. It was time. With a sigh, she unlocked the shed and brought out the loaded wheelbarrow and a shovel. First, she took an empty glass gherkin jar and tossed in three nails. Then she threw the tarpaulin off the wheelbarrow and averted her eyes from their little grey faces. She snipped a lock of hair from each girl and added it to the jar, mixing in a clump of her own. She lifted her

236

skirt, pulled down her knickers and squatted over the jar. Hot urine splashed all over the outside of the glass but enough trickled inside to dampen the hair and nails.

Wiping away her sweat, Agnes swallowed hard and grabbed the brand-new hacksaw. She picked up Molly's left hand. The cold little hand was engulfed by her own. She sucked in a long breath through her teeth. 'I'm sorry,' she sniffed and bile bubbled up her throat. 'I didn't know this would happen...'

Agnes didn't hear the back door open.

'Oh my God,' Jackie screeched. 'What are you doing?'

Agnes had forgotten Jackie had her own set of keys to open the shop. She staggered back from the body. Tears teemed down her cheeks but her fingers stayed wrapped around the saw. 'I'm sorry,' she sobbed.

'You. You're the one. You killed them. Why would you do something like that?' Jackie turned for the door. 'I'm going to the police.'

Dropping her saw with a clatter, Agnes lunged forward and grabbed the teenager by the hand. 'No, I can explain. They made me.'

'Keep away from me!' Jackie tore away from Agnes's grip and slapped her hard across the face. Agnes reeled backwards and stumbled to the ground.

'It went wrong,' Agnes pleaded. 'Let me explain. Please.'

Jackie's eyes bulged. 'You're crazy.'

White noise blurred her thoughts as her mind descended into chaos. She raked her fingers through her hair as Walter's instructions rang in her ears again. 'No,' she cried but now she had no other option. She would have to include Jackie in her plan.

Jackie turned for the door again and Agnes dashed for the shovel. She lifted it high and smashed Jackie across the back of the head.

Like a felled tree, Jackie toppled to the ground, out cold. Agnes clipped a lock of Jackie's hair and dumped it into the bottle with the others.

'I'm sorry,' Agnes blubbered.

237

As she wept, she picked up the saw to finish what she'd started.

2018 – NANCY

'Where is it?' Mafalda said. She marched down the centre aisle towards Nancy and the others.

Pastor Vanhanen clapped his hands and stepped up onto the low stage alongside the lectern. Nancy gulped, unable to tear her eyes away from the book under the Bible. 'Welcome. It's so nice to see new faces at our humble little church. Please take a seat.'

Mafalda, along with Stella, Dajana and Miles joined the three police, encircling Nancy, forcing her back a step and pinning her against the stage.

'We need it, Al,' said Stella. 'Now.'

'You're just in time, Stel. Our new friend, the pastor is about to hand it over. Aren't you, mate?'

The pastor shrugged once again. 'I still don't know what you are talking about.'

Mafalda gasped and pointed to the lectern. 'There it is!'

The old man was swift. He grabbed hold of the book before any of the others could move. But Nancy was close behind. She leapt up on the stage and hurtled herself at him like a rugby player. They both fell and hit the carpet hard. The blow loosened the old man's grip and the book toppled onto the ground.

Scrambling on her hands and knees, Nancy lunged for the book as it bounced and tumbled, resting a few anxious feet from her fingers.

'Get it,' the pastor yelled.

Brouwer charged towards her but Stella slipped in front of him. She jabbed Nancy with a sharp elbow and shoved her out of the way. Nancy groaned and clutched her temple while Stella grabbed the book off the floor and pulled it close to her chest like a lover.

'Finally. Finally, you're mine,' she said dreamily. 'I've waited so long.'

'Good,' Mafalda said, hurrying to her daughter's side. 'Give it to me. Let's destroy it.'

'No,' Stella said firmly, then began to caress the front cover.

239

Nancy swallowed hard. Stella's eyes glimmered with an unnatural light, the same light she'd seen in Pastor Vanhanen and Lorraine, the woman obsessed with her muffins. She shuddered. Had her face looked the same way?

'What are you doing? This is not what we agreed. We have to get rid of it.'

'But Mama. Think what we can do with this book. We can ensure prosperity forever. For all of us. We can stop scraping out a living. Rebuild the community. Make Hopetoun a paradise. We can all get what we want.'

'Don't be an idiot,' Mafalda barked. 'Don't you remember your father? Your sister?'

'It's been calling to me in my dreams ever since we put them back in the ground. The book needs me.'

'It's dangerous,' Mafalda said. 'It takes more than it gives. Hand it over. We need to tear it up so no one can ever use it again.'

'She didn't do the spell properly. Don't you realise, Mama? She tricked us.'

'They didn't want to come back. We stopped their entry into Heaven.' Mafalda shook her head with a sigh. 'When I think about what I did to them…every day I must repent for the sin.'

'I can make it right. All I needed was the book. And now I have it. I can perform the spell properly this time and bring them back to us.'

'No.'

'While you've been wallowing in guilt, I've been preparing myself. I am strong. I can fix this.'

Nancy bit her lip. The strange hum of Stella's touch, it hadn't been her imagination, there was already power in her fingers. With the book, what was she capable of? And what would the book ask her to do?

'I have been waiting so long to touch these pages.' Stella opened the book and tilted the pages under the light. 'It looks so innocent but its power crackles like a fire. All the possibilities inside are begging to come out and play.'

'Stop this. Hand it over,' Mafalda said, her palm out flat.

240

'No. Mum. No. Why won't you listen? I'm doing this for you. For all of us.'

'Alessandro? Talk some sense into your sister.'

Caruso stood back, his gaze darting between his sister and his mother.

'Make a choice, Al,' Stella said through gritted teeth and as she glared at her brother, Mafalda swiped the book from her arms. Nancy laughed out loud as Stella cried out.

Stella chased after her mother but Mafalda was already dashing towards the fire brazier blazing in the corner.

'No, you don't.' Nancy pushed over a row of chairs, knocking Stella off her feet. Then Nancy jumped on top of her, pressing her into the floor.

'You bitch,' Stella grumbled as she kicked and struggled to get out from underneath her.

In the corner, Mafalda dropped the book into the fire pit. Gasps of horror filled the room until Dajana jumped down off the stage and snatched the book from out of the flames.

'Ha,' Dajana said as she dashed down the side aisle along the wall, a feverish gleam in her eyes like all the others.

Nancy launched herself off Stella with a grunt and followed the book.

Miles hurried through the row of chairs to meet Dajana in the aisle. 'Nice work. Hardly any damage at all,' he panted and rubbed his hands together. 'Let's go.'

Dajana scoffed. 'Out of my way, fat boy. This is mine.'

'But...' Miles wheezed as he struggled to keep up with her. 'We had a deal.'

Nancy and Brouwer rushed up the centre aisle to block Dajana's exit.

'This was never about the money.' She stopped and rifled through the slightly charred pages, her jaw clenched.

'Don't you get it? A real grimoire with this provenance could be worth hundreds of thousands of dollars,' Miles said. 'Maybe more. I've already got buyers lined up.'

She ignored him. 'Where is it?' she scowled but her filler-filled face stayed baby smooth. 'It should be here. The fountain of youth. The answer has to be here. I can't turn into a sack of potatoes like my mother. I can't. I won't.'

Nancy inched towards Dajana, hands outstretched as if approaching a wild animal. 'What are you looking for?' she said.

'Where is it? You're supposed to be a real witch,' Dajana shouted back at the oblivious Agnes sitting in the front row.

'Maybe I can help? Give it to me,' Nancy said calmly.

Dajana scoffed and turned until she hit a brick wall, a wall in the shape of Constable Brouwer. 'Out of my way.'

'Hand it over,' he replied.

With one hand clutching the book to her chest, Dajana clenched her fist and jabbed Brouwer in the chin. The big man reeled back, more in shock than in pain. He rubbed his chin but quickly recovered. She came at him again, hurtling towards him with a battle cry. He stood stoically, unflinchingly, until at the last moment he thrust out his meaty forearm. Dajana kept coming and her neck slammed into his arm, sending her collapsing to the ground, gasping.

Wincing at Dajana's fall, Nancy ran up as Brouwer snatched up the book. Then something from Dajana's shoulder bag on the floor caught her eye.

'What the—?' Nancy's mouth hung open.

A large ziplock bag had tumbled out onto the carpet, the clear plastic bag filled with red liquid. Nancy bent down and picked it up between two fingers. In amongst the blood, there was something white. She peered closer. It was a whole human hand, severed at the wrist. 'Janet?' she spluttered and held the bag away from her body.

'No. No. No.' Dajana scurried away on hands and knees. 'What's that doing there? I've never seen that before.'

'I knew it was you.' Stella appeared behind them. 'I knew you and Miles were up to something. Trying to take the book for yourself.'

Miles opened and closed his mouth like a fish.

'You framed me, you bitch,' Dajana spat at Stella.

'I don't know what you're talking about.' Stella folded her

arms.

'I'll take that,' Brouwer said to Nancy and this time, she readily handed it to him. He tentatively held the bag in his fingertips while at the same time, he hugged the notebook close to his chest. He turned to Dajana huddled on the floor beside a chair. 'You're under arrest.'

'It was her. Not me,' Dajana cried, pointing at Stella. 'Arrest her.'

'Trinh? Detective Caruso? Cuff her, will you?' Brouwer called out and the two cops rushed over.

'First things first,' Caruso said. 'Hand over the book, Brouwer.'

Pastor Vanhanen joined Caruso's side, his hand similarly outstretched. 'Yes, my son. Hand over the book,' he said. 'To me.'

Brouwer stood statue still, his mouth open. Book in one hand, bloody plastic bag in the other. 'Um.'

'That's an order, Constable.'

'Do what you know is right. God is watching.' the pastor nodded.

Brouwer said nothing as he glanced from face to face.

'No!' Agnes screamed like a banshee. The old woman picked up a chair and smashed the big man across the back of the head. With a grunt, he toppled forward and Agnes leapt on top of him, clawing with knotted fingers. Nancy elbowed the others out of the way and joined her aunt. She threw herself on Brouwer and began wrestling with the fallen policeman.

Her glasses flew from her face as the three of them writhed and growled on the carpet, everyone grabbing for possession of the notebook. Agnes had the advantage, despite everything Brouwer would never injure an old lady, and as he tried to deflect Agnes's sharp fingernails, Nancy tugged the book out of his hands. She scrambled to her feet.

But Brouwer had no qualms about Nancy. His reactions were lightning quick and he lunged out and grabbed her by the ankle. Nancy stumbled, almost falling but she kept her balance. She stamped on his fingers and started running with the notebook securely in her arms.

This time she felt nothing. It was an ordinary notebook like any other. The infection was gone.

1992 – AGNES

Piercing daylight streamed through the window and onto Agnes's face. She prised open her eyes and squinted at the clock. It was almost 9 o'clock. She clutched at her throbbing head. Her muddy shoes were still on her feet and the curtains were wide open.

With a groan, she rolled out of bed. She stumbled through her flat and kicked through the papers strewn on the floor like autumn leaves. A half-finished sherry glass sat on the bathroom sink and she found more sticky glasses tucked under the couch. Did she have a party last night? Agnes scrubbed her hand across her forehead and tried to push her brain back into place. The last thing she remembered was walking up Mafalda's front path with a plate of raspberry tarts. Had Mafalda fed her some of her uncle's lethal grappa?

A loud knock sounded on the shop door. With a sigh, she shuffled down the stairs, the muscles in her arms ached as she gripped the balustrade.

The knock sounded again, a determined rap on the glass. She didn't bother to check her reflection or tidy her bed-hair. From the sour taste in her mouth, she knew she'd look a fright and she didn't care.

'Coming,' she croaked and opened the door to a twenty-something woman in a trouser suit with a bright orange shirt, and a uniformed fresh-faced policeman with thinning fair hair.

'Agnes Bittesby? I'm Detective Lennart and this is Constable Brouwer. Can we speak with you?' The woman in the suit held up her identification card and the words wriggled before Agnes's face.

'That's me. How can I help?'

'We'd like to ask you a few questions,' the detective said.

'Come in.'

'Not open today?' Lennart said flatly as she stepped through the doorway, glancing at the empty bread racks on the wall.

'I'm not feeling very well.' Agnes shaded her eyes, the sunlight like needles into her eyeballs.

'Is the back door this way?' The balding Constable pushed

past her and headed through the swinging door.

'Wait a minute,' Agnes said and followed the cop through the kitchen and out towards the back door. He stopped by the row of windows looking out into the backyard and cupped his hand to peer through the glass.

'Do you mind if I have a look outside?' he said.

She shrugged and unlocked the back door and Brouwer sprung out into the back yard like a fidgety dog.

'What's he looking for?'

'Let's have a chat,' Lennart said. 'Is there somewhere where we can sit, Miss Bittesby? You look like you need a cup of tea.'

'Upstairs.' Agnes pointed and the detective followed her up to her flat.

Black clouds swirled in front of her eyes as she climbed, and halfway up, Agnes had to pause to grip the handrail.

'Are you OK?' the detective said.

'I'm fine.' She gulped and continued upstairs, ushering the detective into the kitchen.

'We're here about the Sheridan girls,' Lennart said as she took a seat.

'Jackie?' Agnes frowned as she filled the kettle with water. 'Oh no. Has something happened to her?'

The detective raised an eyebrow. 'No. Not Jackie. Her sisters. Molly and Bridget Sheridan. You know they're missing, don't you? You were part of the search party.'

Agnes pinched the bridge of her nose. It seemed familiar but her head was so hazy.

'They've been gone since Saturday night and there's been no sign of them.'

'That's terrible,' Agnes said. 'I don't mean to be rude but what has it got to do with me? I know Jackie, of course, she works here. She's a nice girl. Reliable.'

'Where were you Saturday night?'

'Last night?'

'No, Saturday. It's Monday today.'

'Monday?' Agnes's voice trailed away. How could it be Monday already?

'Before the police were notified about the missing girls, I understand you were driving Jackie around the streets in your car.'

'Do you take sugar?' Agnes rose to her feet and switched off the screeching kettle. 'What did Jackie tell you?'

'Jackie is in hospital.'

Agnes gasped. 'What happened?'

'She's under heavy sedation. She hit her head after drinking a bottle of vodka. She was babysitting them at the time they disappeared. But you know that, don't you?'

'Poor thing. I hope she gets well soon. Can she have visitors yet? I should get her some flowers. Will the Constable want a cup too? How does he have it?'

'Miss Bittesby, were you with Jackie or not?'

Agnes squinted and scoured her brain. She could vaguely picture herself sitting in the car with Jackie but it was blurry, like a movie she'd seen a long time ago.

'We also received an anonymous report. Someone heard shouting coming from your backyard. An argument about murder.'

'Me? Murder?' Agnes guffawed and poured the kettle. 'You know how people overreact when children go missing. Mass hysteria or whatever they call it.'

She placed two mugs of tea on the table as Brouwer appeared in the doorway and shot a brief nod at Lennart.

'We'd like you to come down to the station with us,' Lennart said.

'But I've just made tea.'

'Help us with our enquiries, Miss Bittesby. Consider it a community service.

'OK.' Agnes shrugged. 'I'm happy to help but I don't know anything. You'll be wasting your time.'

The view from the backseat of a police car was different than Agnes expected. A wire cage separated her from Lennart and Brouwer and she traced the lines with her eyes, looking for ways to escape, wondering how many murderers and rapists had sat here before her. The cops didn't speak to her and she rested her woolly head against the cool glass. But something niggled at her like an invisible splinter in her foot. There was something Agnes was forgetting.

Inside the police station interview room, they asked the same questions over and over again in different ways and she answered the same way each time. She didn't know. She couldn't explain the argument her busy-body neighbour heard. She couldn't remember.

In frustration, Lennart fanned photos of the missing girls on the table top. Her stomach skipped when she looked at their smiling school pictures.

'I want to help. Believe me I do,' she said. 'But I can't. I don't know anything.'

After a few hours, Lennart let her go. But the police returned to the bakery in the coming days and weeks, always asking the same questions. Sometimes she'd spot a figure watching her shop, standing by the railway line, across the street, day or night. She didn't know what they expected to find. But the cops weren't alone with their suspicions.

Each day, fewer and fewer customers came to buy bread. At first she held her head high, confident the police would catch the culprit and forget all about her. There was talk of the estranged father and another man, a local pervert known to police, helping them with their enquiries.

But a sour taste lingered in her mouth. Whenever she tried to remember, whenever she reached into the vacant space inside her mind an iron fist clamped around her skull. Something was wrong but what?

She tried to convince herself it would all blow over soon, and she almost succeeded until the night of the monthly Traders Association meeting at the pub.

She arrived at the Railway with a smile and a plate of chocolate caramel slice in her hand. It had been years since her last meeting, she was looking forward to a giggle and a natter, reuniting with her shopkeeper friends. But as soon as she crossed the threshold of the back room, everyone hushed and every head turned.

'Hello,' Agnes started.

Like a train, the ageing Valjoy hurtled towards her and grabbed her tightly, her lolly pink nails sinking deep into Agnes's skin.

'You have some nerve,' Valjoy hissed.

'Sorry?' Agnes blinked in confusion as Valjoy tugged her towards the door. She glanced over Valjoy's padded shoulder and spotted Mafalda. Their eyes met for a millisecond before Mafalda slunk away into the background.

Fred took Agnes's other elbow and they bustled her out into the corridor like bouncers.

'The police might not be able to prove anything,' Valjoy spat. 'But we know.'

Agnes ripped her arm away from Valjoy's claws. 'I've been through this a million times with the police. I had nothing to do with their disappearance. It's all malicious gossip.'

'Rubbish,' Valjoy snorted. 'We know what you're capable of.'

Memories of the Brough Street fire and the train derailment squeezed Agnes's heart in her chest. 'That was different.'

'Do we have to spell it out for you?' Russell said, as he joined the circle around her in the corridor. 'You're no longer welcome here.'

'Consider yourself lucky,' Fred said. 'We don't always take so kindly to strangers.'

'I've been here for fifteen years.' Agnes said and jammed her hands on her hips. She stopped and squinted at them. 'OK. Now it all makes sense. It was you. You lot dobbed me in.'

'Take my advice, darl. Pack your bags and leave Hopetoun,' Valjoy said. 'No one wants you here.'

'Thanks for the pearls of wisdom, Valjoy, but I'll do as I please,' Agnes said. 'You can't force me from my home. None of you!'

She stomped away with her plate of chocolate slice under her arm and pushed through the side door out into the evening air. Hot tears stung her eyelids and she lifted the plate high in the air and smashed it onto the footpath. Chocolate, gooey caramel and broken china scattered everywhere and she crushed the remnants into the concrete with her heel.

'I won't run away again,' she muttered, threading her fingers through her hair. 'I won't.'

From that night on, Agnes was all alone.

The days turned into months and eventually years. Agnes continued to bake, but her cakes and breads were never the same. Every time she tasted another disappointing batch, she wracked her brain. Was there something she'd missed? Had she forgotten an ingredient? But her method and her recipes were exactly the same, perfected over years, but even her award winning white bread tasted bland. At first she wondered if it was her own palate playing tricks on her but then her customers began to turn up their noses, the few customers she had left.

Most of Hopetoun hurried past the bakery with their head bowed, not wanting to even look at the witch shop. All except for the brash teenagers who only came inside on a dare. Agnes stopped venturing into the shop front to serve customers. Even after she came out of hospital, Jackie never came back, she never returned Agnes's phone calls, and Jackie was replaced by a run of shop girls whose names Agnes could never remember. Agnes stayed upstairs out of sight and hoped her absence would bring the customers back but the shop bell no longer tinkled and the shelves were full of unsold bread at the end of the day. At least the birds were happy, they were Agnes's only friends now.

Then one day Agnes didn't bake. She didn't open the shop. She sent the last shop girl home and stayed upstairs. She shut herself inside and hid away, only the niggling blank space inside her head for company.

2018 – NANCY

Nancy pelted down the centre aisle, away from everyone clustered around the protesting Dajana. Stella lunged for her as she passed but Mafalda grabbed her daughter by the shoulder, and yanked her away.

Nancy sprinted to the blazing brazier and held the book over the fire.

'No,' cried Stella.

Nancy smirked as she folded back the cover and dumped the pages into the flames. The fire gobbled up the old paper greedily. The red sparks crackled with delight, spewing a cloud of bitter almond and dill into the room.

As the cleansing power of fire took over, Nancy stared transfixed. In pretty reds and yellows, it was a destructive force greater than them all.

From behind, a skinny arm fastened around Nancy's throat, grappling her in a headlock. It was Stella. Nancy choked and struggled, her kicking feet knocking over the brazier.

The metal brazier thudded to the ground. Burning coals and embers tumbled out, singeing the carpet with a toxic plume of melting plastic. Sparks and a flurry of grey ashes flew into the air, and the blackened book cartwheeled across the floor. But the fire had already completed its task, the book was useless. All that was left was a charred spine.

She'd won.

Nancy scoured the room for Agnes, hoping to see relief and lucidity in her great aunt's face. 'Agnes?' she called.

'You stupid idiot!' Stella kicked a chair. 'What have you done?'

'Quiet,' Mafalda spat.

'But Mum,' she pleaded like a child. 'It was for you.'

'Don't lie to me. I did what I did for our family. And I will regret it forever. This was only ever about you. You wanted power. You disgust me.'

Her mother turned away and Stella's face crumpled.

Finally Nancy spotted Agnes sitting on the floor, squeezed between two chairs, hugging her knees with her grey-head bowed. It appeared the destruction of the book had changed nothing.

Mafalda had found Agnes too. She strode over to her old friend, reaching her first, and laid her hands on Agnes's shoulder.

'I am sorry,' Mafalda said with a choke. 'This is all my fault. All of it.'

Staying back, standing a few feet away, Nancy listened with a painful smile.

'You wanted a quiet life here. But I forced you to turn to your book again. You wanted to start a new life but I pushed and pushed. I was so selfish. And then I blamed you when it all went wrong.'

Nancy held her breath. Mariel, Agnes's care nurse, had once said dementia patients respond better to emotion than words. But the old woman didn't move.

Unperturbed, Mafalda continued. 'I understand if you can't forgive me. I'm happy with that. After what I did, I don't deserve your forgiveness. But I promise I will make it up to you.'

Nancy's throat thickened.

'Agnes?' Mafalda said quietly and kindly. She shook Agnes gently by the shoulder. 'Agnes?'

Concern rippled across Mafalda's face.

'Aunty Agnes?' Nancy rushed to Mafalda's side and touched Agnes's arm.

Her great aunt's head lolled on her neck. Her hair shifted, revealing her face and her tightly closed eyes. Everything in the room, the whole world, suddenly slowed down.

'Is she asleep?' Mafalda asked.

Nancy pulled out Agnes's hand and gripped her wrist, her fingers searching for a pulse. She gasped, then pressed her fingers against her aunt's throat but felt nothing.

'Is she…?' Mafalda said.

Nancy slowly nodded and got down on her knees. She wrapped her arms around Agnes's thin shoulders. Mafalda joined her in her embrace, and this time, they both cried.

There was a flurry of movement and voices around them. Nancy looked up through her tears. Trinh was coming towards her. Stella and Caruso were arguing in the corner, while Brouwer carted the hand-cuffed Dajana towards the door. Miles stood alone, open-mouthed.

But there was one person missing from the room.

Pastor Vanhanen. The old man must have slipped away during the confusion.

'I'm sorry,' Trinh said with a solemn nod, standing over them.

Then an announcement blasted out from the two-way radio on Trinh's belt. 'Fire blazing out of control on Station Street, Hopetoun,' the dispatcher said.

'Station Street? Don't tell me,' Nancy sighed.

'A woman has been arrested at the scene,' the dispatcher continued.

'Jackie finally took her revenge,' Nancy mumbled to herself.

Maybe it was for the best, too many bad things had happened inside the shop. This way everyone could start fresh. Without the book, they could all begin again. All except one person.

Shakily Nancy got up to her feet. 'It's over, Aunty Agnes. It's finally over.'

Epilogue

2019 – NANCY

The shop bell tinkled. A plump woman in heels stepped inside with three wriggling kids in school uniforms close behind her. The two boys and a girl made a quick detour to pat the big black dog lying by the door before they raced to the display cabinet and pressed their greasy fingerprints on the glass.

'Finger buns, Mum!' they said in a chorus.

'OK then. Three finger buns and a chocolate caramel slice please, Nancy,' the round-faced woman said. 'How's business going?'

'Not too bad.' Nancy smiled as she glanced over at the almost empty bread racks. 'How was school today, kids?'

'Good,' said the gappy-toothed Maya. The two boys grunted in reply and went back to wrestling over a Minecraft figurine.

The Earl Street Bakery had been open six weeks now and Nancy had already gathered a set of regular customers, like Paula. The day after Agnes's funeral, she and Wolfie left Hopetoun with a single bag. The service had been quiet, only Mafalda, Nancy and Mariel the nurse came to farewell Agnes and witness her last journey.

After the funeral Nancy considered returning to Sydney but she'd always liked the wilderness and history of Tasmania, so she took her own journey across the sea.

Drifting around the island for a few months taking odd-jobs, Nancy baked, picked potatoes and bored herself to death with data entry until she landed in leafy Launceston. On a crisp clear winter's day, she and Wolfie walked past a shop with a 'for rent' sign in the window. Something clicked. It was time to try again.

These days it was hard to hide from the news and so Nancy couldn't help but read about Dajana's committal proceeding for Janet's murder and her public protests of innocence. But the surveillance footage of a blonde woman breaking into Janet's home seemed damning.

In the intervening months, she'd had no contact from the police. Nothing more was said about the Sheridan girls and she presumed that with Agnes's death, the case was closed. And there was still no sign of Pastor Vanhanen.

The only remaining shadow which hung over Nancy's head was Jackie. After the fire, she'd been sent to a remand centre, awaiting trial.

The guilt, not only about Agnes and her sisters, and the stolen lemons, but now with the charges of arson, ate away at Nancy. She wrote a letter filled with heartfelt regret and mailed it to the generic prisoner address at Corrections Victoria, in the hope her atonement would find its way into Jackie's hands. After a few weeks and no reply, she sent another, and then another one month later. When she was on the verge of writing letter number four, she received a strange email from the Naarm Remand Centre, confirming her details for Jackie's approved phone call list.

Her belly curdled with dread for weeks after the email and she flinched every time her mobile rang. Then one day, an unknown number appeared.

'Yes,' she answered. Her heart beat like a trapped bird in her chest.

'It's me,' Jackie said flatly.

'Jackie,' Nancy said with a sigh. 'How are you?'

She'd rehearsed this call a hundred times but all her carefully scripted words disappeared at the sound of the familiar croaky voice.

'Ha,' Jackie barked. 'What do you think?'

'I'm sorry,' Nancy said. 'I can't even begin to tell you how sorry I am.'

'Good,' Jackie spat. 'How does it feel?'

Nancy's lip trembled.

'Well?' Jackie continued. 'What did you expect? Some kind of kumbaya forgiveness? That old bitch killed my family and ruined my whole bloody life.'

Her words were a slap across Nancy's face. In her letters, she'd tried to explain about the thrall of the book. About Lorna and Walter, and Mafalda's role too, but Jackie was right, nothing could excuse what Agnes did to her and her sisters. And the sin stained Nancy's hands too.

'My lawyer said I shouldn't talk to you. But I wanted to tell you myself. You see, I'm honest. Not like you.'

'Please—'

'No, you listen. Don't ever write to me or try to contact me again. I don't want anything to do with you and your evil family. When this is all over, I'm getting as far away from Hopetoun as I can. I'm closing the fucking door and getting on with the rest of my life. Stay away from me. OK?'

Before Nancy could reply, the call ended and she slumped into a puddle on the floor. From that moment on, she put a little money aside each week for Jackie in a piggy bank shaped like two cherubs. She'd taken to calling the angels Molly and Bridget. It was the least she could do, even if Jackie never accepted the money.

'Oh, I meant to ask, do you do catering?' Paula asked. 'We've got a work event next week. And I got lumped with organising morning tea.'

'Absolutely. Let me get my order sheet.' Nancy handed over four individual paper bags. The bags rustled as Paula and her kids tucked in straight away. The satisfying sound of chocolate cracking as Paula took her first bite.

'These are so good. You're an evil woman,' Paula moaned. 'You should be on one of those cooking shows.'

Nancy shook her head with a chuckle. She grabbed her clipboard and a pen to take Paula's morning tea order. Her hand gracing over a notebook sitting amongst her papers.

'Or at least write a book. A recipe book,' Paula said as Nancy returned to the front counter.

Nancy tapped the side of her nose. 'Family secret.'

THE END

Author's Note and Acknowledgements

Folklore, urban legends and folk horror were the primary inspirations for Black Soil White Bread, including the tale of Black Annis, the life of Rosalee Norton and spooky stories told in the school playground. Thank you, as always, to the Folklore Thursday community for leading me down many fascinating rabbit holes.

I have to thank my early readers, the amazingly thorough EJ Dawson, Nathan Jesse Hoffman and the Melbourne Writers Group (Ste, Claire, Tonia, Mark and Jake).

Also, thanks to the D'Este Advisory panel; Maureen Traughber (baking) and Aaron Smith (trains and mechanical stuff), as well as the Monthly Twitter Writing Challenge community for their encouragement and support.

About the Author

Originally from Tasmania, Madeleine D'Este now lives in inner-city Melbourne surrounded by books.

After studying law and seeing the world, now she writes speculative fiction and mysteries at night — female-led, of course.

In 2019, her supernatural mystery novel, The Flower and The Serpent, was nominated for the Australian Shadow Award's Best Novel. Her Australian gothic novella, Radcliffe (Deadset Press), received a 2023 Aurealis Award nomination for Best Horror Novella.

When not writing, Madeleine enjoys podcasts, knitting, forteana, indie films, kettle bells and likes her coffee as 'black as midnight on a moonless night.'

Find Madeleine at www.madeleinedeste.com, on Goodreads or on Bluesky @madeleinedeste.bsky.social

Books by Madeleine D'Este

Radcliffe
Bloodwood
The Flower and The Serpent
Women of Wasps and War
Evangeline and the Spiritualist
Evangeline and the Mysterious Lights
Evangeline and the Bunyip
Evangeline and the Alchemist